TORP

TORP

A NOVEL

MICHAEL MIROLLA

Cover design: Debbie Geltner
Author photo: Salvatore Mirolla
Book design: WildElement.ca

Acknowledgement: A mighty thank you to Linda Leith for taking this on. It takes courage to be a publisher in this day and age.

Library and Archives Canada Cataloguing in Publication

Mirolla, Michael, 1948-, author
　　Torp / Michael Mirolla.

Issued in print and electronic formats.
ISBN 978-1-927535-90-5 (paperback).--ISBN 978-1-927535-91-2 (epub).
--ISBN 978-1-927535-92-9 (mobi).--ISBN 978-1-927535-93-6 (pdf).
　　I. Title.
PS8576.I76T67 2016　　　　　C813'.54　　　　　C2015-908478-4
　　　　　　　　　　　　　　　　　C2015-908479-2

Printed and bound in Canada.

The publisher gratefully acknowledges the support of the Canada Council for the Arts.

Linda Leith Publishing Inc.
P.O. Box 322, Victoria Station,
Westmount Quebec H3Z 2V8 Canada
www.lindaleith.com

To Jackie, for believing

ONE
NICOLE

What then is the good of each?
Surely that for whose sake everything else is done.

—Aristotle,
Nicomachean Ethics,
Book 1, Chapter 7

The first time I laid eyes on that apartment, I almost turned right around and demanded to be taken back to Montreal. It was so fucking dark and depressing. And dank. And it smelled of ... I don't know ... dead things, I guess. Rotting things.

"Too too nice basement," the landlord said, waving his arm. He was a squat and solid-looking man in his mid-sixties I guessed, with an accent almost as thick as his chest. "Yes? You must think so, no?"

I looked at Giulio. Giulio did his usual thing, shrugged and turned the other way, pretending to inspect a crack in the wall. The landlord, a Mr. Harold Bedner, as he'd proudly introduced himself, had already said the same thing at least three times before we'd even got into the place. I was starting to think those were the only English words he knew.

"Bedroom," he said, standing in a room the size of a walk-in closet. And maybe it had been a closet once because you stepped right into it from outside.

"Nice bed," he said.

I looked around. I couldn't see any bed. The only furniture in the room was a ratty-looking sofa. And a peeling puke-green dresser that looked like it had been standing in a puddle for too long.

"I show," he said, laughing. "I show."

He knelt down in front of the sofa. Then reached under and yanked at it. The sofa squeaked and popped open, sheets already in place.

"Bed," he said again. "Good, strong bed."

He sat on it and gave it a few bounces.

"Hey, that's a neat idea," Giulio said, putting on that blank-faced beam of his. "Good way to save space. Don't you think, Nicole?"

"Nice," I said through gritted teeth. "Too nice."

I walked over to the window. It was one of those basement-type openings placed just a bit above ground level. Sealed shut with paint and caulking. And with a little plastic curtain that had been obviously jerryrigged in place. Through it, I could see a piece of Mr. Bedner's front lawn and sections of one-storey houses that you wouldn't be able to tell apart if it weren't for the different-coloured front doors. This was getting more depressing by the minute. Where was the ocean everyone said you could smell in the air? Where were the mountains everybody was always talking about? Never mind that. Where was the fucking sky?

"Lots of sun," Mr. Bedner said, motioning with his hands as if that was going to bring the sunshine in. "Too, too bright."

As he said this, I heard a gurgling flush and Giulio came out of a cubicle to one side of the so-called bedroom.

"Toilet works," he said. As if it had come as a surprise. And then the gurgling kept right on going. Mr. Bedner rushed in and jiggled the handle until it stopped—or almost stopped anyway as a small trickle decided to push on. I followed him in.

"Oh yes," I said, beating Mr. Bedner to the punch. "Too, too nice."

I didn't mind so much that the washroom was little more than a drain area for the shower. Or that the toilet bowl and the basin had rust spots from the constantly dripping water. I didn't even mind that, if a person stood over the sink to wash her face, her ass would hang over the toilet. What got me was the thick layer of green mould growing along the bottom edges of the shower area. And the black splotch on the ceiling where the water had splashed up and caused the plaster to sag. It got me to thinking about one of those really bad movies where the aliens are slime balls that seem completely harmless. Until they start to crawl around and suck the humans dry. Slurp.

"Fix," Mr. Bedner said when he noticed me looking up. "Paint. Plaster. Quick job."

"Yes, quick job," I said. "Too too quick."

"You see rest now, yes?"

I started to shake my head. I'd seen enough and was ready to try some other rat hole. But Mr. Bedner didn't give me a chance. He took Giulio by the arm and led him into the next room, which was only a little bit bigger than a walk-in closet.

"Kitchen," Mr. Bedner said. "Everything here."

Yeah, I guess it was. Or there was. A torn and stained

card table and four folding chairs held together with grey duct tape. A two-ring heating element with the wires showing through where the electric cord had frayed. A bunch of bent cutlery and cracked cups and glasses that had been left to dry in the sink—oh, maybe twenty years before. A blackened tea kettle. And a half-fridge that looked like it had been built in the Stone Age.

"Window, too," Mr. Bedner said.

I'd forgotten the window—this one right over the kitchen sink. Though I'm not sure it really made it as a window. It was about two feet wide by a foot high and you couldn't actually look out through it, what with the shrubs and weeds and wild flowers right up against it. Not to mention this huge spiderweb on the outside that made it look like the glass had cracked and had never been repaired.

"It's a little dark in here, isn't it?" Giulio said.

God bless Giulio. What a guy. When he wasn't in philosophy la-la-land, his grasp of the obvious was beyond fucking parallel.

"Dark?" Mr. Bedner said. "Prison dark. Dungeon dark. Cemetery dark. This no dark."

"Well," Giulio said, "if you put it that way, maybe—"

"I'm sorry, Mr. Bedner," I said, cutting him off, "but I think we'll—"

"I like you," Mr. Bedner said, cutting me off in turn. "You look nice people. Like children, yes. Come, come."

"Mr. Bedner," I said, looking at Giulio for support, "I don't think—"

But the landlord had already climbed back outside, standing near the steps that led to his own first-floor living space. And Giulio ... well, he was as supportive as he'd ever be. I'd learned in a hurry not to rely on him for a decision. Too busy weighing the pros and cons to actually make up his mind about anything.

"Come, come," Mr. Bedner said. "You meet wife. Yes?"

We were stuck. Shit! Maybe if Giulio had said something, lied maybe like we had other apartments to see, we might have been able to get away. But somehow I doubt it. I don't think anything would've got us away from that guy. Mr. Bedner was determined not to let us go. He waved for us to follow him up the steps. On the other side of the door, half-hidden behind it, was a tiny, hunched-over old woman, a black shawl wrapped around her shoulders. The first thing I noticed about her face was the moustache and the start of a thin goatee.

"Mrs. Bedner," the landlord said proudly, introducing us. "Irena."

Mrs. Bedner smiled, revealing a strong set of dentures, and then backed up so that, as the door opened, most of her body disappeared behind it. All we could see was that wrinkled face peeking out.

"Hello," I said. "How are you?"

She smiled again.

"English not too good," Mr. Bedner said, thumbing his finger back at her without even looking. "Never learn. But I Canadian citizen." He pounded on his chest and his face reddened. "Canada my country. Proud Canadian. Swear oath. To Queen. Like empress, no? Those Quebecers, they crazy, yes? Separate here, separate there. Like snip snip scissors. No separate. I come from country where everyone want to separate. Make more food for big red bear."

"Red bear?" Giulio said, puzzled. "You mean brown bear, don't you? Or black bear?"

"No, no," he said. "Red bear; red star." Then he growled and slashed at the air. "Kill father, kill mother. Come, I show you."

With his wife shooing us from behind and Mr. Bedner leading us on, we were pushed into the living room. But it wasn't your ordinary, everyday living room. This was like one of those sitting rooms you see in paintings. Or like at that museum in Paris. Everything was in red, a deep velvet red: the thick curtains held down by lead weights; the carpet with the design of a castle in it; the sofa and chairs with those funny claws instead of regular legs. There was even one of those tassels that you can use to let people know they shouldn't be going into the room without your permission. And right in the centre of the room, just a little above head level, was a real honest-to-goodness chandelier—and I mean genuine. One of those with candles instead of lights, though there were real lights in the room. And the walls were covered with these huge portraits of the ugliest, meanest-looking men and women you'd ever want to see. Some you couldn't tell the difference. They were wearing these starched-up collars and each had a little gold nametag underneath. I tried to read the names but I couldn't make them out. They were in some weird writing, Russian or something.

"That's fantastic," Giulio said, standing in front of one of the portraits. "How old are these?"

"Old," Mr. Bedner said, as he pulled out a bottle from a cabinet and poured out several glasses of a thick liqueur. "Very old. From old country. From old house. Before revolution, yes?"

"And where's that?" I asked, catching a peek of Mrs. Bedner behind me. "The old country, I mean."

"Bah," the landlord said, waving his hand. "No talk of that. Old country dead. Eaten up. Dinner for red bear. Now, we drink, yes? To new country! Canada! Vancouver! To ocean!" He pointed one way. "To mountains!" He pointed in the other.

And he gulped down his drink in one shot, indicating Giulio and I should do the same. I took a sip. It wasn't half bad. Not bad at all. I drank the rest down, feeling it warm up my insides.

"What is it?" I asked, holding up the glass and watching the dark leftover liquid slide back down the side.

"Brandy," Mr. Bedner said. "Plum brandy. I make! Here. Drink! Drink more."

Before we could protest or pull our glasses back, he'd refilled them.

"Sit, sit," he said, patting the sofa. "We talk. You nice people. Nice couple."

"Thank you very much," I said, putting the glass

down. "But I think we'd better get going now."

"Going?" Mr. Bedner asked. "Where go? This new home for you. Very nice home. Too too nice."

"It is a nice place," Giulio said. "But—"

"Ah, bathroom," Mr. Bedner said. "No worry. I fix. Quick fix. Now, sit and we talk. You like politics?"

"Not really," I said.

"Neither me! Politics stupid! Separatists stupid! Bomb people stupid! Trudeau—"

"Stupid!" Giulio said.

"Ah," Mr. Bedner said, touching the side of his head with his finger. "Only pretend stupid. Trudeau smart. He know old country proverb."

He leaned back, placed his hands across his stomach and shut his eyes.

"And what proverb is that?" I asked when it dawned on me he wasn't about to say without some coaxing.

"Give man enough rope—"

"—and he'll hang himself," Giulio finished for him.

"No, no," Mr. Bedner said laughing and slapping his knee. "He tie you up with it."

After that, there was no holding Mr. Bedner back. With every drink he gulped down, he became louder and harder to understand. Several times, we tried to stand up to leave, but he wouldn't hear of it. And Mrs. Bedner stood at the doorway, blocking any quick exit.

"Shower," he said at one point.

"Shower?" both Giulio and I said at the same time.

"Yes. Shower. You know? Like bath, only different.

9

I never have shower before. No shower in old country. No shower here. But my brothers. They carpenters. They make. Seven feet by four feet. Then I wash—standing up!"

I don't know how he went from showers and making soap-rubbing motions all over his body to what he did for a living. But the next thing we knew he was telling us about his job as a night watchman at a lumberyard.

"Good job," he said. "Too too good. But I retire soon. Tomorrow, no. Next week, no. Next year—yes! Then I sleep at night. Sleep like baby!"

And, with that, he stretched out full-length on the sofa. Mrs. Bedner burst into giggles behind us.

"Like little baby again," Mr. Bedner said.

You know what? That's exactly how I pictured him at that moment. Like a pink chubby little baby all curled up on the sofa. It wasn't a pretty sight.

"So," he said, sitting up and rubbing his eyes. "Where suitcases? You bring?"

"We don't have very much," Giulio said. "We left our bags down at the train station."

"You stay tonight then," Mr. Bedner said. "No problem. Then you get bags. Tomorrow, you get bags. Good idea, yes?"

"Mr. Bedner," I said, sighing. "I think we should ... you know ... look around first."

"Look around?" He seemed confused. Really confused. "What for look around?" He looked first at me, then at Giulio. Finally, he turned to his wife, who was still standing in the corridor, head tilted so she could see into the living room. "You understand: Look around?"

Mrs. Bedner shook her head, then turned and vanished.

"Nicole," Giulio said. "Maybe ...."

That second fucking "maybe" sank us. I wasn't about to play the heavy. No fucking way. I wasn't about to stomp all over an old man who was obviously desperate to rent the place out. Which from the looks of it hadn't had an occupant, at least not a human occupant, in years.

"Okay, Mr. Bedner," I said with a sigh and a not-too-cheerful sideways glance at traitor Giulio. "We'll give it a try. But you've got to get that bathroom fixed."

"No problem," Mr. Bedner said. "My brothers carpenters, plumbers, electrical guys, you know. Too, too good. They fix just like that. Quick fix."

He snapped his fingers.

I'd been looking for something different. Something with a little more class. With a lot more class actually. Like an apartment in one of the modern highrises that were being built all over Vancouver. You know, something 1970s instead of something nineteenth century. I'd seen them from the train on the way in. The type with a doorman maybe and laundry service on the same floor. A place with real furnishings and kitchen appliances that didn't look as if they'd been picked up from a pawnshop. Or a junkyard. Instead, here we were, three thousand miles from home, and we'd landed in the same shithole kind of neighbourhood we'd just left behind. Working-class drab, I called it. I wouldn't be surprised to see the worn-out discoloured underwear hanging on the clotheslines. And the hairy hot dogs standing at the top of the stairs in those ball-busting jeans, sucking away on their cigarettes and scratching their crotches. Each one thinking he was God's gift.

"The moment you get a raise," I told Giulio, "we're out of here. You hear me? Not a fucking moment longer."

"It's a promise," he said, reaching up to sweep away another cobweb.

"Oh well," I said, sitting on one of the kitchen chairs. "To tell the truth, I've seen worse. A lot worse. And at least I won't have to sleep with a knife under my pillow."

"Shit, look at this."

Giulio had opened the side door that led from the kitchen to the rest of the basement. I peered in.

"It smells like a cave," I said.

"Dark like prison," Giulio said, imitating the landlord.

"Dark like cemetery," I said.

We laughed, hands over our mouths to keep the noise down. Giulio found the light switch. A single naked bulb came on, but it kept flickering as if it couldn't decide whether or not to stay on. But it was enough to make me want to pull the door shut again and maybe hammer it closed from the inside. There was no real flooring except from some packed-down earth. The ceiling beams and wall two-by-fours were exposed. Great hiding spots for all kinds of vermin, I said to myself. A set of rickety stairs with plenty of missing steps led up to the first floor. And planks had been placed from the foot of the stairs to a washer-dryer area at the back. Another door, looking as if it hadn't been opened in ages, led to the backyard. I couldn't decide what smelled worst: the mouldy carpeting piled up in the back, the chairs with rotting legs, or the moth-eaten clothes—all tossed into one heap. I got the shivers thinking what pleasant little fuckers waited underneath that heap.

"And here I thought the side we were on was bad," I said. "It seems like paradise now."

"Yeah," Giulio said. "I hope he doesn't get the notion to rent this side out, too. That would make for some pretty weird neighbours."

There was a sound in the walls—like scratching.

"I think we've got neighbours already," I said, taking a step back into the kitchen. And Giulio was quick to follow.

"Look at that hole under the door," he said, pointing to a one-inch gap between the door and the floor. "Looks like we're going to have some uninvited guests."

"Not if I can help it," I said.

I went into the bathroom and brought back a rag that had been hanging against the side of the shower stall. I stuffed the rag under the door and jammed it tight.

"There," I said. "That'll have to do for now."

But Giulio wasn't satisfied. He must have thought it was his duty to protect me, so he tied a cloth to the end of a broom handle and went searching every corner of the place for cobwebs. He was even brave enough to poke around the insides of the kitchen cupboards. And under the sink. When he pulled the broom handle back, there was a spider stuck to it, a big fat brightly-coloured red and black thing. Its guts had been busted open and all it could do was wiggle its legs in the air.

"Ugh!" Giulio said, holding out the broom handle as far from himself as possible. "Look at that thing."

"You look at it," I said. "I've seen enough fucking spiders to last a lifetime."

Giulio couldn't take his eyes off the creature. He tried to squeeze it with a Kleenex but only managed to knock it to the floor. There, it started to go around in circles, dragging its guts behind it. I could tell Giulio was nervous. He couldn't stop talking about the spider and how "it had desperately fought our attempt to bring light to the dark spots, to the places where damp, decay, and corruption were entrenched." He always talked that kind of bullshit when he got nervous. Like everything had some deeper meaning or something like that.

The truth was he just couldn't stand the thought of insects or rats and that kind of stuff in the flat. He had been brought up in a home that was spotless, a place where not even the dust dared enter. During the few months we'd spent there, I'd actually seen Mrs. di Orio on her hands and knees first thing in the morning polishing the stairs. And sweeping the sidewalk was a daily routine. Including the cracks in the cement. Don't get me wrong. I couldn't stand spiders or rats either. But that was because I'd seen too many of them. Shit, I even had a rat crawl across my feet once while I was trying to sleep at my grandmother's place during one of my parents' tries at making a go of things. I didn't get much sleep after that, let me tell you. And when I told my grandfather in the morning, all he said was: "Nicole, you missed a great chance there. That rat would have really spiced up the pea soup." I've had a thing about pea soup ever since.

"There," Giulio said, holding up a broom handle covered in cobwebs. "Those little buggers won't be back for a while."

But it wasn't the end of his cleaning for the night. He had to do the same thing with the bed. Giulio insisted we strip it down and check it out from top to bottom. I warned him he probably wouldn't like what he found.

"There are things best left alone," I said. "Take the word of someone who knows."

Giulio is the kind of guy, I figure, who would pull a dressing away to see the pus underneath—and then, after glancing at it sideways, rush off to the bathroom to vomit. But it wasn't as bad as I thought it would be. Sure, there were a few holes where the material had been torn—or maybe eaten—away. And a few mouse droppings. But that was about it. Giulio whacked the sofa hard several times with the broom handle, hoping to scare off any inhabitants still stupid enough to stay behind. He didn't find any.

"I think they heard us coming," I said, replacing the sheets and pillows on the sofabed. "That's probably them in the walls right now."

"Yeah," he said, putting his ear against the nearest wall. "I can hear them."

"So, what are they doing?"

"They're huddled around their children and telling horror stories about us. They're saying: 'Look out for those turkeys. First they did in the spiders. And now they're gunning for us.'"

I started to giggle, and then I couldn't stop. Giulio tried to shush me up and pointed at his watch to say it was late. But I couldn't help myself. I fell back on the sofa and buried my face in the pillows. Giulio lay down beside me and passed his hand through my hair.

"So is this paradise?" he asked. "Or what?"

He bounced up and down on the sofa.

"What the hell are you doing?" I asked, turning to face him.

"Did you hear anything?" He bounced again.

"No. What am I supposed to hear?"

"The squeaking of bed springs, of course," he said, as he rolled over onto me.

"Shit, you're right."

"And no one listening in the next room, except maybe a couple of frightened mice."

"Now what are we going to do?" I said. "We don't have any more excuses."

Giulio leaned down to kiss me. Soft lips. That was one of the first things I had found out about him. I could feel him hardening against my stomach. Then, he suddenly rolled off me and stood up.

"I'll be right back," he said. "Wanna brush my teeth."

"Screw it," I said. "I want you—now!"

"Hold your horses. Or whatever you hold in a situation like this. I won't be long."

I didn't say anything else. I knew that once he'd made up his mind about something, no way could I change it—especially when it came to getting clean. I think he had a ... what do they call it? ... a fetish about it. Like, after a certain point, he couldn't stand the smell of himself or something. Hey, there are worse things a man can have a fetish about, right? Like that sick pervert my mother brought home one night. Claimed he liked to do the laundry—until I caught him with his face buried in a pair of my unwashed panties. And then he grinned and wanted to hand them back to me.

"Uh, yeah," I had told him, "it's okay. You can keep them."

I sat on the sofa and took off my clothes. There was a mirror on the outside of the bathroom door. Hmm, not bad, I told myself as I posed sideways in front of it. Getting a little thick around the thighs and ass. But I breathed in, letting my breasts pop straight out. Kazoom! How do you like them knockers! I'd always been proud of them. Giulio's brother liked to say that what you couldn't get into your mouth was wasted. Another of Raf's expressions was: "Why buy the whole cow when all you wanted was a little milk?" Yeah and I'd tell him right back: "Why put up with all that bull when all you needed was a little

17

meat?"

"Giulio," I said, finally knocking on the washroom door. "What the hell's taking you so long?"

"I'll be right out," he said.

"Don't tell me you're playing with yourself again," I said.

"No, of course not!" He sounded indignant that I would suggest such a thing.

"Well, you'd better not be," I said laughing. "I want you all to myself."

I turned out the light and went back to lie down on the sofa, not bothering to cover up. It was perfect. There was just enough moonlight coming through the curtain so that he'd be able to see me. Or my silhouette anyway. I rubbed my nipples and gave them a little tug. Then I squeezed my breasts. My body was starting to tingle.

"Giulio," I called out again. "Please hurry up."

"Coming, coming."

Giulio came out at last, carrying his clothes on his arm. I knew then he hadn't just brushed his teeth. No, that wouldn't be my Giulio. Knowing him, he'd probably scrubbed his ears and cut his toenails—and even pulled back his foreskin to make sure there wasn't any crud underneath.

I almost said: "Hey, what do you know. All fresh and scrubbed and ready for a good, screw-the-sounds, no-holds-barred fuck."

But I bit my tongue. Giulio was sensitive that way. He didn't like to have the mood, as he called it, broken.

"Come over here," I said instead, holding out my arms. "Momma's got something for you."

"For little old me?"

Giulio put down his clothes and walked towards me. The moonlight made him glow: a skinny, long-legged creature with a slightly-curved back, shadow prick standing straight out. He stopped at the edge of the sofa and looked around.

"Now, what are you doing?" I asked.

"Hear that?"

"What? I don't hear anything."

"Exactly!" he said, as he lay down beside me. "No snoring from the next room. And no nosy mother getting up in the middle of the night pretending to get a glass of water."

"Of course not, silly." I rubbed my fingers across his chest. "But maybe if we make enough noise they'll hear us clear across the continent. Wouldn't that be fun?"

Wishful thinking. When my fingers slid down between his legs, I discovered he had gone limp again.

"Hey," I said, laughing. "What's this? A second ago, you were sticking out like a flagpole."

"I don't know," he said. "The moment we started talking about my mother—"

"For chrissakes!" I said, turning onto my back and letting out a sigh. "Maybe we should've brought her with us. Yeah, like stuffed her into one of the bags or something!"

"I'm sorry, Nicole. It's not like I wanted this—"

"Forget it, okay. Just forget it." I took his hand in

mine. "You're probably just nervous about starting your job."

"Yeah, I guess that must be it," he said, turning towards me. "I'm not sure what to expect. And I hate that."

"Get some sleep," I said, kissing him on the lips. "See you in the morning."

He turned his back to me and curled up. Within minutes, he was asleep, making soft shuddering sounds. But I knew it wasn't going to be as easy for me. Every part of my body twitched and jumped—like someone was jolting it with electricity. And, when I started to hear the sounds in the walls again, that was it. Screw that, I said. I reached over and turned Giulio back towards me. If I wasn't going to sleep, he wasn't going to sleep either. I started licking his nipples and reached down to stroke him. He let out a gasp as I buried my head beneath the sheets and worked my tongue down past his belly button to the base of his prick.

"Umm," I said, licking gently. "Looks like it's decided to stand up for itself again."

I lowered my lips onto him and he started to buck. I was careful to time his motions as I had no intention of letting him come in my mouth. No, I wanted him inside me. When I felt he was getting too wild, I made my way back up his body.

"So," I said. "Do you still want to go to sleep?"

He rolled over on top of me and arched up to get himself completely inside me.

"Here comes the train," he said. "Choo! Choo!"

"That's not what it's saying," I said.

"What's it saying?"

"Fuck me! Fuck me! Fuck me!"

A few moments later, I felt Giulio getting ready to shoot his load. I reached behind and gripped his buttocks, holding him tight against me. He bucked a couple of times and then fell on top of me, breathing hard.

"It's nice not having to pull out," he said.

"Well, aren't you the lucky one," I said. "No condom and no worries."

Hadn't been much fun being told I couldn't have children but it sure made it easier in the heat of the moment.

"Yeah, nice and cozy in there."

"Good," I said. "Now, my turn."

I grabbed his hand and slid it down between my legs. He started to rub awkwardly, one finger sliding up and down and occasionally making contact.

"No," I said, rising up to meet him. "Circle. You have to rotate. You have to—"

He wasn't very good at it and it felt kind of rough where he'd bitten his nails. But I didn't care at that point. When I came, I let out a shrill moan and bounced crazily. And then I started shivering: coming had always left me cold.

"Brrr!" I said, wrapping myself around Giulio, trying to feed off his warmth. "Good night, lover boy."

"Good night, Nicole."

We were still tight against each other in the morning when

a loud knocking on the front door startled us awake.

"What the hell——?"

Giulio gathered up his clothes and went off into the bathroom while I put on a robe and answered the door. How come I wasn't surprised when I was greeted by Mr. Bedner's smiling face? He was holding a tray with a coffee pot and two cups on it. To the side was a basket with some pieces of dark bread and a plate with butter.

"Mr. Bedner," I said, rubbing my eyes. "What brings you——"

"Hello, hello," he said. "Mrs. Bedner, she know you have no breakfast. So she tell me: 'Bring some to the nice tenants. Tomorrow they buy.' Yes?"

"Mr. Bedner," I said. "You shouldn't have."

"Harold, please. And pleasure all mine," he said, holding out the tray for me to take. "Now, you eat, yes. I go sleep."

He turned as I called thanks after him.

"Room service?" Giulio said as he came out of the bathroom.

"I guess he's really desperate for us to stay."

I sat down at the kitchen table and looked around. There was actually some sunlight getting in. "What the hell. Maybe things aren't so bad after all."

"You might not say that after you've seen the bathroom in daylight. Not a pretty sight. I think some of that green stuff has moved."

"You leave it to me," I said. "I've had plenty of experience with that sort of thing. And if worst comes to worst, I'll just do what a friend of mine did once."

"What's that?"

"Paint the whole thing black!"

But I didn't need to do that. Some heavy-duty cleaner was enough—at least to remove the green scum around the shower area. The ceiling I didn't even try to clean, as I was afraid it might come down right on my head. After I'd done my best with the bathroom, I decided to clear away the shit behind the kitchen window. But first I had to get into the backyard, and that wasn't as easy as I thought it was going to be. The back door had been nailed shut. I found an old crowbar on the other side of the basement and used it first to remove a foot-wide layer of dust and webs and then to yank the nails out. Let there be light, I said as I threw open the door. The backyard was just like I'd imagined it, more jungle than anything else. The grass and weeds were waist-high. There was an old trellis but it was rotten and covered in dead ivy. And whatever path there might once have been was completely overgrown now. I had to search around near the wall before I could find where the kitchen window was. I put on a pair of work gloves I'd found in the basement and started tugging at the nettles and milkweed plants. Let there be even more light, I said after I'd finished and could actually see into the flat. Not only that but from here the tips of the mountains were visible. White and pure. Maybe we'll stay here for a while after all.

I spent the rest of the day cleaning out cupboards and even decided to tackle the fridge, which wasn't as bad inside as the outside made you believe. No rotting food, at least. Or anything that was about to spring out and attach itself to your face. At one point in the late afternoon, Mr. Bedner showed up, carrying a cardboard box.

"Here," he said. "We don't need. You take, yes?"

He opened up the box. It was filled with cutlery and glasses and delicate coffee cups. Some of it looked like it had never been used.

"Mr. Bedner …Harold," I said, getting ready to protest. "There's no need—"

"No, for you," he said, holding up his hand. "We bring from old country but we never use."

"But," I said. "What about your children? Don't they want it? Save it for them."

"No children," Mr. Bedner said, lowering his eyes. "Not possible."

"I'm sorry."

"No," he said. "No problem. In old country, children not healthy. Many die. Disease. Killing. We lucky no children. You?"

"I guess we're in the same boat," I said. He looked at me as if he hadn't understood. "I can't have children either."

"Who say?"

"The doctor told me."

"Ah, no listen," Mr. Bedner said. "Doctors full of poop." He clapped his hands. "You have children. I see it. You have lots and lots of children. And you buy nice house. Maybe even here. Nice neighbourhood. And then

24

you have plenty visits from grandchildren. I see it all. Right here in my head."

"That's very sweet, Mr. Bedner."

"Harold, please."

"Harold."

After Mr. Bedner left—I just couldn't picture him as "Harold"—I showered and then went down to the train station to get our bags. The station was in a weird part of town. The buildings were falling apart and there was writing all over the walls. Stuff like: "Anarchy Is The Only True Government" and "Up With Chaos." Some of them were signed with the letters: PFRG. I wondered if they were the Vancouver section of the FLQ. To top it all off, there were bums all over the streets. I had to step over some who were sleeping right in the middle of the sidewalks.

"Lady, lady, lady," one of them said from where he lay on the street covering his eyes from the sun and looking up at me. "You look like my mother."

"I don't think so." I started to walk away.

"You're right," he said, squinting to get a closer look at me. "You're cute. She was nothing but a fucking whore." He grinned, showing me a mouth without bottom front teeth. "How about a few cents then?"

I looked at him. Hard to tell but he seemed young, way too young to be lying on the street wrapped in a torn blue ski jacket that smelled like … like he was on top of a mound of dog shit.

"Here," I said, fishing out a quarter and tossing it to him. Then, I moved away quickly before my lunch came up.

"Thanks, lady," he said. "And if you see my mother …."

By the time Giulio came home that night, I had managed to put our clothes away—after lining the dresser with paper. I'd also had time to set out a supper of chicken, fries, and coleslaw—thanks to the local fast food takeout. And I'd found a couple of candles for the card table.

"Wow," Giulio said, whistling as he looked around the flat. "I'm impressed. And supper, too. All that's missing is something we can use to toast the start of our life together."

I reached down beneath the sink and pulled out a bottle of red wine I'd picked up at a liquor outlet near the train station.

"Will this do?"

"You bet. All we need is a corkscrew."

I searched through the cutlery drawer. Not a fucking corkscrew in sight. Of course not. That would have made life too easy.

"Give it here," I said as Giulio examined the bottle as if looking for another way to pour out the wine. "I've done this before. My mom was always losing her corkscrew. Among other things."

I used a knife to slowly push the cork into the bottle, making sure it didn't come spilling out the top. The things you learn during a childhood spent fending for yourself.

"Voilà," I said, filling our brand-new glasses, compliments of Mr. Bedner.

"Umm," Giulio said, taking a bite of the fried chicken. "A gourmet meal. Here's to us."

We clinked glasses.

"Now," I said. "You're supposed to tell me about your day. Isn't that what working husbands are supposed to do when they come home to their wives at night? I want all the juicy gossip you get from hanging around the water cooler."

Not that I could ever imagine Giulio hanging around the water cooler.

"Well, let's see," he said. "When I walked into the philosophy department office this morning, there was a big brass band waiting for me. Then, I was handed the keys to the executive washroom—"

"Yeah. I guess they figured out pretty quick you're full of shit."

"Hey, that's not nice." He held out his glass. "Give us another drink."

"So," I said, "what are you really supposed to do there? Seriously."

"I'm their resident genius, what else. I correct mistakes made by the other profs and I clear up any confusion that may arise. And, believe me, when you're dealing with things like The Mind-Body Problem, Fate, Time and the Existence of God, and The Aristotelian Substratum in the Scheme of Reality, confusion is bound to come up."

I kicked him under the table.

"Alright, alright. You want serious, you'll have serious. I get to run some conferences for first-year students for the real professor who teaches the course. And I correct their term papers because that same professor finds it beneath him to do so."

"I don't know what you're complaining about," I said. "At least you don't have to pick up garbage from morning till night. Or have to stay awake nights keeping an eye on a lumberyard. And maybe one day, if you play your cards right, you might be that professor."

"Yeah, I suppose you're right," he said, suddenly looking glum. "What about you? What are you going to do once the flat's all fixed up?"

I hadn't thought that far ahead.

"I don't know," I said. "Maybe I'll look for a job, too. There must be work for secretaries around here—especially with all this real estate going up."

"Why don't you go back to school? That might be fun."

"Me?"

"Yeah, why not?"

Not that I hadn't thought of it. I once had had a dream of becoming a nurse. But that kind of went down the drain when my mother and I moved to Montreal. Now, I still had this idea of maybe caring for the sick or something like that. But I wasn't interested in going to school to study for it. I guess I could try volunteering at a hospital. Or a nursing home. Learn to push old people around in wheelchairs and stuff like that.

"I guess getting a job makes more sense," Giulio says.

"Come on," I said. "Let's go for a walk. We'll discuss this later. And, from now on, you'd better have some stories to tell me when you get back in the evening. Otherwise, I might not let you in."

Those after-dinner walks became practically a nightly event for us, until the weather turned bad. There were a lot of parks and playgrounds in the neighbourhood, but most of them were abandoned and didn't have very many children in them. I guess at one time there must have been a bunch of young families living in the area. But now it was mostly older people, like Mr. Bedner and his wife. They were probably those same young couples actually— just grown old. Giulio and I used to sit on the park benches huddled together. Giulio had never been a great talker, so getting him to spill about what had happened during the day was like pulling teeth. Besides, the things that interested me—what one person was doing to another and who was stabbing who in the back—left Giulio cold. Or maybe a better word would be confused. Like he didn't have a clue why human beings did some things. And the stuff he liked to talk about ... well, you could just forget about that, unless you had a higher degree in philosophy. It was like—whoosh—way over my head. So I had him tell me about his students.

"Some of them are real characters," he said one night as we shivered together on the bench, watching an old man yanking his dog along. "I don't really know what they're doing at the university. Some of them look like they just wandered off the streets, you know. They're dressed in rags and don't smell that good. And they beg. They beg for money, cigarettes, food—anything they can get, I guess."

"Sound more like bums than students to me," I said, thinking back on the mother-hater in the torn ski jacket.

"Well, they're young enough to be students, and some of them actually attend classes. Although I don't think they ever sign up officially because they can't afford the tuition."

"So why don't the security people keep them away? That's what I'd be doing."

"Hey, the age of the flower children may be coming to an end, but that doesn't mean we should set up a police state."

"Flower children," I scoffed. "Just an excuse to do drugs. I know their type."

"I suppose," Giulio said. "But there's not much we can do about it. Besides, they're harmless."

That's when he told me about one of these characters who attended his conference in introductory philosophy. At least, he showed up whenever he felt like it, according to Giulio. Often halfway through the class, dirty, hair all matted, and barefoot.

"He lives on the beach with some of his friends," Giulio told me. "They sleep there from what I can gather. They use the driftwood to build bonfires and they eat whatever they can get from tourist handouts. I don't know. When I was younger, I used to fantasize about becoming a monk—"

"A monk!" I said. "That's a good one."

"Yeah, you know. Living all by myself. But I just can't imagine doing what those people do: not having a hot cup of coffee in the morning, a solid roof overhead, not knowing where the next meal is coming from, not being able to bathe or brush my teeth. Ugh!"

"Hey, don't I know it. You get confused just sleeping on the other side of the bed."

"Exactly," he said.

"What's this guy's name?"

"Torp."

"Torp? What the hell kind of dumb name is that? What is it, short for torpedo or something?" Right away, I pictured this real kook. Maybe one of those guys who'd done too many drugs a couple of years back and now had a whole bunch of brain cells missing. I'd run across a few of those in my time—a few too many. Hey, my mother brought one home once from the restaurant where she was waitressing. The guy claimed he'd just come back from San Francisco. The "scene" as he called it. Full of idiots walking around with flowers in their hair. He was always grinning like a retard and walking around the house in his bikini briefs. Shit! What is it with men and bikini briefs anyway? He was okay I guess—until he came into my bedroom one night and suggested he could teach me a few tricks. That's when I started sleeping with the kitchen knife.

So you can just imagine how pleased I was when, a couple of weeks later, Giulio showed up at the door with who else but this Torp in tow. He was everything Giulio had described: slobby, scruffy, dirty, with clown-hair like he'd stuck his finger in an electric socket.

"Hello, Nicole," Giulio said, a stupid smile on his face. "This is Torp. Remember I told you about him."

I grinned at Torp who was still standing in the doorway—then shot a nasty look at Giulio.

"Uh," Giulio said, lowering his eyes. "I asked him to come over because has something he needs to discuss with me."

"I guess it couldn't have waited till tomorrow," I said sweetly.

"Maybe this wasn't such a good idea," Torp said. "Maybe I should go."

He started to turn.

"No, no," I said. "Now that you're here you might as well come in." I looked at Giulio again. "We were just about to have supper anyway, weren't we, dear?"

"You're sure now," Torp said. "I don't want to inconvenience you."

"I'm positive," I said.

Besides, I knew that look on Giulio's face. It was like he'd just found this wounded animal on the street and had to bring it home. No matter what. He would have been really disappointed if I'd said no. But the first thing I did was to suggest the washroom to Torp. Politely, of course. Then, while Torp was cleaning himself up, I told Giulio that it was okay for that evening but I didn't want it to become a fucking habit. Knowing Giulio, he'd provide bed and board for every stray cat in the city if I let him. I told him this was our home, a private place for the two of us. Not some commune for street people and free love loonies.

"It won't happen again," Giulio said, grinning and nodding. "Cross my heart and hope to die. Now, what's for supper?"

"Homemade soup and pork chops," I said. "I was hoping for a nice, quiet dinner—just the two of us."

"This is a great pad," Torp said as he came out of the washroom. "You guys are really lucky to have found it."

"The department secretary recommended it," Giulio said. "Come on, sit down."

Torp sniffed the air.

"Wow! What a great smell. Homemade chicken noodle soup, right?"

"You got it," I said. "Let's eat."

I had to admit Torp wasn't as disgusting as I thought he'd be. And at least he knew how to use a knife and fork. But I wasn't about to let him off that easily.

"These are delicious pork chops," he said.

"Supermarkets," I said, drawling. "They're a great invention."

Torp grinned at me and did a thumbs up, letting me know I'd scored one.

"I hate supermarkets," Giulio said, taking me seriously. "I think they're a prime source of modern-day paranoia. If not *the* prime source."

"Oh, stop it," I said. "Supermarkets are places to shop, that's all. And they're much better than some dirty corner store where you don't know what the hell they've done with the food."

"But that's precisely it," Giulio said. "Supermarkets fool you into thinking they're harmless—and then they take you prisoner. They make you a captive of the consumer society. All that hypnotic music and those loudspeaker sale announcements—they're meant to keep you in there forever." He turned to Torp. "What do you think?"

Torp put down his knife and fork and wiped his mouth and fingers. Then he smiled, looking first at Giulio and then at me. When he did that, I thought for sure he was going to come up with some high-sounding bullshit. I said to myself: "Oh shit. Here it comes. One more know-it-all above-it-all philosophy student getting ready to shoot his mouth off." I'd heard enough of that crap during the few times I'd met Giulio's fellow students from McGill. Diarrhoea of the mouth. And oh so weary and worn out. Like they'd lived a hundred years of horrible torture.

"I happen to agree with you," Torp said, looking at me. "Supermarkets *are* just places to shop."

"But you can't be serious," Giulio said, taken aback by what he must have thought was a betrayal. "We're talking here about a pernicious symbol—"

"Quiet," I said. "Let the man speak."

"Fear of supermarkets, skyscrapers, eight-lane

highways, etc., that's exactly what the forces that control us want. They want us to believe there's more to them than meets the eye. But really there's nothing wrong with supermarkets. In fact, they can be fun—if a person takes them in the right spirit and ignores all the propaganda crap."

Well, you can imagine my surprise. It was such a sensible thing to say.

"So tell me," I said, clearing away the dishes, "you don't sound Canadian. Where you from?"

"Oh so you picked up on my accent," he said. "Or is it because I don't end every sentence with 'eh'?"

"Both," Giulio said, taking out our bottle of cheap brandy and three glasses.

"I'm from south of here … California," Torp said, holding the brandy glass with both hands.

"California!" I said. "Wow. I've always dreamed of going there."

"You and The Mamas and the Papas," Torp said.

"So, why …"

"Why did I leave?" He took a sip of his brandy and smacked his lips. "Same old story. Didn't get along with my folks—my dad being an ex-Army man and all. Left home the first chance I got. That was six years ago. Travelled around the States mostly. Haven't seen them since."

"You haven't seen your parents in six years?" Giulio asked, eyes opening wide. For Giulio, brought up in a family that would rather smother you to death than let you go, that was close to sacrilege.

"Couple of years back, I called from Seattle to say

hello. My dad, he got a great kick out of telling me my draft notice was waiting for me. That's when I decided to get the hell out of the States. And Vancouver was the easiest place to cross the border. In fact, I couldn't even tell I'd crossed until I saw a Canadian flag near an RCMP station."

"Vietnam's been good to Canada," Giulio said. "Reversed a bit of the old brain drain."

"What about you guys?" Torp asked. "What brought the two of you together? And, more importantly, are you happy?"

Giulio and I looked at one another. I reached over and took his hand. Maybe it was the brandy or some shit like that. But at that moment, I really did feel good. And it didn't matter if he sometimes talked silly and made no sense. It didn't matter if he tossed big words around and would never come straight out with something. Like he was always hedging his bets. For a long time, I had been happy just getting out of my mother's house. Just putting my childhood behind me. Just getting rid of all that fucking useless baggage. But, now that I did think about it, I had to answer that I was happy. Maybe Giulio wasn't the kind of guy who expressed emotion easily. And he wouldn't be caught dead in the middle of a belly laugh. Or clowning around. Those things were beyond him. But I could honestly answer Torp that things were better now that the two of us were together. Sure, Giulio occasionally fell back into his old habit of thinking too much about things. Shit like the meaning of life and suicide and that kind of crap. Stuff that solved nothing and only gave a person a nasty headache. But, as long as I was around to help, I wouldn't allow it to go too far. No fucking way.

"Well," Torp said. "I can see you're a couple who should be envied."

"Are you pulling my leg?" I asked, ready for a fight.

"No, no," he said, holding out his hands. "I'm serious. It looks like you two have found what you want out of life. Me, I've been groping around blind for years and I'm still groping around blind. And right now it doesn't look good for the future either."

"Hey," I said. "You're young. You'll get it straight."

He stood up.

"Well," he said, "I think I've intruded on you guys long enough for one evening. Time to head home."

"Where's that?" I asked.

"You're not thinking of walking back to the beach," Giulio said. "That's at least two hours away."

"Hey, I'm used to it."

"No, we can't let you do that. Right, Nicole?"

Oh, oh. I knew how Giulio's mind worked.

"Well, if he has to get back, honey," I said.

"But you can ... you can stay here for tonight!" Giulio exclaimed. "I saw an old mattress—you can sleep on that." He turned to me. "Can't he, Nicole?"

"It might get a little uncomfortable," I said, feeling my teeth starting to grind.

"After you've slept on wet sand," Giulio said, "anything feels good. Right?"

"That's true," Torp said, looking first at Giulio, then at me.

"It's settled, then," Giulio said. "You'll sleep here tonight—and get back to your beach friends in the morning."

Oh shit, I said to myself. I wanted to shout out: "No! I don't want some stranger sleeping in the same house with us. I've had enough of that." I wanted to take Giulio by the throat and choke some sense into the idiot. I mean, what fucking right did he have to do something like that? But he just stood there looking at me with his stupid puppy eyes, like he'd just done his good deed for the day. His second good deed for the day.

"Yeah, sure," I said, not feeling up to a fight. "Just make yourself at home. As for me, I'm going to bed."

"Hey," Torp said. "Thanks."

"I'll be right in," Giulio said. "I'll just help Torp set up the mattress."

I lay on the sofa, listening to the two of them talk as they tried to find a spot for the mattress.

"Do you ever get involved in politics?" I heard Giulio ask.

"Politics? No fucking way, man. Politics is red tape. Power to the people is my motto. Direct power. Let the folks decide what's to be done."

I heard the sound of the table being pushed aside and the mattress plopping down. Hope they shook it first, I said to myself. Otherwise, he's going to have a few friends sharing his bed.

"Yeah," Giulio said. "But don't you think that's a bit dangerous?"

"Hey, no more dangerous than allowing the politicians to run the country."

"You're right about that." Thudding sounds. "There you go—sleeping arrangements fit for a king."

"I don't know how to thank you guys," Torp said. "I guess now I've got to change my opinion of you."

"Change your opinion? What do you mean?"

"No offence. But in class I always thought you were a tight-ass kind of guy—"

He is, I whispered, giggling. Tight as they come.

"That's okay," Giulio said. "Everyone thinks I'm that way. Mostly, I'm just shy."

"You and your wife are great. I really appreciate it."

You'd better, I said to myself. No one else would have allowed a guy like you to sleep over.

"Listen," Giulio said. "If you need to use the bathroom, just knock on the door."

"Okay—but I think I can wait until morning."

Giulio said goodnight and came into the bedroom. He was humming to himself as he undressed.

"Nicole," he said quietly as he slid in beside me, "you still awake?"

I didn't answer, hoping he'd just leave me alone. No such luck.

"Nicole."

"What!"

"I just wanted to say thanks for not getting too upset

with me tonight. If you'd caused a scene about my bringing Torp here, I wouldn't have blamed you. In fact, I thought you'd give me a much bigger fight about him. All the way home on the bus, I was preparing myself for a scene, and I was determined not to get angry no matter what you said or did. But you were very polite and nice to him."

"Are you finished?" I asked.

"Yeah, I guess."

And then he started right up again.

"I wonder how long it had been."

"How long had what been?" I asked with a sigh.

"Since he'd eaten. It must've been at least a couple of days. Did you hear his stomach rumbling as he swallowed the soup?"

"No, Giulio. I really wasn't paying much attention to his stomach."

"Well, he tried to hold it back but he let it slip out a couple of times."

"Maybe, if he got himself a job, he wouldn't have to go days on end without food."

"There are more important things than jobs—or food," Giulio said.

"Oh yeah? Like what?"

"Like—"

"Like philosophy, maybe?" I was getting a little pissed off. "That's a great stomach filler, isn't it?"

I was definitely spoiling for a fight. But Giulio wasn't taking the bait.

"I wonder what it's like to be truly hungry," he said. "Forced to eat boiled chicory plants and birch bark. Or, even more desperate, parts of yourself. Homo autophagous. Has there been a paper done on the moral implications of eating your own leg? I'll have to check it out."

"Why don't you check out the moral implications of eating your own bullshit? That's something you know about."

Jeez, now why did I say that? It was like I couldn't help myself.

"My parents are always talking about being hungry in the old country," Giulio said, as if he hadn't heard me. "Especially during the war. Trying to sneak food and hide from the Germans at the same time. But they eat so well now—pasta and steak and roast lamb and all kinds of other goodies—it's hard to believe anything like that ever took place. But Torp's hunger is unavoidable. He was right there before me. Did you see the way his hand trembled as he brought the spoon to his mouth? I got the feeling he wanted to swallow the soup all at once, to gulp the plate down as fast as it would flow down his throat. Instead, he ate politely and even took time to compliment you on it."

"What a man!" I said. "Now, can we get some sleep?"

But Giulio wouldn't let me sleep. For some reason he decided he needed to have sex. He started to rub himself against me, trying to ease himself between the cheeks of my ass.

"Giulio," I hissed, pushing away. "Stop that! I don't

feel like it tonight."

"Oh yes, you do," he said. "You always feel like it. Or at least I've never known you not to feel like it."

And I guess he was right. Soon, I was pushing back against him, allowing him to slip into me from behind. He reached around and slid his fingers down to my clit. We came together—and I had to bury my face in the pillow not to make too much noise.

"So tell me," I said, after I'd cleaned myself off. "Why is it tonight you were able to have sex with someone in the next room?"

"Wait a minute," Giulio said laughing. "I didn't have sex with someone in the next room. I had sex with you."

"Don't be a wise ass. You know what I mean."

"I don't know," he said. "I hadn't even thought about it."

"Sure, sure. The day you don't think about something is the day I'm declared a genius."

"Go to sleep," he said.

I was practically gone when I remembered the letter.

"Oh shit," I said. "You got a letter from back home. I forgot all about it. I guess it'll keep until the morning."

No. Giulio insisted on reading it right away. He just had to know, saying he was worried something was wrong.

"If there's something really wrong," I said, "they'd send a telegram. Don't you think?"

But he'd already switched the light back on.

"It's on the dresser," I said.

Giulio took the letter and went into the bathroom. He came out a few minutes later.

"You were right," he said. "Everything's fine. From my mother. She had Raf write it for her."

He handed the letter to me:

My Dear Dear Son.

How are you? We are all fine here. Your father's back hurts but will he go see a doctor? Oh no. Not him. And his back didn't stop him from making the wine. When he dies, he's going to ask St. Peter if he can make the wine in heaven. In the evening, I have to make sure he doesn't watch the news. Because then all he does is yell about the stupid separatists and why don't they learn to speak English like the rest of us. That's your father.

Your brother Raf is doing good. He just sold a house in Westmount. No, not a house. A mansion. And he says he is going to sell another one soon ('You bet—Raf!'). Me, oh I'm fine, too.

Sometimes, I cry a little when I think of you so far away. But I know Nicole is taking care of you. She is, right? And I'm so proud of you and I tell all the neighbours what a smart man you are.

Giulio, do you remember Cosmo, that

friend of yours from high school? You always said you didn't like him because he
didn't wash. Well, he died, poor man. His car
fell off the Metropolitan in the middle of the
night. Thirty feet down it went. It's so sad.

Anyway, it's getting cold now. It won't be
long before Montreal is full of snow again.
Raf tells me there's no snow in Vancouver. Is
that true? I think sometimes Raf likes to make
fun of me. Giulio, please take care of yourself.

Love, your mother.

I was about to fold the letter back in the envelope
when I noticed more writing on the other side. It was a
P.S.:

Say, Giulio. Raf here. How's it hanging?
Don't be surprised if I decide to pay you
guys a visit some time soon. Say near the end
of October or the beginning of November.
Yeah, that's right! Well, I'm thinking about
it anyways. I gotta take some of my holidays
before the end of the year—or lose them for
good. So what's it going to be: Atlantic City
or a visit to my younger but wiser brother?
Atlantic City's mighty tempting—beaches,
casinos, chicks on every street corner. On
the other hand, I only got one brother
and I've always wanted to visit Lotusland

North. Besides, if Quebec closes its borders (ha ha!), they might not let me back in from the States. Come to think of it, they might not let me back in from Vancouver either.

"Giulio," I said. "You didn't tell me your brother might be coming out here for his holidays."

"What!" he said, reaching for the letter and flipping it over.

All the blood drained from his face.

"What does he want to do that for?" he said. "I don't need him around."

"Jeez," I said. "It's your brother. Not some monster. Besides, I don't think you have anything to worry about."

"What do you mean?"

"You don't really think Raf's going to come all the way out here when he can drive down to Atlantic City, do you?"

"That's true. That's true."

The next morning, I was standing on the front lawn saying goodbye to Giulio and Torp when the landlord, lunchbox in his hand, came around the corner.

"Mr. Bedner!" Giulio said. "How are you this morning?"

"I fine," Mr. Bedner said. "Too, too fine. I smell the ocean. I see the mountains."

"And it's a beautiful morning, isn't it?" I said, squinting up at the sky.

"Vancouver fall," Mr. Bedner said. "Beautiful, yes. But rain come. Soon. And then no stop."

"This is our friend Torp," Giulio said.

"Hi," Torp said.

Mr. Bedner nodded abruptly in Torp's direction.

"I go sleep now," he said, as he turned and headed up the front steps to his house, stopping once to look back.

I saw Mrs. Bedner in the living room window, half-hidden by the red curtain. The reflection of the sun made her face glow. I waved at her but she didn't wave back—I guess she couldn't see me because of the sun. Then, Mr. Bedner himself showed up behind her. They stood there for a moment looking out before Mr. Bedner drew the curtain shut.

"Well," I said, "I'd better get busy. Mr. Bedner said I could clean out his backyard for him. Maybe next spring I'll get a garden going back there."

Giulio looked at his watch.

"Oh shit. I have to get going." He turned to Torp, patting his briefcase. "I've got your paper. I'll have a look later today."

"No rush," Torp said. "My statement on Aristotle. I think you'll find it different."

"I wouldn't expect anything less from you."

Giulio was about to walk away when he stopped.

"What are your plans for today?"

"Not sure," Torp said, pulling out a map of Vancouver. "Maybe, I'll just wander around. Scout out some locations."

"Locations?" I said, spotting a bunch of red "X" marks on the map.

"Yeah," he said, folding the map again and putting it into his pocket. "Big project coming up. Hush-hush for now. Soon all will be revealed. Powerful stuff. Should blow some people's minds."

"Is it something you need to do today?" Giulio asked.

"Why, what do you have in mind?"

I couldn't believe my ears when, out of the blue, Giulio suggested that, if Torp had nothing urgent to do, he might like to hang out. Maybe help with the shopping or something. After all, he pointed out, the two of us did have an "affinity" for supermarkets. Oh sure. I mean, all I needed was this guy following me around everywhere. Like a puppy dog or something. A puppy dog that had been dragged through the mud. And I could just imagine him in the produce section with the other housewives going out of their way to avoid him. He'd have every security guard in the place down his throat the moment he picked up a cherry, for chrissakes. I nudged Giulio but it was too late. The damage had been done.

"Yeah, sure," Torp said. "If you didn't mind. Actually, I'd love to lend a hand with the shopping. I'm very good at that."

Yeah, I bet, I said to myself. You have to be to pick out the good shit from the rotten at the bottom of a garbage can. But what the fuck could I do? I couldn't very well say: "Uh, no thanks, Torp. I've got a reputation down at the supermarket. And I don't think they'd be too happy with you copping a feel of the lettuce. But just let me know if you want to go looking for shells down at the beach. I'll be glad to come down and lend a hand." No, all I could do was smile and curse stupid old Giulio under my breath—as he walked away towards the bus stop, all puffed up with another good deed he'd just pulled off.

"Come on," I said. "We might as well have a cup of coffee before getting started."

At first, I felt kind of nervous having this guy—this stranger practically—hanging around the house. There I was, taking a shower, and he was sitting in the kitchen not twenty feet away. And wouldn't you know it—there was no way to lock the stupid bathroom door. I had to jam a piece of wood against it. Then, when I came out, I found him scribbling stuff into a blue folder. And he quickly shut it when he noticed me.

"Something important?" I asked.

"Not really," he said. "It's like my security blanket. Here, you want to see it."

"Sure. If you don't mind."

It was filled with a bunch of these silly sayings like: "Actions speak louder than words" and "Haste makes waste".

"Jeez," I said. "I don't know too much about this shit—but this doesn't sound too original."

"You're right," he said, laughing. "My motto is to keep things simple in my life. Besides, I'm here to help you with the shopping, right?—not to give you lessons in philosophy."

Thank God for that, I thought. If he had started on any of that philosophy bullshit, I think I would have thrown him out on the spot. Shit, maybe I should've anyway. It would have made things a lot simpler.

"So," he said, "are we going to shop till we drop—or what?"

It happened just like I thought it would. When the other shoppers got a load of Torp, they kind of eased away from him. Like he had some sort of contagious disease. At first, I felt embarrassed to be seen with him. Especially as he was so enthusiastic and loud, pointing out sales and items being cleared at low prices. But then I started to notice that he was really good at what he did, that he really knew what the real bargains were and how to test for good fruit and shit like that. That's when I decided: *Screw it! I'm going to be just like him—and not give a shit about these losers.*

And I was kind of sorry to see Torp go when the shopping was done. I invited him back to the house but he said he had things to do.

"Otherwise," he said, "my friends might think I've gone over to the other side."

"The other side? What other side?"

"The side of decency and manicured lawns."

"Oh, that side," I said, trying to decide if I'd been insulted.

"Anyway," he said, as he started to walk away down the street, "I'll probably see you again sometime."

"Yeah, sure. And thanks for helping with the shopping.

That was great."

"It's nothing," he said. "Spent two years at a Safeway checkout in Seattle. Anyway, you'd better get inside now before the rain starts."

I started to walk away. Then, I stopped and almost called out for Torp to forget about his friends and have supper with us again. But I chickened out at the last moment. Who knows. He might have taken it the wrong way.

TWO
GIULIO

For moral excellence is concerned with pleasures and pains;
it is on account of the pleasure that we do bad things,
and on account of the pain that we abstain from noble ones.

—*Nicomachean Ethic*s,
Book 2, Chapter 3

On the bus to the university, I took the opportunity to take a peek at Torp's "paper." I knew from the title—*Anarchy: The Only Natural Condition*—that it wasn't going to be your usual discussion of Aristotelian logic. And I was right. Inside the plastic folder were several newspaper clippings ("Pinkville Incident to be Investigated," "FLQ Releases Manifesto"), some fragments of glass glued to a cardboard cereal box, and, in a separate plastic bag, what looked like a piece of dried flattened-out dog turd. The "paper" itself consisted of a set of equations: "Patriarchy + Coverup = Crap; Crap = Anarchy; Anarchy = Freedom; Ergo, Patriarchy + Coverup = Freedom (Eventually)." The professor's not going to like this, I said to myself. It seemed childish, almost a prank. At the same time, there was a tradition in skepticism that said the search for knowledge was destined to be a fruitless one.

I had just replaced the folder in my briefcase when the bus screeched to a halt. I looked out the window. There was shattered glass and office equipment all over the sidewalks and streets. And some people were walking around as if they were stunned while others just sat on the curb with their heads down. I could hear ambulance and fire truck sirens as they converged on the area from all directions. Police cars had blocked off many of the streets, slowing and diverting traffic. Men in yellow plastic suits and oversized rubber boots had already started to check over the rubble, here and there picking up little pieces and examining them. Just like archaeologists. I gathered this was only the latest in a series of bomb blasts in the Vancouver area, blasts that until now had caused a lot of property damage but no serious injuries. Scrawled in dripping black paint on a nearby wall was the word: PFRG. The Pro-Form Radicals For The Good, according to letters written to the newspapers claiming responsibility. But just who these guys were, no one seemed to know. It was certainly an unusual name for a terrorist group. And what they were fighting for also wasn't very clear.

I gathered there was some sort of battle going on— Native rights, jobless rights, logging rights, fishing rights, student rights. Maybe all five. The only battle I knew that wasn't raging out here was for language rights. That was imported from another country, something those "crazy Kebekers" out east fought about. But it looked like these battles were becoming just as vicious and dangerous. And everyone said it was only a matter of time before someone did get hurt. I hadn't understood what the fuss had been back in Quebec, and I didn't understand any of it any better now. It all seemed so senseless and petty. As if blowing up a few buildings and killing a few people would make any difference. As to who was in the right and who at fault, that to me was like trying to untangle one of Kant's moral parables: the deeper you got into it, the more confused you became. Until, in the end, you just opted for the simplest solution. Shoot the guy as he comes rushing through the front door looking for sanctuary. That solves everything, I guess. No, I still believed what my father had told me in one of his rare moments of expansiveness: "Son, remember what happened to Mussolini. He was a great man who tried to pull the Italian people up by their bootstraps, and what did he get for his troubles? He got himself hung by his own bootstraps. Whatever you do, son, never ever get involved in politics." Don't worry, Dad. I'll try not to.

A policeman directed the bus around the barriers. Then, it picked up speed again and soon I couldn't see any trace of the damage behind me.

"What a bloody waste of time," my colleague Pamela Goodall said, when I mentioned the latest bombing to her. "If you want my advice, you shouldn't be concerning yourself with that kind of shit. It's all a load of bollocks. What's important is the new job posting in the philosophy office."

Pamela was the department's other assistant lecturer, and we shared an office. She'd just come over from England, and she liked to point out how easygoing and relaxed things were here compared to her previous posting.

"It was sodding intense," she told me one day. "Like the first thing they did back there was to sharpen their blades. Not that it doesn't happen in this department. But you needn't worry yourself about that, di Orio. Right now, nothing's going to happen to us because we don't exist, you see. We don't count. At least not yet. You'll know you're important when that first blade is aimed your way. But I don't plan to have that happen to me. No bleeding way. I'm going to make sure I strike first. Pre-emptive strike. Sodding right."

I was confused. Was this the way offices were supposed to work? And, even so, weren't philosophers supposed to be different? Weren't they supposed to be above that sort of thing? Weren't their minds set on the higher planes of being, trying to discover the Unmoved Prime Mover, teleological proofs for the existence of a perfect creator, what is matter, reality, appearance, morality, etc.? It came as quite a shock to discover that professors of philosophy also hung around the water cooler, eavesdropping on conversations and waiting their chance to stick the knife in.

"Come on," Pamela said. "Let's go see that job posting."

We walked over to the posting board. A full lecturer's position had come open, and they were looking to fill it from within.

"He just up and quit," Pamela said, back in the office. "Can you believe it? Barely lasted a month before he packed it in. Word is he signed on to crew on a cruise ship to Alaska. Or maybe it was off to explore the bird sanctuaries of Micronesia. Now, isn't that a romantically ballsy—and utterly stupid—thing to do? Are you going to apply?"

I shrugged—and ducked my head, pretending to examine the papers I'd started marking in the morning.

"Well, you can fucking well bet I am. I didn't spend six sodding years memorizing sodding categorical imperatives for the fun of it. No sir. Not me." She laughed and puckered her lips, making kissing sounds. "Shit, I've got to practice my ass-kissing techniques. They're a little rusty."

That evening, as I walked across the front lawn towards the door of my flat, Mr. Bedner suddenly came out of his house to intercept me. He didn't look in very good shape. His eyes were bloated, his face all puffed up and his hands shaking.

"Giulio, yes," Mr. Bedner said, smiling awkwardly, while at the same time looking back and forth between me and Mrs. Bedner whom I'd suddenly spotted in the window. "Something to say to you."

"What is it, Mr. Bedner?"

"I wait all day," he said. "I no sleep. I no want to miss you. You understand?"

I didn't really, but I nodded anyway. Simpler that way.

"Important," Mr. Bedner whispered. "Very important."

He rubbed his eyes and glanced furtively towards the window of my flat. I looked as well, to see if anything was amiss. But everything seemed in order. The curtain had been drawn back and the bed had been converted to a sofa again.

"The rent?" I said. But that couldn't be it. It wasn't anywhere near the first of the month.

"No rent," he said. "This too, too important."

"Is it something to do with Nicole and me?" I asked. "Something we're doing to disturb you?"

"No, no." He shook his head vigorously. "No trouble.

Good tenants, you and wife. Very fine, very clean. No trouble. Too, too good tenants."

Well, that was nice to hear. But I didn't know what else to say, really, when Mr. Bedner suddenly stepped up closer to me and gripped my arm. I winced. It was a strong grip for a man his age, the kind of grip that would leave a neat blue mark if held for long. And he was now close enough so I could tell he'd been drinking. More of that homemade plum brandy.

"Who strange fellow?" Mr. Bedner asked. "In morning? Strange fellow with dirty hair like no good bum?"

"That's no strange fellow," I said, laughing. "Or maybe he is in some ways. Not to worry, Mr. Bedner. He's just a student of mine. He means no harm."

But, instead of calming Mr. Bedner down, that only served to get him more worked up.

"No student," he whispered harshly. "Devil!"

As Mr. Bedner said this, he looked around as if a horde of malevolent spirits was hovering nearby, just waiting to pounce.

"Devil?" I said. "What are you—?"

"He stay today," Mr. Bedner said. "In house. All morning. Then him, your wife, they go."

I tried to explain that I had asked Torp to remain behind so he could help Nicole do the grocery shopping. Mr. Bedner's grip tightened and his face flamed red.

"You ask?" he said, eyes wide. "You?"

"Mr. Bedner," I said, by this point getting more than a little fed up. "There is nothing wrong with that. Besides being a student of mine, he's also a friend. Look. Nicole sometimes gets lonely staying all day in the house by herself. She needs someone to talk to once in a while."

"Talk!" Mr. Bedner exclaimed. "Satan no talk. Satan trick. Pull down to hell."

He pointed downwards between his feet. I glanced at the spot but saw only lush grass that needed a trim.

"Mr. Bedner," I said, trying to be patient. "Torp—"

"Torp!" he said, shaking even harder. "What name that? No name. More like sign. Of devil."

"It's just the name he goes by," I said. "A name he likes to call himself. It's not his real name."

"Aha! Real name Beelzebub, yes. *Teufel. Szatan.*"

I tried to interject, to explain once more that he was just a poor student down on his luck.

"See!" Mr. Bedner said, pointing at Mrs. Bedner in the window. "My wife fear. Very much, she fear. Hands shake when she see. Like leaf in wind. Like this."

He held out one of his hands and made it tremble like he imagined a leaf in the wind would. By now, I had given up trying to talk sense and simply kept nodding my head. All I wanted to do was to get away from him. But that seemed to make Mr. Bedner even more passionate and incoherent.

"When my wife fear," Mr. Bedner said hoarsely, "we all fear. She fear little. No rats. No snakes. No people—no fear even dirty Commie reds. Only devil, she fear. She know things. Many things. Listen!"

"I'm listening, Mr. Bedner."

Suddenly, his stubby finger jabbed at my chest. "You good boy. Nice boy. Friends, you, me. My wife she know. Tell your wife. Lock up cookies."

"Lock up cookies?" I said, scratching my head.

"Yes!" Mr. Bedner said. "Or he steal. The devil steal."

"Sure, Mr. Bedner. I'll tell her to lock them up. I'll see to it right away."

"Good, I sleep now."

Mr. Bedner glanced once more at the basement window, then turned and walked slowly up his steps. I watched him disappear into the house and saw the slow drawing of the curtains by Mrs. Bedner. Then I shrugged and continued to my own door, thinking: "Oh, oh. Mr. Bedner seems to have dropped a few of his marbles."

When I told Nicole what Mr. Bedner had said to me, she laughed and said I'd probably misunderstood.

"Most of the time, I only get half of what he's trying to say."

"I don't think so," I said. "He seems really upset about the fact we allowed Torp to sleep over last night. And he kept saying that I should make sure you keep the cookie jar locked up."

"He's probably worried Torp will steal his old country valuables," she said. "I mean, I had the same kinds of thoughts about him when I first saw him. He doesn't exactly inspire a lot of confidence, does he?"

I had to admit he didn't. I was about to start in on how you can't go by appearances when Nicole beat me to the punch.

"But I gotta tell you," she said. "He's a great shopper. I think he saved me about ten dollars today. He's got a real nose for finding the best products at the cheapest price. On our budget, that's a godsend."

"So," I said, ever so slyly, "you won't get mad if I invite him over again for supper?"

"Funny," she said, "I was going to suggest the same thing. When?"

"Well, I was thinking tomorrow evening. There's something he wants to discuss with me."

"Sounds good. We'll do pasta. Just like your mother makes."

"I just hope Mr. Bedner doesn't go into his devil routine again."

"Hey," she said, "I like Mr. Bedner. He's a nice guy. But he can't tell us who we can have in our flat."

The next day I approached Torp after class, and he agreed to come over. When the two of us entered, the kitchen window was steamed up from the boiling water, filling the flat with a feeling of warmth and generosity. I sat across from Torp, admiring the way he'd managed, on one hand, to avoid being bogged down in "the deadly dull of daily life" and, on the other, how he'd kept a safe distance from those twin pits I so feared and loathed: introspection and loneliness. Thanks to his example, I could see myself, superhuman, walking boldly between the two fierce monsters that had haunted me and threatened to make my life a slaughtering ground for hope.

As if taking up the general drift of my thought, something akin to my spirit (or what I would imagine it to be) suddenly pulled itself away, floating up to sit cross-legged and Buddha-like just above the table. I watched Torp twirling the pasta awkwardly; I watched Nicole leaning over to show him how it was really done; I watched the eyes of my spirit as they sparkled. My humble home had become a wayfarers' inn, with the lantern in the kitchen window, offering aid and comfort to the creatures of the night. And to those of the day as well: for weren't those the remaining members of my family—mother, father, brother—come a full three thousand miles to sit at my table (suddenly grown large), to smile radiantly at one another, glad to be reunited on this occasion of no great feast but of general happiness? To pat me on the back, congratulate me for my good fortune, my choice of home, wife, job? For my intelligence and my good nature?

I cursed myself for never having seen them in this light before, for having made them the reflections of malevolence. My spirit blushed mightily as I thought back to that night when the job letter from the university had arrived and my mother had insisted on reading it first, that kindness I had taken for perversity. My mother had just wanted to siphon what she thought was bad news through herself, to take some of the poison out of it. Besides, it had turned out to be good news. All the evils to which I had felt subjected suddenly seemed less than calamitous. They were only trying to be helpful, to toughen me up. I, in my blindness, had refused their help or twisted it around.

I had, in particular, misunderstood the intentions of my father whose only wish, in his taciturnity and uncommunicativeness, was to show me the nature of the world outside his cool walls, was for me to become a man as soon as possible. And my brother. Why, now that I looked more closely and they were sitting side by side rubbing shoulders, trading beach stories and occasionally blending into one another, Torp and my brother resembled twins. Or was Torp a younger version of my father? My mother? Nicole? The conversation turned to street survival: where to find food, shelter, clothes, how to protect yourself from young punks, when to—

"Giulio," Nicole said, tapping my hand with her fork. "Your pasta's getting cold. Is something wrong with it?"

Not so much Nicole's voice but the quick shutting and re-opening of my eyes caused both the family and the spirit to vanish. From past experience—I used to indulge in these exercises while deep in Aristotelian logic or Platonic dialogue—I knew it was no use trying to get them back. They always returned in distorted form or as negative afterglows.

"No," I said, pouring myself the last of the wine. "It's fine. I guess I just let myself wander off for a moment."

"That's not unusual," Nicole said. She turned towards Torp: "Before Giulio met me, you know what he did?" Torp shook his head. "He used to spend all his time locked inside a tiny room and thinking deeply, as he put it. Not for a second would he allow himself to be happy."

"Not for a moment?" Torp said. "Is that true?"

"Unfortunately," I said, "it is."

"I'll never forget the first time I saw him," Nicole said. "A birthday party for your brother, wasn't it?" I nodded. "Well, he had the gloomiest expression I'd ever seen on man or monkey. And everyone else around him was having shitloads of fun. Dancing, drinking, making out. I said to myself: 'Jeez, I'm not asking him to start belly-laughing and acting like a clown. But at least he could smile.' I taught him how."

"When we got married," I said, "I told Nicole that, at last, I'd found something more powerful than all that stupid deep thinking and brooding."

"He'd found you," Torp said.

"I had," I said. "And that was the end of my tiny room filled with lonely thoughts."

"That's interesting," Torp said, mopping up the last of his pasta. "I had the same choice and ended up going in the opposite direction."

"And have you fallen into any pits?" Nicole asked.

"Pits?"

"Yeah, you know. When a person thinks too much, he sort of, you know, gets caught up, you know—"

"I think I see what you mean. Like suicide and all that crap. Absurdity, the quest for meaning in life, metaphysical rebellion, the impossibility of obtaining any answers worth obtaining to questions worth asking?"

Torp startled me. The words he'd used so lightly and freely, throwing them aside like dead and gutted insects, had been the very subjects of my long-discarded brooding, icons I once worshipped so dearly. Especially when all my dreams were of becoming the hermit monk in the desert, St. Simeon Stylites.

"Yeah," Nicole said. "That kind of crap. Does it bother you?"

"Nope," he said, patting his stomach. "I've developed an immunity to it."

"An immunity?" I asked.

"You mean like a vaccine or something," Nicole said.

"Yeah, you might call it that. I like to call it life. I find that, when you're forced to sleep on a beach and eat what others toss out, you ain't got much time to brood about the so-called higher mysteries of living."

"Fucking right!" Nicole said, pumping a fist and opening up the second bottle of wine by pushing the cork into it. "Shit, we've got to get ourselves a corkscrew one of these days."

For dessert, Nicole had a special treat: canned peaches smothered in ice cream. The only thing I liked better was fresh strawberries and whipped cream. But I made one mistake. One fatal mistake. I ate the whole thing too fast and, before I knew it, my teeth were aching. And, from past experience, I knew the ache would last at least for the rest of the night and would probably spread to fill my entire mouth.

"You should chew on an aspirin," Torp suggested. "I have a friend who swears by those things. He pops them in like that guy in that movie."

"Perry Smith," Nicole said. "*In Cold Blood*. I really

cried when I saw that movie. Especially the ending where they're hanging him and it's raining and the raindrops get all mixed up with his tears. Speaking of which, maybe we should go see a movie tonight. We haven't been to a movie since we've been out here."

I thought that was a great idea. But I could hardly concentrate with the throbbing in my mouth.

"A shot of brandy might do the trick," Torp said. "You swirl it gently around the mouth to deaden the nerve endings. It's always worked for me."

Nicole poured me half a glassful, and I swished it around my gums and teeth.

"How's the brandy doing?" Torp asked a few moments later. "It should have kicked in by now."

The throbbing was still there.

"Listen," I said, "maybe I'll just go lie down for a while. If I feel better afterwards, the three of us could go to that movie together."

I guess the brandy started kicking in after all because I managed to doze off. And I might have slept all night if Nicole hadn't tapped me on the shoulder.

"Giulio, dear," she said. "We've found a movie."

"Yeah," Torp said, standing behind her. "*The Adventurers*. Lots of moral dilemmas—and plenty of action, too."

"You two go ahead," I said, pushing a fist against my jaw. "I couldn't enjoy myself with this toothache anyway. You know how I get with pain. I'd just make things miserable for everyone else."

"Well, in that case," Torp said. "Maybe it's best if I head on home and leave you in peace."

"No, no," I said. "You must stay. I insist. It's your duty to stay. Nicole just hates going to movies by herself. Don't you, Nicole?"

"I can't stand it," Nicole said. "It makes me feel all sad and lonely."

"Well," Torp said, "if you put it that way .... What the hell! My friends can wait another few hours."

"That's the spirit!" I exclaimed.

Nicole kissed me on the forehead; Torp patted me on the back. Then, the two of them left. Lucky stiffs, I told myself, all pain-free. As for me, I'll continue to stare out the window, this 18- by 10-inch vision of the world outside. It's important that I concentrate with every fibre in my body. It's important that I try to understand intellectually the nature of pain, the way a physical blow can also cripple the mind and leave it utterly dysfunctional. And vice versa, although that's something I've never experienced. I think back on the saints and their myriad tortures. Turn me over, I'm done. Stick a hot poker where it hurts the most. Bless me, but I'm not only a saint but a virgin as well and if you shove that broom handle where you're intending to shove it, well .... Isn't it wonderful how a reflecting upon cosmic ills—no matter how far removed—can help put personal pain behind you? At least for a few moments. Because the mere thinking upon the personal pain brings it back full force, doesn't it?

As I looked out, who should fill my window but the

landlord, good old Mr. Bedner. At first, he was nothing but a pair of unconnected legs, then the rest of him came into view, red-eyed and puffy as he stooped down in search of weeds. The sight of him recalled our conversation. At this point, my toothache took over the debate, its pulses like binary signals controlling my thoughts: on one side, the idea that what Mr. Bedner had said was just talk, and silly talk at that, the kind of superstition naive, uneducated peasants carry with them to the grave, never understanding that the world has passed them by, leaving them in a rut where they circle like stubborn mules till they drop from weariness; on the other, the idea that feelings are more important than logic, that certain psychics can sense things, understand the inner meaning, the underlying essence behind the world of appearance. And I thought about Torp and how appearance can be deceiving. Can even mask the essence within.

On one of his stoops, Mr. Bedner noticed me on the sofa and waved. I waved back, not wishing to seem impolite. Mr. Bedner then took hold of a huge milkweed plant that had fastened itself against the base of the wall. He yanked with both hands and the plant burst out of the ground, roots and all. Clinging to the clumps of earth was a writhing night crawler, immense, a splotch of dark red against the dull brown of the rest of it, swinging desperately in the air, trying to find some way back to the safety from which it had been so unexpectedly pried. But it never got the chance as Mr. Bedner plucked it from the roots and tossed it on to the sidewalk—where its fate would be to dry out and then to be swept away by the street cleaner. Mr. Bedner threw the plant aside, rubbed his hands together and disappeared from view.

A few moments later, there was a knock on the front door. I got myself up, pain and all, to answer it.

"Mr. Bedner!" I said. "What brings you—Come in, come in. Please."

"No time," Mr. Bedner said, swinging his lunch box. "Go work soon."

"Yes," I said. "It must be terrible going to work when others are just settling down for bed."

"Wife, she go out?" he said, looking about the bedroom.

"Yes, Mr. Bedner. She went to a movie. Being cooped up in the house all the time isn't good, you know. I would've liked to go too but I've got this terrible—"

"With that Trop guy?" Mr. Bedner said, cutting me off. "Both go?"

"Yes, Mr. Bedner, and his name's Torp," I said, hoping there was an edge to my voice. "Now, is there anything I can do for you?"

"My wife, she right."

"Right about what?"

"I no believe," Mr. Bedner said, shaking his head. "I no believe."

"What don't you believe, Mr. Bedner?"

"She see, yes. My wife see. And you—you allow?"

"I wish I knew what you were talking about, Mr. Bedner. It's perfectly legal in this country for me to choose the friends I want and for my wife to go out with whomever she pleases."

"But this Torb. Bad smell. How you say it? *Czlowiek obey*. Strangler, yes?"

"Strangler? You mean a person who chokes others?"

I made choking motions with his hands.

"Chokes?" Mr. Bedner said. "No, no. Stranger, I mean. Torb a stranger."

"Oh, a stranger," I said. "First of all, the name's Torp and Torp's a friend—not a strangler ... stranger. Secondly, Mr. Bedner, I understand your concern—and it's appreciated. Believe me. Very much appreciated. But right now I have a horrible toothache that's getting worse by the minute and I really can't stand here—"

I held my hand against my face and grimaced.

"Yes, yes. Sorry. I go now."

Mr. Bedner backed up, apologizing, and then turned to vanish down the suddenly dark street. At the same time, the light in his living room, which had cast a long shadow across the lawn, went out.

I pulled open the sofa, slipped between the sheets and, thanks to the alcohol and pills, quickly fell asleep.

By morning, my toothache had subsided, and I was able to see the world again without the blur of pain like a jagged red stripe across it. As I lay in bed, I could hear Nicole humming in the kitchen. Then laughter. Hm, I said to myself, she must have read something funny. But no. When I threw open the bedroom door, there were Nicole and Torp sitting at the table.

"Hey," I said. "What a surprise!"

"Torp walked me home," Nicole said, getting up and giving me a hug. "It was late. So I told him to stay."

"Great," I said.

"How's the toothache?" Torp asked.

"So far, so good," I said. "Just have to be careful with the hot and cold."

"Isn't it a fantastic day?" Nicole said. "Sunny for once."

"And Saturday, to boot," I said, sitting down.

After breakfast, during which I made sure to avoid extremes, Nicole suggested that Torp and I should go out to enjoy the last of the good weather before the winter rains came. She wanted us out of the house in any case as she was going to give it a thorough cleaning. I don't need those nasty spiders getting a foothold in the place again, she said.

"Good idea," Torp said. "And I know exactly where to go. Kill two birds with one stone."

That's how Torp and I ended up spending the day at Stanley Park, the second most talked-about spot in Vancouver next to the mountains. Torp, acting as tourist guide, gave me the highlights: the roadside art exhibits, many of which had been set up by his friends; the statues of founding fathers and lost explorers; the clowns and other performing artists; the lagoon reputed to be bottomless.

As Torp spoke, something suddenly rose up out of the cattails around the lagoon's edge. At first, it looked like some type of animal. But it turned out to be a man, huddled in an oversized ski jacket, ripped down the sides with some of the stuffing hanging out. He stumbled towards us, zigzagging till he stood swaying in front of us.

"Hey man," he said, looking at me. "Don't I know you?"

"I don't think so," I said, holding my breath as the odour wafted from him.

"Yeah," he said grinning, revealing huge gaps between teeth. "You're the man on the moon."

"If you say so," I said, hoping to speed him along.

"Do you know how old I am?" he shouted, twirling on one leg.

"Be cool, man," Torp said. "You don't want the fuzz showing up."

"Yeah. Shh!" he said looking around and placing a finger to his nose. Then he whispered: "Twenty-two. Can you believe it?"

"That's cool," Torp said. "But we've got to move along. Take care."

"Yeah," he said. "I dig it. Appointments to keep. Places to be."

"You got it," Torp said.

"Listen, man," he said. "Got any change? I need to call my mother."

Torp held out his hands to indicate he didn't have any money on him. I searched my pockets and pulled out a dollar bill and a few coins.

"Here," I said, dropping the money into his

outstretched palm. "Go make that phone call."

"Thanks, man," he said, stumbling off towards his next victim. "If you ever need anything, let me know. I'll be there for you. I'll be fucking there."

"Glad to hear it," I said.

"You've made a friend forever," Torp said.

We walked through the forested part of the park, an area thick with underbrush that provided a certain amount of privacy for the beach beyond it. Then we broke out sweaty and tired to the roar of the ocean. There were sailboats in the distance and a mist-enshrouded bridge that seemed to hang in the air, that seemed to be only half there. The beach itself was more slimy rock than sand, littered with broken bits of shell and seaweed. Lining it was a massive seawall.

"Home," Torp said. "And there's the family now."

Torp pointed to a group of young men and women who had formed a circle further down the beach. Those not in the circle were busy collecting driftwood and spreading the pieces out to dry on the sand.

"Come on!" Torp shouted.

He ran up and greeted each with a yell and a handshake that looked like the start of an arm-wrestling match. I stood back, ready to be introduced. I wasn't, and it took me several seconds to realize no introductions were necessary. All I needed was a similar handshake. That handshake, however, was beyond me. The others tightened their circle. One of the women, wearing nothing but a pair of rolled-up pants and bra, was framing each separate piece of wood with her hands. I edged forward to listen to their conversation.

"The name's important," Torp said. "It has to catch the eye. Otherwise, people won't even pick it up."

"How about 'Driftwood'?" the woman in the bra said. "Picked clean to the bone?"

"Not bad," one of the men said. "But it's like too ... too hippie. People will think it's a beachcomber mag. Or some shit like that. They won't take it seriously. And we want to be taken seriously. Right?"

"Fucking right!" the entire circle yelled out.

"*A Journal of Universal Ethics*," I suggested.

Everyone turned to look at me, as if seeing me for the first time. I smiled weakly. "I guess that's a bit too pretentious."

"Yes, rather," Torp said with an upper-class British accent. "The white man's burden and all that."

The others laughed and then turned back. I moved further away so that I could no longer hear them. The woman resumed her driftwood framing. I stared through the frame. It may have been the noon sun—but the pieces started to move, to vibrate, as if they were being energized. The illusion was destroyed by a large, iridescent beetle crawling over the surface of the wood. I rubbed my eyes, which had started to water. The beetle loosened its wings for a moment, all red and black, and then lost itself in a deep crack. Torp now had his arm around the bra woman and they passed a joint back and forth, laughing sharply. The others were also laughing—or playfully tossing sand at one another. I spotted the beetle as it re-emerged and headed out towards the water's edge. It whirred away as a wave splashed against the shoreline. Torp came over and squatted down next to me.

"Listen, man," he said. "Thanks for everything, you know. That's really great what you and Nicole have done for me."

"What are you talking about?" I said. "We haven't done anything."

"No, no. Listen. You've been good to me. Now, I want to be good to you—by not coming back with you."

"I don't understand," I said.

"Don't make any sudden moves," Torp said. "You see that guy standing on top of the seawall?"

I kept my head straight while glancing sideways. I nodded. The man had a pair of binoculars and was looking out at the ocean. Or so it seemed.

"That guy's a cop," Torp said. "An undercover cop. They've been keeping an eye on us. I know that, if I come back with you, he's going to follow me. And then you'll get into trouble, too. I don't want that to happen. So I'm just going to stay here, at least for now. And you go on home. Maybe I'll see you in a couple of days."

Nicole was disappointed when I went home without Torp. She said she was getting used to having him around. Besides, he was a lot of fun. I had to agree with her. And there seemed to be something missing that evening at dinner. The two of us just sat there glumly, picking at our food. Things didn't improve much when there was a knock on the door that led to the other part of the basement.

"You answer that," Nicole said. "I'm going to the bathroom."

It was, of course, Mr. Bedner. Oh God, I said to myself, not another of his harangues.

"Mr. Bedner!" I said, smiling. "What a surprise. And no, Torp isn't here. Would you care to come in?"

"Not here?" he said, stepping in. "Good, good." He looked around. "And Nicole? Not with him, I hope."

"No, Mr. Bedner," Nicole said, coming out of the bathroom.

"Good, good," he said.

"So what brings you here at this time of night?" I asked.

"Walls," Mr. Bedner said, a serious look on his face. "You have noise in walls. Yes? Scratch, scratch."

"Yes," Nicole said. "Plenty of scratch, scratch."

"Mice," Mr. Bedner said. He turned to me. "You come. I show."

We stepped into the unfinished part of the basement. He switched on a flashlight and aimed it at one of the walls. There were small holes in the drywall.

"Mice," he said again loudly.

Then he leaned towards me and gripped my arm. I turned away. His breath smelled of newly-dug earth; his nose was ripe with blackheads that seemed about to burst; his yellow eyes were filled with mucus.

"Really not there?" he whispered.

"See for yourself," I said.

"No, no. I believe," he whispered. "Good, good. I happy man. Wife happy, too." Then more loudly as Nicole appeared at the door: "I go now. Wife, she wait."

"We can't have that," Nicole said.

"I get traps, okay," he said. "I get good traps. Snap! Eek-eek!"

And he disappeared up the stairs. Nicole and I looked at each other—and we burst out laughing.

"Snap!" she said, her hands around my neck. "I got you!"

"Eek-eek-eeeek!" I said, letting my tongue hang out the side of my mouth. "Devil mice dead dead dead!"

The next morning, an ambulance pulled up in front of the house. Nicole and I stood outside watching as Mrs. Bedner was taken away on a stretcher. Nicole went over to ask Mr. Bedner what had happened, but he just turned away and closed the door behind him. We only found out later—and then through the milkman—just how serious Mrs. Bedner's condition had been: she was dead.

"Poor poor man," Nicole said. "It must be awful. Maybe someone should go up to console him. Why don't you go see if there's anything he needs?"

I had a few moments before heading off to classes, so I decided to pay him a visit. But, though the living room curtain was wide open and I could see him standing there, he either couldn't or wouldn't answer the door. I leaned over to knock on the window but I just couldn't get his attention.

He kept staring out, and acting like he couldn't see.

"Poor fucker," Nicole said when I told her what had happened. "It's obvious he lived for her alone. What the fuck is he going to do now? I remember what happened to my own grandfather after my grandmother died. It wasn't even a month before we were back up there for his funeral. We've got to pay our respects."

I tried to persuade her that I wasn't sure "paying our respects" was a good idea. After all, we weren't relatives or anything like that. But Nicole insisted, he'd treated us like family, she said. At least at the beginning. She found out from a neighbour where and when the body was being shown. It was one of those funeral parlours that's divided into a series of rooms which can be made smaller or larger with folding doors on tracks. Mrs. Bedner, with only a dozen or so others gathered, was in one of the smaller cubicles. Although there were several mourners who resembled Mr. Bedner in an uncanny way, the landlord himself didn't put in an appearance. I was glad of that as I could just picture him starting to harangue us in front of his dead wife. As it was, I found it hard to endure the sight of her in the half-opened casket, grown suddenly younger because of her paleness and makeup and the process of embalming.

I had often imagined my parents' death—in my fantasies, they always died together—but it hadn't been like this. Things were too still. As I constructed it, there had always been a twitching in the bodies, a feeling that if one said the right words, the proper incantation, the two of them would rise again with a wan smile and ask for a glass of homemade. Or demand to read my mail. Or make fun of my inability to dance. Or put the sauce on. Here, there was only stillness and whispers. I knew I wouldn't get an answer. Nevertheless, there was no harm in trying. So, as I stood over her coffin, I whispered her name under my breath. Ah, strands of her hair moved! Floated lightly into the air. No, it was only a ladybug, wings spotted red and black, emerging from beneath her hair and crawling along her forehead. I tried saying her name backwards. Nothing. But perhaps that wasn't her real name, her secret name. The bug slithered into her left nostril before quickly emerging again. I wanted to flick it away but feared the move might be misinterpreted. The others who filed by either didn't notice it or were reacting in the same way.

No one offered a reason for her death. From what I could gather, for most of them spoke in the same cryptic manner as the landlord, it (whatever disease it was) had been working on her throughout her life, eating away from the inside like some voracious animal till the outer shell of skin and bone collapsed under its own weight. I had always pictured her as only half-there and even the half-covering of her body in the casket was in keeping with this. On my way out of the funeral parlour, I noticed several more ladybugs flitting along the walls. Maybe they were part of the ceremony, a Biblical reminder. Or used to keep maggots at bay. I had read somewhere that ladybugs are voracious carnivores. And that, given the chance, they'll even eat their own young.

"Did you see them?" I asked Nicole once we were back home.

"What are you talking about?" Nicole said. "What was I supposed to see?"

"The ladybugs," I said with a shudder. "One right there in the casket, crawling right alongside the body. And some more climbing the walls."

"No, I didn't see them," Nicole said, looking at me in a strange way. "Are you alright?" She placed her hand on my forehead. "You're not coming down with something, are you?"

"I saw them," I insisted.

"Okay, okay," Nicole said. "So you fucking saw them. It's possible. They might have flown in while the door was open. Why not?"

We sat at the kitchen table for a while, not saying anything.

"They did a good job on the body," Nicole said at last. "I really hate it when they don't shut the eyes properly, you know. That really grosses me out. And they left her mouth open just a little bit—that made it look like she was still breathing."

"I always wonder about the clothes myself," I said. "Do they dress the body completely or just put on the part that shows?"

"Yeah—and the shoes. You never know about the shoes. I bet you they switch them if they're new. I bet they have a pile of old shoes from the cremated bodies."

Nicole stood up and walked over to look out the window. I continued to sit at the kitchen table, drumming my fingers along the top. Once again, we'd run out of things to say. When did this start happening?

"Stop that," Nicole said.

"Stop what?"

"Stop drumming on the table."

"Sorry," I said. And continued tapping my leg instead.

Nicole decided at the last moment she didn't want to attend the burial, so I went by myself. Mr. Bedner was there this time, being held up by two of the men from the funeral parlour. I was once again struck by the resemblance—they had to be relatives, I thought. Most likely the brothers who were building Mr. Bedner's shower stall. In fact, they might have passed for triplets if it weren't for a noticeable difference in age, with Mr. Bedner the youngest of the three. He looked at me only once during the burial, and that was at the moment they were lowering the coffin. I looked back at him but didn't know what would be most appropriate: a sad smile, a nod of my head or a gentle shaking motion perhaps. Should I remain absolutely still and let my eyes do the talking or should I go over to him and firmly shake his hand? In the end, I did none of these things, as the landlord chose that moment, with chunks of earth bouncing off the casket, to unleash a flood of tears. They slid down the natural grooves of his face and he sobbed.

"Irena, Irena," he cried out—and lurched forward towards the open grave. "Sorry, sorry, my love."

The two men tightened their grip on him. One of them leaned over and whispered something in his ear. Mr. Bedner straightened up, took out a handkerchief from his back pocket and blew his nose loudly.

When I returned from the burial, I caught the whiff of an odour I hadn't noticed before.

"I don't smell a thing," Nicole said. "Unless you're talking about that musty stuff. It's all the rain around here. Sometimes I feel like I'm in a boat or something. A fucking ark with just me and the mice."

But it didn't smell like must to me. More like putrefaction. Something dead and decaying. I took off my jacket and began to examine the entire flat: the cupboards, the kitchen sink, the bathroom, beneath the mats and carpets. I found nothing except for the hollowed-out shells of insects.

"Maybe you're looking on the wrong side of the basement," Nicole said. "There's enough garbage over there to have it declared a bloody dump."

I checked the other side. But I knew right away the smell didn't come from there. As for the mousetraps Mr. Bedner had set up, they were empty, although several had been triggered.

And then suddenly the smell was gone—only to come back so strong in the middle of the night it woke me up. In the end, Nicole started to get upset with me and said I was imagining it and that maybe, between the ladybugs and the smell, I should have my head examined. That's when I decided not to mention it anymore. But it was there. In the air. Lingering.

And it was still there several days later when, while Nicole and I were about to sit down for supper, there was a timid knock at the front door. I looked out the window.

"It's Mr. Bedner," I whispered.

"Well, let him in. He's getting soaked out there."

"Mr. Bedner," I said, pulling open the door. "Come in, come in. Long time no see."

I stepped back into the flat but Mr. Bedner just stood there in the rain.

"Mr. Bedner," Nicole called out behind me, "please come in for a moment."

"No," he said, shaking his head. "You come upstairs. Both. We talk."

Nicole said we could talk just as well in our flat—and maybe he'd have some supper with us. But Mr. Bedner was adamant, saying he couldn't leave his house empty for too long. Nicole and I looked at each other.

"Sure, Mr. Bedner," Nicole said, taking him by the arm. "Let's go up to your place. It's nice and cosy up there, isn't it?"

The moment we entered, Mr. Bedner locked and bolted the door. I kicked something on the floor. It was the rent money envelope still lying where I'd slipped it under the door after Mr. Bedner didn't answer. I picked it up to hand to Mr. Bedner but he brushed it aside and instead led us into the living room.

"Sit," he said, pointing at the sofa. "Please, sit. Then, we talk. Okay?"

I placed the envelope on one of the beautifully-carved end tables and sat down, sinking into the sofa. The curtains were open and the setting sun slanted right across into our eyes. Mr. Bedner walked slowly, almost floating, to one of the portraits on the wall and then stood there—as if he'd forgotten that Nicole and I were in the room. He stayed that way for more than a minute. I was beginning to get nervous when he suddenly took two quick steps to the window and pulled the curtains shut, bathing the room in the murky red light of sun through velvet.

"You do right thing," he said smiling.

"Sorry?" Nicole said.

"You get rid animal. Good. I glad."

"Oh," I said. "I see. You're talking about the mice. Well, to tell you the truth, those mousetraps—."

"Mousetraps!" Mr. Bedner roared, laughing not at all pleasantly. "Mousetraps useless."

"They sure are, Mr. Bedner," Nicole said. "They haven't caught a fu- ... a goddam thing."

"That because it rat, not mouse." He sat down in his oversized chair. "My wife, she right. Wife, she always right. Nothing but trouble."

"Mr. Bedner," Nicole said. "Don't get yourself so worked up. It's only a few rodents."

"Trouble. Trouble. Trouble. You know trouble? Trouble bad." He stood up again. "My wife, she know. She know all. Sin. Truth. She see and she say: 'Evil. Face of evil.' And I think: 'Giulio, Nicole. They like little children. No understand.' But you understand. You get rid. I very glad."

"That's good, Mr. Bedner," Nicole said. "We're glad that you're glad." She turned and patted my knee. "Now, I think we'd better get going. Supper's getting cold."

We stood up and headed for the front door.

"But too late for my Mrs. Bedner," Mr. Bedner said. "Not soon enough."

"I beg your pardon," I said. "What was too late for Mrs. Bedner?"

"You tell me," he said. "What she die? You tell please. Who kill? You think disease? She no disease. I disease. Bad heart, bad liver, no stomach. I disease, not wife. She die for me."

"Mr. Bedner," Nicole said, taking a deep sigh, "don't talk that way. You're not to blame. These things happen."

"No, no," he said, shaking his head violently. "She die because devil here. Too close. She woman of God. My fault to wait. First day out. Wait too long. But I forgive." He turned to me. "You nice young man. Like my son. I no have son." Then he took Nicole's hand. "And you like daughter."

"Thank you, Mr. Bedner," she said, giving him a hug. "If there's anything we can do—"

"You do already," he said. "You remove rat. Now when she return everything okay. Like before. We drink plum brandy, laugh. Go now. Have supper. I make everything ready here."

"What the hell was all that about?" Nicole asked once we were back in our own flat.

"I'm not really sure," I said. "But I think he thinks we got rid of Torp."

"If it weren't so sad, it would be downright funny," she said. "That poor man's about to lose it."

The following Monday, I arrived at the office to find Pamela whistling loudly as she cleaned out her desk.

"I've got the fucking job," she shouted, pumping her fist in the air. "They gave it to me. Can you believe it? My own office; my name on the door; a real title. I still can't believe it."

I congratulated her and held out my hand. To my surprise, she hugged me instead.

"A celebration's definitely in order," she said. "Yeah —and I know exactly what kind. A bottle of champagne; some cheese and fancy crackers; an ocean view; soft music."

"Doesn't sound like the venerable philosophy lounge to me," I said.

"Sodding right it doesn't," she said, slinging her stuff into a bag. "Come on. You've never been up to my place, have you? Well, it's about time."

Pamela's apartment was on the eighteenth floor of one of the new complexes built along the beach—the kind Nicole and I had first looked at but quickly discovered we couldn't afford. There was an intercom system and a doorman and laundry service for the tenants. Because it was still morning, the view was of blue sky, ocean waves, sailboats and the famous bridge connecting the two arms of the bay. This was the second time I'd had a view of the bridge, and again I couldn't make out the far end, shrouded in mist. Later in the day, it would vanish entirely, hidden in the rains that, at this time of year, arrived regularly in the early evening. One of my more poetic colleagues told me:

"Ah, the Vancouver rains. They blow in from the ocean like waves of disembodied barbarians, piled one on top of the other. And just when you think you can't stand it anymore, February's civilized legions sweep clean the air."

"Wow," I said, looking around. "This is some place."

"Compliments of a good divorce lawyer," she said, removing her jacket and tossing it on the floor. "From the proceeds of the settlement when I unloaded that excess baggage known as my husband."

"You were married?"

"Unfortunately, yes," she said, putting an LP on the record player. "*Let It Be*. Hope you like it." I nodded, although I'd never heard it before. "Yes, Trevor and I met at uni. Same Wittgenstein tutorial. Lust at first sight. Lasted all of six months."

"Sorry to hear it."

"Don't be," she said, handing me a glass of sparkling wine. "Turned out his family was loaded. Paid a sodding handsome sum to get rid of me." She laughed and held out her glass. "Here's to philosophy. May it always be so opportunistic." She downed hers and poured herself another. "Come on, come on, we're supposed to celebrate. Get it down. It's real champagne, you know."

I took it in one gulp.

"That's better," she said, as she refilled it. "Once you open a bottle of this, you've got to finish it. That's the law."

We sat on her sofa. As promised, Pamela had set up a plate of a bunch of different cheeses and, from what I could tell from the label on the box, Danish thins.

"Oh God, what a miracle," she said, downing another glass. "What sweetness and delight! I thought for sure they'd give it to that dour-faced Kierkegaardian—what's his name, the one who does nothing but suck up to the chairman. But they gave it to me. Me! Hot damn! Hot fucking damn!"

And with that she kissed me. Not a celebratory peck but a kiss that had her tongue deep in my mouth and her crotch rubbing against my thigh.

"So," she said, "how do you feel about fucking me?"

"I'm married," I stammered, breaking into a sweat. "I've ... never made love to anyone but my wife."

"Hey," Pamela said. "Get with it. We're on the cusp of the swinging sixties and seventies. Everybody fucks everybody else. I bet your wife has no compunction. Come on. You can tell me."

"I don't know. I've never asked her."

"Hey, who gives a shit really? I won't tell if you don't."

But try as I might, I couldn't do it. It was as if I was back in my little room at home—and there was my mother holding a glass of water and with her ear to the wall. In the end, Pamela had to give up.

"Jeez," she said, rolling off the sofa. "You're serious. Well, I gotta admire you—even if you are leaving me one sodding horny mess."

"I'm sorry," I said.

"That's alright," Pamela said. "No harm done. But listen. Even if we didn't get it on, you have to leave me something of yours. Anything you can spare. It's a tradition around here."

She pulled out a laundry hamper from the closet. It was filled with men's clothing: from checked shirts to underwear. There was even a dirty overcoat and several ascots, one of them identical to those favoured by the chairman of the department. I didn't really want to leave anything of mine, but she insisted—and threatened not to let me out if I didn't. So I finally took off my tie and handed it to her. She tossed it casually into the laundry hamper.

"You're sure now," she said, rubbing herself against me again while sipping yet another drink. "We could always give it another try, you know."

"I don't think it would do any good."

Pamela drove me back to the office just in time for my conference. Most of the students were already seated when I entered, carrying their marked-up papers.

"I'll put these on the side here and you can pick them up after the conference is over," I said. "I've tried to be fair, but if anyone's unhappy with his or her mark, or needs some clarification, I'll be available in my office right after class. Now, if I remember correctly, last time we were trying to make sense of Aristotle's notion of chance. You've had a week to mull it over. Any thoughts?"

"I'm not sure I understand what Aristotle means by chance," one of the students said. "Is he saying there are things in the world that happen by accident?"

"It all depends what you mean by accident," another student said.

"Well, I don't know, but it seems we should let our intuitions be our guides in this matter. When we say that someone getting run over by a steam shovel is a tragic accident, do we mean the actual act of being run over or the circumstances surrounding it? For example, would we call it an accident if the steam shovel deliberately ran the unfortunate over? Would we call it an accident if a person deliberately threw himself or herself in front of a steam shovel?"

"But ... but isn't that a kind of superficial way of looking at it—I mean, just through local, efficient causes that don't lead to the desired final cause? Couldn't we argue that, no matter what, if we were able to reduce things to their primitive cause and effects, there would strictly speaking be no such thing as chance?"

"But what about free will?"

"Aha, you choose to have it."

"Seriously, doesn't a billiard ball model of the universe predetermine everything, thereby squeezing out any notion of free will? That's the reason for Aristotle's defence of chance—so that necessity doesn't roll over everything."

"Like a steam shovel?"

I leaned back, leaving the students to argue among themselves. I was still shaken by the advances of my colleague, trying to get it clear in my own mind what the consequences would have been if I'd been able to follow through. Probably no consequences. So why hadn't I been able to go along with Pamela?

"I can't believe it," an angry voice suddenly shouted. "Here you are discussing a world by rote, concept, and definition—and forgetting that it's actually out there. That it's something real and dirty. I mean, trying to break down fluid motion into mechanics, motives into discrete particles of chance and necessity, matter into basic components—isn't this a waste of time and energy? Why not just enjoy it? It's there. Period. Go with the flow. Know what I mean?"

I looked up to see who was speaking. To my surprise, there was Torp standing at the back of the class. He hadn't bothered showing up for several weeks, and I hadn't seen him since the day at Stanley Park. I was about to say something in Aristotle's defence but thought better of it. I figured someone else would jump in. Maybe talk about the importance of understanding the world instead of just living in it. The essential difference between humans and animals, etc. But nobody spoke up, and the only thing that came to Aristotle's rescue was the bell.

"Torp," I said, after the other students had filed out, "what brings you here? I thought you'd abandoned philosophy."

"I've got some bad news," he said. "I went over to your house to pay you guys a visit. Nicole—"

"Is Nicole alright?" I said, feeling as if someone had me by the throat. "What's happened?"

"Nicole's fine," he said. "She's fine. It's her mother. She's suffered a heart attack."

"Oh Jesus. I'd better get home. Nicole must be devastated."

"There's no rush," Torp said. "I convinced her to take the first flight out. She's on her way to Montreal right now. She asked me to bring this note to you."

I sat at my desk and read the note while Torp checked the bulletin board:

> Oct. 6. Giulio, I'm sorry, I couldn't wait any longer for you to get home. My mother's had a mild heart attack. I wanted to catch the last flight of the day so I'm rushing off to the airport right now. I don't know how long I'll be away but it shouldn't be more than a week. At least, I hope not. I don't think I could stand being with my mother for longer than that. We'd probably end up trying to kill each other. Ha ha. But, if it's going to be longer, I'll let you know. Take care of yourself and don't do anything I wouldn't.
>
> Love forever, Nicole.
>
> P.S.: I left some sauce for you if you want to make yourself some pasta. Otherwise, I guess it's pizza."

"So, Mr. Torp," I said, as I folded the note and put it in my pocket, "what have you been up to?"

"Me? Not much really. We've found an abandoned warehouse near the edge of False Creek. You know where that is?"

"Can't say I do."

"It's not a creek really. More like a pool of sludge right in the middle of the city. You've probably seen it from the bus on your way to the University."

"Okay, yeah. I think I know what you're talking about now."

"It's not exactly the Waldorf-Astoria," Torp said. "You get to fight spiders and mice. Do battle with rats the size of cats. The water stinks; the roof's made of tin and leaks; the windows have been blasted away; and the only heat's if we light a bonfire. But it's perfect for what we want to do."

"You mean stay out of the cold and wet?"

"That—and put out a magazine."

"A magazine?"

"We were talking about it on the beach that day with my friends."

"Oh yes, now I recall. You were trying to decide on a title."

"Yeah—"

Torp was about to say something else when Pamela stepped into the office doorway.

"Don't you have another conference, Mr. di Orio?" she said, barely looking at Torp. "You'll never get anywhere if you keep on showing up late for your classes."

"Shit," I said, looking at my watch. "Look, Torp, I'd love to hear more about this magazine. Why don't you come over tonight? I'll pick up a pizza or two."

"Should be safe," he said. He leaned close: "I think that undercover cop has got tired of watching us."

The flat was dark and silent when I entered. It felt strange, like the first time Nicole and I had seen it. At the time, I remember thinking how I'd never felt so naked. There we were, amid the markings for other people's furniture: the ghost limbs of stereos long gone, the flickering images of TV sets, the pale impressions left by portraits and posters. My entire life till then had been a navigation of stuffy rooms, packed so tightly one had no thought of vacuums, of space where nothing happened, where, as someone once said, "the bumps of existence actually flatten out to nothing." In fact, in these places, the opposite was true. There was so much there one had to worry about one's own existence. Was there enough room to co-exist? Could inert matter make way for you—the sofas, loveseats, end and coffee tables, pianos, pillows, cushions, massive paintings in scrolled frames?

On the other hand, these two rooms were positively bare, almost agoraphobic. "Come on," they seemed to be saying. "It's up to you to define us, to tell us what we are." Of course, that's only what they seemed to be saying. In reality, they were mute and full of a reproachful dead-clunky existence, like all things. I could understand my emotions then, but why was I suddenly feeling the same way now? Maybe it was because it had started to rain again— a fine mist that soaked right through you—and left you slightly disoriented when the usual landmarks vanished.

I switched on the light. There, that was better. I placed the pizza on the kitchen table and reached beneath the sink for a bottle of wine. We had started buying screwtop. Saved a lot of trouble, even if my father would have gagged at the thought. Well, he gagged at the thought of any store-bought wine. Full of chemicals, he said. I sat down, poured myself some of the chemical wine and opened up the newspaper I'd started to read on the bus. The big news again was the series of bombs that had rocked the city, the aftermath of one which I'd seen with my own eyes. The explosions had knocked out several electric utility sub-stations as well as damaged stores and offices. Once again, there had been no casualties, but police officials quoted in the story said it was only a matter of time. Maybe not, I said. Maybe these guys know what they're doing. The PFRG—I still didn't know what it was all about. No one in the philosophy department had been able to enlighten me, that's for sure. The police said in the article they had a good idea who the PFRG people were—and were close to making arrests. But they weren't releasing any other details.

The other front page story was the investigation into the FLQ kidnapping of James Cross the day before. When I'd been living in Quebec, I hadn't really believed the FLQ had the courage to pull off something like that. They struck us—the English-speaking people there—as a bunch of clowns. Nasty clowns, but clowns nonetheless. Now, it seemed just one more piece of sinister news from a distant shore. Except that Nicole was headed straight there. Still, I couldn't see her being in much danger. She wasn't the type to get involved in politics.

I flipped through the rest of the paper quickly and was about to put it aside when I saw a small headline below the Births & Deaths notices: "Park body found bludgeoned to death." According to the ten-line article, a young man had been discovered in a wooded area of Stanley Park with his head caved in. Nearby, the police had found the murder weapon—a bloodied two-by-four, studded with nails. Normally, I would have paid little attention to such an item. But the conjunction of the area and the description of the victim—"a runaway who frequented the beach area and had been picked up several times on begging and disturbing the peace charges"—made me pause. Perhaps it was one of Torp's friends. I folded the article so I'd remember to ask Torp about it.

I was about to give in to my hunger and grab a slice of pizza when there was a knock on the front door.

"Sorry, I'm late," Torp said, shaking the water off a makeshift raincoat—a large garbage bag with two holes for arms.

"Hey," I said, "as long as you don't mind cold pizza."

"Bring it on. Bring it on."

I poured a glass of wine for him. Then I asked him if he'd heard about the person being killed in Stanley Park.

"Yeah, isn't that wild?" he said.

"Did you know him?"

"No, not really. He used to hang around at one time, but I hadn't seen him for quite a while. Although I wouldn't really know because I haven't been hanging around the beach myself these days. Spent most of my time looking for locations."

"Right," I said. "The magazine. How's it going?"

"Well, you know. When you have a bunch of people all trying to decide something, it takes a long time to get

95

anything done."

"I know what you mean," I said. "Decision-making by committee. Not always the best."

"But we're getting there. I think we've got some sort of editorial policy now. We've just gotta put it all together."

"I look forward to seeing the first copy."

"I'll make sure to autograph it for you."

We were silent for a moment. I watched him chew on his pizza, holding the end up so the cheese and pepperoni wouldn't spill on his shirt.

"Kind of different without Nicole around, isn't it?" he said.

"Sure is. You get used to having someone else around the house. After a while, it's like you're two halves of the same person really."

"Wow," Torp said. "That must be a great feeling. Haven't had the opportunity myself."

"Yeah, I guess it is a nice feeling." I paused—and something came over me. Maybe because of what had happened with Pamela. "Nicole's the only woman I've ever been with."

"No kidding," Torp said. He clinked glasses with me. "Here's to the last faithful man in the entire fucking universe."

"No," I said, taking another drink and starting to feel lightheaded. "I don't think it has much to do with being faithful. I've discovered I just can't do it with another woman, that's all."

"Maybe you just haven't met the other right woman yet," he said.

"Maybe." I poured myself another glass. "So, tell me. How many women have *you* slept with?"

"God, I don't know," Torp said laughing. "A couple of dozen maybe."

"Why? Just out of curiosity."

"I really don't know why," he said, shrugging. "Or maybe it's because there's a different reason for each one. Sometimes, I sense a longing in the woman. Sometimes the longing is in me. Sometimes I do it just for the fun of it. Sometimes because I find myself attracted to the woman. And sometimes for no reason at all. It just seemed a good idea at the time."

"So maybe you haven't found the right woman either."

"Hey," Torp said, clinking glasses again, "you could be fucking right, man."

I emptied the rest of the bottle and stood up to get the other one under the sink. I had to steady myself against the table.

"Jeez there, sailor," Torp said. "You're sucking it back pretty hard, aren't you?"

"Hey, that's alright," I said as I sat down again—hard. "You know the old expression: while the cat's away ...." I refilled the glasses. I wasn't really watching and spilled some wine on the table.

"Oops."

"Oops," Torp repeated—and laughed.

I started to rub the spilled wine with the bottom of the glass.

"Do you know what my father always says when he wants to insult someone?" I said.

"No. What does your father say when he wants to insult someone?" Torp repeated, leaning back in his chair.

"I'll tell you," I said. "He says: 'That jerk can't even make a zero with a glass.' But I think he's wrong. The real jerks are those who think they can change things. The guys who think they can make the world better. It's all a bunch of crap, really. A real bunch of crap. You can read all the books you want, but it's just reading books. And you can blow up all the buildings you want, and it's just blowing up buildings. It's when the book readers try to blow up buildings and then spend their courtroom time explaining why they did it for the good of society that the real trouble starts. Know what I mean?"

By then, I was feeling very dizzy and didn't really know what I was saying. And it came out all confused and slurred.

"Hey, is that an insult?" Torp said.

"I'm sorry," I said, my head on the table. "I didn't mean you. I wasn't talking about you."

"That's alright," Torp said, patting me. "You're forgiven."

"Can I ask you another question?"

"About what?"

"About sex?"

"Hey, ask away," Torp said. "We're among friends, right? And I've got nothing to hide."

I lifted my head from the table for a moment, then leaned back down.

"Forget it," I said.

"Come on, man. If there's something you want to say to me, get it out."

"Okay, then," I said, the slur in my voice now very pronounced. "What about Nicole?"

"I beg your pardon," Torp said.

"Have you ever slept with Nicole?"

"Giulio," he said. "Now, I know you're very, very drunk. I make it a policy never to sleep with the wives of my friends. It's my one iron-clad rule about sex."

"Did you ever think about it?"

"Think about it?" Torp said. "To tell you the truth, I have. Nicole is a very attractive woman."

"Very attractive," I said, or at least that's what I tried to say.

Suddenly, my stomach heaved.

"Oh shit," I said. "I think I'm going to throw up."

"Not all over me, you don't," Torp said, moving back from the table.

I pushed my chair aside and stumbled to the washroom. I barely made it to the toilet bowl before my pizza came right back up. I wiped my face with a towel, rinsed my mouth out, and went back into the kitchen.

"I'm sorry," I said. "That's the first time I've ever thrown up in my adult life."

"Hey, don't sweat it, man. Happens to the best. Maybe you should go lie down though."

"Yeah, maybe you're right." I stumbled again, and he managed to hold me up.

"Come on," he said. "I'll give you a hand."

He put his arm around me, and we staggered to the sofa.

"Here," he said, "see if you can't hold onto the wall while I pull this out."

I leaned against the wall—and then slid slowly to the floor. I could see Torp pulling out the sofa. Suddenly, I burst out laughing.

"What's so funny?" Torp said.

"I don't know. I felt like crying—so I laughed."

"That makes sense." He pulled the sheets back. "There, time to tuck you in."

He lifted me up and brought me to the bed. I sat down and struggled to undress myself. Halfway through, I did what I had wanted to do in the first place. I started crying.

"Giulio," Torp said, "are you okay?"

"No, I'm not okay," I said, practically shouting as the tears rolled down my cheeks. "I'm lonely and confused and all fucked up. So why don't you get the hell out of here and leave me alone!"

I curled up in bed, feeling so sorry for myself. Torp switched off the light. The next sound I expected to hear was the door closing behind him, the door that would probably mean I'd never see him again. Instead, he slid into bed and, even in my drunken haze, I could feel his naked body pressing against mine.

In the morning, he was gone—and it was all a dream, right? It had never happened. He had never been there. I'd never got so drunk I didn't realize what I was doing—or whatever other excuse I was going to make. But none of that was true. I knew it. Just like I knew that my head was pounding for a very good reason. I got up and made my way to the bathroom. I turned on the hot water in the shower and soaked under it for a good fifteen minutes. I thought of Nicole, the only woman I'd ever slept with. And I thought of Torp. And then I turned on the cold water full blast.

Torp had left a note on the kitchen table, further proof it hadn't been an illusion:

> Giulio, sorry I couldn't stay last night. Had to get back to the warehouse. Much work still to be done on the magazine. We print next week. I probably won't be seeing you before then. Say hi to Nicole when she gets back.
>
> PS: thanks for the pleasant evening.

I looked out the bedroom window but couldn't see much because the lawn was so overgrown. What the hell was that Mr. Bedner thinking about, letting the weeds get that bad? I went out and yanked out as many as I could. I guess some of them were flowers, but how was I to know the difference? And why didn't Mr. Bedner come out to guide me? Or to berate me for killing his flowers?

When I got to school, there was another surprise

waiting for me—a new assistant lecturer. I was introduced to Reginald Worthington III, Esq., who described himself as "not just a specialist in pre-Socratic Skepticism, but the foremost specialist from the world-renowned University of Buenos Aires, Facultad de Filosofia y Letras." But what I noticed about him was the God-awful polka-dot bowtie he was wearing. Combined with a falsetto delivery and a cherubic face that would have suited a Valentine's Day cupid, it made it hard to take him seriously. There he was, talking so knowledgably and intensely about the "criterion crisis" and the "vicious circle debate"—and all I wanted to do was giggle. There I was, picturing Reginald's bowtie suddenly starting to spin, propelling him through the roof as it hypnotized everyone else around him.

To keep from laughing in his face, I wandered over to the bulletin board. The University of Auckland in New Zealand was offering a replacement junior lecturer's position for a recent graduate. Starting in the second term. Possibility of assistant professorships, full tenure track. Philosophy in the South Pacific—now wouldn't that be a gas? I took down the details—not that I'd ever make a move like that. Especially not now.

After listening to Reginald Worthington III describe his philosophic exploits and list every single paper he'd ever published, I was glad to get away. The note from Torp had said he wouldn't be back for at least a week. But maybe he'd changed his mind. Maybe he'd be waiting for me on the sofabed, ready to continue from the previous night. Come, Giulio, I have much to show you now that you're sober. Together, we'll fulfill the Socratic ideal, the manly joys, the dreams of true Platonic love ....

He wasn't there. I felt a sharp sense of disappointment, as if I'd been jilted or something. I held the note he'd written in my hand and re-read it. My body started to tingle. What's happening to me? What's going on here? Why am I—?

My self-questioning was interrupted by the loud, grinding sound of a truck coming to a stop before the house. It was hard to see through the heavy curtain of rain, but I did make out a red van with the words Bedner & Bedner stencilled crudely on its side. As the truck pulled up, Mr. Bedner came out of his house and down the stairs. He was carrying an umbrella to protect himself from the rain. Two men, one in black and one in red rain gear, came out of the truck. They motioned for the landlord to come to the back with them. Then, the three of them pulled out a large object from the truck. It was covered with plastic, so I couldn't really make out what it was. But it was definitely heavy and I could tell the three of them were struggling to haul it up Mr. Bedner's stairs. I almost went out to lend a hand, but then I thought better of it. Perhaps the landlord didn't want me to see what it was. But when they turned it sideways up the path and I could catch a glimpse of it three-dimensionally, I knew exactly what it was. There was little question about it. A coffin. What else could it be? The two men—even their appearance, faceless, featureless, hidden deep within their raincoats, reminded me of a romanticized notion of death—held it on either side while the landlord guided the front and opened the door for them.

This is getting more crazy by the minute, I said to myself. What the hell does the landlord want with a coffin? Jesus, I hope he's not planning to kill himself, too. That's all I needed—a body rotting in the house above me, juices dripping through the floor. No, I told myself, there must be some other explanation. Some more logical and reasonable one. Wasn't there always?

As if in answer to my question, I heard a sharp rap. And then another. It took me a moment to realize they were coming from the door that led to the other side of the basement. Ah, Mr. Bedner, here to explain. But it wasn't Mr. Bedner. It was one of the men I'd seen at the funeral. Red or black rain gear? I couldn't tell, as he had on a grey suit and striped vest.

"Hi," I said, brightly. "Can I help you?"

"Harold—he wishes for you to come upstairs."

"Harold? Oh, you mean Mr. Bedner?" The man nodded. "Sure. After you."

"Giulio!" Mr. Bedner exclaimed—just as if he'd discovered a long-lost friend after many years apart. He gave me a hug and patted me on the back. It was obvious he hadn't noticed Torp in the house. "Where wife? I no see."

I told him the story as he walked ahead of me towards the living room.

"Trouble, trouble, trouble," he said. "It come in threes, yes."

"And even more."

The other man I'd seen holding up Mr. Bedner at the

funeral was standing in the living room. He was dressed in identical style to the one who'd come to get me—and I couldn't tell them apart when they stood beside each other. Their rain gear was hanging in the hallway, dripping water on the floor.

"Giulio," Mr. Bedner said. "These my brothers. *Fratelli. Frați* in my language."

The two brothers bowed in unison. Then, one of them took a card out of his pocket and handed it to me:

> Bedner & Bedner Inc.
> Deluxe Woodwork Done to Specifications.
> Plumbing. Electricals. Flooring. Roofs.

"Retired now," he said.

The other nodded.

"Yes," Mr. Bedner said with a laugh. "I young man—they old. Work only for me."

Mr. Bedner seemed much more his old self and, taking hold of my arm, entreated me to stay. They were just about to share a little vodka.

"Few moments," he said.

"Alright," I said. "I guess I've got a few moments to spare."

Mr. Bedner left to fetch the vodka, leaving me with his brothers. The two of them sat there, one on either side of me. Just smiling. Suddenly, the one who had been doing all the talking turned to me.

"You do what Harold ask, yes?" he said, placing a

hand on my thigh and squeezing. "He not well. Not well at all."

"I'm sorry, but—"

"Yes," he said. "Not make him angry. Or sad." I looked at the other brother who nodded as if to confirm. "Heart very weak."

I was about to say I had no intention of making their brother angry, when he returned with the bottle of vodka and four glasses. He seemed in wonderful spirits.

"You're happy, today, Mr. Bedner," I said, glancing at his brothers as they nodded approval.

"Of course," he said. "No need for sad face. I have important announcement to make. Most important."

"And what's that?" I asked.

"Wife soon back."

"Soon when?" the brother who spoke asked, his face lighting up.

"Soon, soon," Mr. Bedner said. I got the impression he was looking at me when he said this. "Now that evil gone."

Oh Jesus, I said to myself, here we go again. He thinks Torp has left for good. And he's got some crazy notion his wife will come back.

"Mr. Bedner," I said, standing up and fully intending to set him straight.

But then I stopped. How exactly was I going to set him straight? Was I going to tell him that dead people don't come back to life? Or was I going to smugly inform him that Torp hadn't left after all. In fact, he'd been in this very house only the night before—beneath this very room.

"Soon, soon, very soon," Mr. Bedner said, pouring the vodka. "But now we drink. When wife back, no more vodka. Wife no like. Only milk. And plum brandy."

Mr. Bedner laughed at his own joke and then held a glass of vodka under my nose. I pulled back, still a bit queasy from the previous night.

"To wife," Mr. Bedner toasted.

"To wife!" the brothers shouted.

I held my breath and swallowed the vodka. Then I thanked him and said it was time to go. Mr. Bedner accompanied me to the basement door.

"You good boy," he said.

"Yes. At least, I try to be."

Mr. Bedner looked back down the corridor. Then suddenly leaned very close to me.

"No worry," he said in a whisper. "All fixed."

"What's fixed?" I asked.

"I know," he said, touching the side of his nose with his finger. "You. Brothers. Everyone. Only play with me. Make me feel good. But I no care. I show you soon. Then you believe. Everyone believe. You see. Go now. We talk again. Soon."

Sure, Mr. Bedner, we'll talk again. Soon.

That night, my encounter with Mr. Bedner and his brothers triggered the first dream I'd had since leaving Montreal. I found myself in a room similar to Mr. Bedner's living room, only the candles had sprouted cobwebs;

the portraits were tilted and worn away; the carpet beneath my feet sizzled like it was on fire; and I was trapped on the sofa. Each time I tried to get up I only succeeded in sinking deeper. In front of me, three people, an older man and woman, and a young man, were engaged in a wild, drunken dance, kicking their legs high into the air like some sort of Can-Can stage. Then, the older man disappeared. The other two leaned on each other and began to walk at a crazy, impossible slant, like vaudevillians. They stepped across the room towards the suddenly flaming curtain, then turned and headed back my way. I tried to warn them that the curtain was on fire but they wouldn't pay any heed.

The older man returned, staggering and bouncing off the walls, holding a bottle of some cloudy liquid high overhead. Sssh, he said, bringing his fingers to his face in an exaggerated effort to get silence. Sssh! Listen. You hear? Rain stop. No more pitter pitter. Pitter, patter, I said. Pitter pitter, he repeated more softly, pitter pitter. The other two joined in the chorus of pitters. Ah, pitter, pitter. No more pitter pitter. I shouted again that the curtain was on fire, that the whole house was in danger of burning down. The ladybugs were flying away. But I could neither stand up nor convince them of what I was saying. And then I thought of Nicole and Torp below, probably sleeping, unaware of the danger. And I saw them in each other's arms, contentment written all over their faces.

The living room spun out. I found myself in a classroom. The students were setting fire to their term papers. I shouted at them: "A categorical imperative! The house is on fire, and the two lovers are sleeping peacefully. I want to save them, but at the same time I feel the sharp pain of jealousy. Or the pain of being left out. Or the pain of not being able to fully understand how exactly one thinks with one's heart. What should I do?" Before anyone had a chance to answer, I was back in the living room, and the danger seemed to have passed. The three people were talking in whispers, words coming from the space where their mouths should have been. I could hear what they were saying but couldn't make any sense of it. They were speaking a language I'd never heard before. It must have been their native language. I made out a few words: *dampne, cunreaden, nigromancien, cuntek, bourde.*

I told the older man holding the bottle that I didn't understand what they were saying. He apologized, and they began to speak English. Big, one of them said, making hammering gestures. Seven, four, three. Not for sleeping. When he said this, all three broke out laughing. Suddenly, the man vanished and there was the sound of rapid hammering from the kitchen. What was he doing? I asked myself. Strengthening the coffin to suit his purposes, of course. And then I was standing in the kitchen, watching him come up the basement stairs with Irena slung across his shoulders. I tried to ask him what he was doing, carrying decaying remains like that. But he simply walked past me and placed her in a coffin, leaning slanted against the wall. It was a reverse burial. He was coaxing her back to life through prayers and promises. And a few kisses. Not enough, not enough, he said as he arose and looked at me. I kill self.

Then she come back. Yes? No, I said, shaking my head.

He smiled and lowered himself into the coffin, beside Irena. You hammer shut, okay? Then, I die, too. I no eat and I die. Be reasonable, I said. Committing suicide won't bring her back. You right, he said. Not suicide—murder. No! You mustn't. I kill him, yes, he said. And I place body in coffin. Who? I asked. Who? But, before he could answer, I felt myself being raised slowly towards the ceiling, as if on a string. The front door opened for me with a whoosh. I tried to react normally and not panic. I realized that the night crawlers couldn't now get at me with their dark lantern jaws, their drooling venomous maws. Then, suddenly, I fell to the ground. I could feel the night crawlers stirring under my feet, slithering away, returning to the earth. I edged along the wall, using it for support. Then I saw a light in the flat. It was coming from the bedroom. I took giant steps across the lawn, hoping to come down on the soaked grass as little as possible. My tracks filled with muddy water. I wanted to be the first to tell Nicole and Torp they were safe. I was safe. We were all safe. But when I threw open the door, it wasn't Nicole and Torp in bed. It was Torp and I. And, on the windowsill, with her hands held high in prayer and self-righteousness and her eyes rimmed with red, sat my mother.

THREE

NICOLE

*Since things that are found in the soul
are of three kinds—passions, faculties, states of character,
virtue must be one of these.*

—*Nicomachean Ethics*,
Book 2, Chapter 5

It was the first time I'd ever been on a plane, and all I could think of was: Shit, what the fuck am I doing here anyway, 35,000 feet up and for what? I should never have let Torp talk me into going back. My mother's nothing but a stupid old bitch who doesn't give a shit about anyone but herself. She was never there for me. Why should I be there for her now? Too late though. I couldn't very well ask the pilot to turn back. Besides, it was pretty down there below us, especially when we went over the mountains all covered with snow. And I liked the part about flying above the clouds. Those clouds reminded me of Little Bo Peep and her lost sheep. So soft. Maybe one day I could live on one of them like a little shepherd girl, bouncing around without a care in the world. Without a mother in the world. The flight attendant asked if I'd like something to drink. So I had myself a couple of beers and slept the rest of the way.

When we landed, there were a whole bunch of soldiers and police hanging around, all armed to the teeth. But I didn't think anything of it, figuring that was the usual thing at airports. Like maybe they had military secrets or something to protect. Or important people coming in. I didn't hear about the kidnapping until the taxi driver taking me to my in-laws' told me about it.

"New in town?" he said in English, looking in the rearview mirror. "Come for the excitement—or what?"

When I answered him in French, he changed his tone.

"Between you and me," he said. "It's about time we get rid of these Brits. These *têtes-carrées*. Don't you think? They've been playing king of the shitpile over us for too long. Don't you think?"

"I'm from Ontario actually," I said.

"Ah," he said. "A francophone in exile."

"Half," I said. "My mother's French."

"And you?" he said. "Are you for or against this? Not that I give my benediction to kidnapping, mind you. But if it teaches these pompous arses a lesson or two, hey, why not? They can't let it go too far, of course. After they make their point, they should let the poor man go. What do you think?"

"I haven't thought about it much," I said. "I've come to make sure my mother's okay. She's in hospital."

"I'm sorry to hear that," he said. "Mothers are the most precious things we've got."

Well, you can have mine, I said to myself. You can fucking have mine.

"Here we are," he said, stopping in front of my in-laws' house. "This is an immigrant neighbourhood, isn't it? I like immigrants myself. I just don't know why they don't like us."

Mrs. di Orio greeted me at the door, dressed as usual in what I called her "mourning" clothes, grieving for a father ten years gone. She hugged me and told me how sorry she was. But now it was in the hands of God.

"Jeez," I said. "I hope it's not that bad. Last I heard, she'd only suffered a mild attack."

"I'll pray for her anyway," she said. "I'll light a candle for her tomorrow morning."

Being in hospital hadn't changed my mother one bit. Not one fucking bit! She was lying there in bed unable to get up, and the first thing she asked me was if I had any cigarettes. She was dying for a cigarette. Ha ha. She laughed at her own statement.

"Can you believe it?" she said. "They won't let me have any because it's supposed to be bad for my heart. What I want to know is what does smoking have to do with my heart, eh? So, com'on, give me one."

"Mom," I said. "I don't smoke. You know that."

"Here then," she said, holding out some money. "Be a good girl and go buy some for me. They sell them downstairs. I know. One of the other patients has her relatives sneak them up to her. Besides, the doctors buy them all the time."

"Mom, you know I can't do that," I said, although I was sorely tempted. Maybe it would speed things up. "It's against hospital regulations."

"So," she said, fluffing up her pillows, "you don't have any cigarettes and you won't buy me any. Is that right?" I nodded, knowing what would come next. "So why did you come to see me then?"

"I've come," I yelled, "to see why you haven't croaked

yet, you miserable bitch! That's what I've come all the way from Vancouver to see!" And I stormed out of the room.

One of the nurses motioned for me to keep my voice down. I almost gave her the finger, but took a deep breath instead. Yes, my mom. She'd always been able to bring out the best in me. It's like we're attached by this cord that's always trying to pull us together—so we can get close enough to rip each other's hearts out. I stormed around in the corridors for a while and then went back in.

"Look," I said, "I'm sorry for yelling. We shouldn't be yelling at each other."

Now, she was giving me her silent treatment. It always worked that way. After she'd made me blow my top, she'd clam up and pretend to be poor little old Gertrude—the person no one in the whole wide world loved.

"Mom," I said, "this isn't doing either of us any good."

She switched on her TV set—she had to have one, even if it cost extra—and pretended to watch *Gilligan's Island*. I tried to be friendly. Honest. I tried to ask her about how she felt and if she thought she'd be getting out of the hospital soon. Then, when she still wouldn't answer, I decided to get out of there before I lost my temper.

"Goodbye," I said. "Maybe, I'll drop in tomorrow—and maybe you'll be in a better mood by then."

I was practically out the door of the ward when she suddenly asked, out of the blue: "Why aren't you staying at my house? Isn't it good enough for you? There's no one there. You could have it all to yourself."

Yeah, sure, I said to myself. Until one of your old boyfriends comes straggling in half-pissed during the middle of the night because he's never bothered to give back your key.

"Mom," I told her. "I've already promised Mr. and Mrs. di Orio I'd stay at their place. I can't go back on my word now. If it'll make you any happier, I'll drop in once in a while to make sure everything's okay at the apartment. Alright?"

I prepared myself for another blast, but she just sighed and went back to watching TV.

"Besides," I said, "the doctor told me it's only a small attack. He says if nothing else goes wrong, you'll be home by the end of the week."

And I didn't want to be anywhere near her when that happened. I wasn't in the mood to become her personal caretaker. And I wouldn't put it past her to pretend she couldn't live on her own anymore. I shuddered at the thought of being chained to her until she decided it was time to croak. Shit, knowing her, she'd probably outlive me.

The visits to the hospital were hell on earth for me. In the mornings, my stomach would knot up and I couldn't get a thing down. Not even a piece of dry toast. And it got worse as the week wore on. Another day of her moaning and groaning, and I swear to God I'd have put her through the wall. Right through the goddam hospital window. When she wasn't carping and bitching, she was whining about how I didn't love her—and after all she'd done for me.

"I slaved day and night to make sure you had a roof over your head," she said. "I worked my ass off slinging hash in restaurants and cleaning toilet bowls. I rented expensive apartments with extra bedrooms so you could have some privacy. And what appreciation do I get? Not even a letter."

Well, I wanted to give her a letter alright—three of them, as a matter of fact: FRO. Fuck right off! I bit my tongue. I almost burst from biting my tongue. I wanted to tell her about the endless line of losers trooping through our house. I wanted to tell her about the bastards who "accidentally" opened the bathroom door—which had no lock—while I was taking a shower. And the ones I could hear jerking off while I tried to sleep in the next room—a chair pushed up against the door in case playing with their own fucking meat wasn't enough. I wanted to scream in her face about the uncles who diddled me and the cool cats who tried to get me stoned or drunk or both so they could do what they wanted with me.

"You were always so high and mighty, weren't you?" she said. "None of my friends were good enough for you. Your nose was way up there, wasn't it?"

And, if that wasn't bad enough, once I escaped my mother, I had to listen to Giulio's blessed and sainted mother giving me lessons on how to be a good wife, how to keep her little son happy.

"Remember my boy Giulio he is very sensitive. You have to treat him gentle. You have to make him nice pasta. With plenty of red sauce. And roast chicken. He love roast chicken."

You can't imagine the number of times I wanted to shout in her smug face: "You stupid ignorant peasant! Your son's nothing but a real jerk. A stupid mama's boy. Who else would be dumb enough to bring another man into the house—and then practically throw his wife into the guy's arms? 'Here, take her. Make sure you fuck her real good, now. We have to keep her satisfied, you know.' And, if it hasn't happened yet, it's certainly not because of him."

No, I didn't really think Giulio was a jerk. In fact, I thought he was a sweet kind of guy—just a little simple when it came to the ways of the street, that's all. But my mother-in-law—"please call me mama, we're all family around here"—pissed me off. Shit, I wouldn't even call my own mother "mama." Why should I do it for a complete stranger? She might have bought her son off with a ladle of red sauce, but it would take a lot more than that for me.

Then I had Mr. di Orio to contend with. Lean and dour-faced, he was always skulking around like someone had just died. And when he spoke, you had to lean over to hear what he was saying—and get a blast of soured-wine breath. And, if he wasn't talking about the good old days back home ("So why the fuck don't you go back there?" I felt like screaming), he was complaining about people who didn't appreciate all they had here in "the new world," as he called it.

"They marry, they divorce," he said. "They say hello,

they sleep together. Back in my little village, you get married forever. And you never get close to the woman until the priest say it's alright. But it's not just the kids to blame. We're to blame, too. We haven't been strong enough for them."

He got that last bit right. I was looking at one of the biggest weaklings of all. No wonder poor old Giulio didn't have much backbone. He had had a father like that as a role model. Why, it made me glad my own father had fucked off into the Northern Ontario sunset before he could do any more damage.

The only one I got along with at all was Raf. He took me out a couple of times—to one of the Crescent Street clubs where we could do a bit of drinking and dancing.

"So, how's married life been treating you?" he asked the first night we went out. "Is that brother of mine showing you a good time?"

"He's got his moments," I said. "But getting him to go out anywhere is like pulling teeth."

"Yeah," he said, laughing. "I'm still scratching my head about the two of you."

"What do you mean?"

"Well, you know. You're like … I don't know … opposites." He laughed and refilled my glass. "If you don't mind my asking, what was the attraction?"

Indeed, what was the attraction? I'd asked myself the same question plenty.

"I guess," I said, "it had something to do with where I'd come from. What I was into. Giulio was different from those other boys I'd known."

"Different might not be a strong enough word," he said. "Weird is more like it."

"He didn't come onto me like they did. He didn't walk around as if he was king of the hill, as if everything centred around the way he combed his hair or wore his clothes. And he didn't mouth off when he had nothing to say. He was so quiet and nervous, always off by himself. Always thinking. At least, that's what I thought he was doing. And his eyes—they were so sad and droopy. I told myself on the spot: 'I'm going to marry him. Just like that. He's going to be the man with whom I'll spend the rest of my life. And there'll be no stopping me. That's a promise'."

"Ah, true love," Raf said, pretending to play a violin amid the background noise of "American Woman." "How well I remember that evening. I had my own designs on you when I invited you to that party."

"I bet you did," I said. "But I had a strict policy about getting involved with my boss."

"Hey, no problem. It all turned out for the best. Even if he couldn't dance worth a shit."

"And he still can't. But who cares, eh? At the time, dancing wasn't high on my list of what to look for in a man. I'd been with too many good dancers already, too many guys who could shuffle their feet and act cool. I wanted someone who would take me away from what was going down at home. Someone who was serious about his commitments and who wouldn't dump me the first chance he got."

"Enter Giulio."

"Fucking right."

"When it comes to having fun, though, old Giulio could use a few lessons. And I'm just the one to show him!"

"Oh yeah. Still planning on coming out?"

"You bet. I've already booked the flight. So you guys had better be ready."

The music shifted. "Wooly Bully."

"Come on," Raf said, standing up. "Let's dance!"

As soon as the doctor gave the okay for my mother to leave the hospital, I packed my bags. I had no intention of spending even one day with her at home, listening to her rant about how that good-for-nothing doctor had ordered her to stop smoking and how she'd rather die than do that. Instead, I had Raf drive me over so I could wait for her in his car. And so he could take me right to the airport.

"These fucking Pepsis," he said when he noticed the FLQ *Québec Libre* scribbled on walls we were driving past. "Do they really think the Americans are going to let them get away with kidnapping and shit like that?"

I shook my head, but I was only half-listening, nervous about what I'd say to my mother.

"Fuck, I wouldn't be surprised if the FBI weren't up here right now, getting ready to blow a few of them away. Rat-a-tat-tat."

"Rat-a-tat-tat?" I said, giggling.

"Yeah, fucking right. Just to teach them a lesson. Anyway, can you just imagine what would happen to property prices if Trudeau allows this to go on much longer? Shit, I might have to move to Toronto. Now there's a shaking and baking place. I've attended funerals that had more action in them."

As soon as the cab arrived, I jumped out of Raf's car and went to greet my mother.

"You're coming in, aren't you?" she said, giving me that helpless look. "You'll stay a few days at least?" She leaned against the staircase. "I'm still feeling a bit weak."

"I can't," I said, not fooled for a moment. "I've got a flight to catch."

Before she could say anything else, before she could appeal to some silly feelings I still had for her, I kissed her on the cheek and told her to take care of herself.

"I'll write you," I said. "Promise."

Then, I got into Raf's car without looking back, and we headed for the airport. It was on the way there that I heard the latest news: the FLQ had kidnapped a second person, some big shot in the government.

"Aren't you glad you're getting out of here?" Raf said. "These guys are going berserk. Fucking out of this world berserk."

"Politics," I said. "I just don't get it. Isn't it bad enough what people do to each other without the politicians sticking their noses in there?"

"Hey, that's right. I hear where you live they don't

have politics—just nude beaches."

"Your kind of place, right?"

"My kind of place—you bet!"

It was mid-afternoon when the cab dropped me off in front of the flat. Even though it was one of those rare sunny days, Mr. Bedner's curtains were shut tight. Still mourning his wife, I said to myself. I have to go up and pay him a visit. Maybe take him out for a walk around the park.

"I'm back," I said as I pushed open the front door. "Hello." I peeked into the bathroom. "Yoohoo, Giulio?" Just where the hell had he gone on a Saturday afternoon? Here I was, all ready for a long, hot greeting, and he was nowhere to be found. There was a note on the kitchen table. That might explain things. But it wasn't from Giulio to me. It was from Torp to Giulio—and it had been written on the same night I left.

I looked around the kitchen. Something was different about it. The mattress—that was it. The mattress was no longer there, leaning on the wall. Giulio must have put it back. And that meant Torp hadn't been sleeping over. Probably hadn't been over since the day I went to Montreal. Oh well, I said to myself. Probably better that way for all of us. I had to admit I had found my resistance slipping. Slipping badly. That last afternoon we'd been together I'd almost suggested something I'm sure I would have regretted. So now he was gone and, knowing his type, he was probably gone for good. Good riddance.

He was too fucking laid-back and too fucking hard to resist. Sooner or later, we would have ended up on that sofa. And that would have been the end of Giulio and me. I couldn't afford that. Still ... the thought of Torp ....

Giulio came home about an hour later, and barely greeted me. He seemed nervous and all tired out. When I asked him what was wrong, he told me he was worried. Very worried. He then explained about the brothers and the coffin—and what Mr. Bedner had said to him.

"But you can't be serious," I said. "No one believes that kind of crap about people coming back to life. Well, except for my mother, maybe. She'll believe anything that has to do with what she calls the spiritual."

"I think Mr. Bedner has definitely gone over the edge," he said. "You heard him, too, before you left."

"So what do you think he's going to do?"

"I'm worried about Torp."

"Torp?" I said. "What's Torp got to do with it?"

That's when Giulio told me about his dream—and how everything seemed to be fitting together.

"You mean—"

"That's right," he said. "I think Mr. Bedner is going to try to kill Torp. And the worst part is that I haven't been able to get hold of Torp to warn him."

"Is that where you were today?" I said. "Out looking for Torp?"

"I went down to Stanley Park, hoping I'd find him on the beach. But no one there has seen him in weeks. One of them told me he was spending all his time at that abandoned warehouse. But I have no idea where that is."

"Maybe we should be going to the police with this," I said. "Maybe we shouldn't be wasting any time."

"And tell them what? That an old man has been mumbling about bringing his wife back from the dead? That we think he might want to sacrifice someone to do it? We've got no proof."

"What about the coffin?" I said. "That must count for some sort of evidence."

"Hey," he said, "people have been known to keep even weirder things in their houses. Shrunken heads, boa constrictors, dead pets. Even dead children. Besides, he could claim he's using it to store old clothes. Or as a place to keep magazines and newspapers."

"You're right," I said. "And you certainly can't rely on the brothers to say anything."

"Well," he said, "I hope it's just a misunderstanding on our part. Maybe he's just talking metaphorically. Some ritual that he has to go through. Part of the grieving process where they come from. Still, until it's cleared up, I'm not too happy with Torp running around without any protection."

"There's not much we can do about Torp until he contacts us. Anyway, if we don't know where Torp is, the odds are pretty good the landlord doesn't either."

"That's true," he said. "In the meantime, we should keep a close eye on Mr. Bedner, don't you think?" I nodded. "For his own protection, if nothing else."

That didn't look like it would be too hard to do.

All Mr. Bedner did was pace back and forth. He was pacing that evening when Giulio and I decided to go out for a pizza at the local greasy spoon. He was pacing the following evening when we came back from a long walk in the park and went straight to bed—and Giulio did something he'd never done to me before: he made me come by going down on me. And he was still pacing the next morning when I kissed Giulio goodbye.

Mr. Bedner, I said to myself, you're gonna wear out the floor if you keep that up. And you're gonna fall right on my head.

Several times, I almost worked up the nerve to go up and see him. Maybe offer him a cup of tea or something. But, to tell you the truth, I wasn't feeling all that comfortable about being alone with him. After that night he'd invited Giulio and me up to his place, and after what Giulio told me about him, who knows? He could crack at any time—and I fucking well didn't want to be there when it happened. In fact, it might be a good idea to lock the two doors from the inside—although they were so flimsy he could probably break through them without any trouble. And me all alone without even a phone.

Nicole, get a grip. You've never been afraid of anything before, and you're not going to start now. Christ, you've fended off drunken truck drivers and idiots gone on speed. You're not going to let a little old man scare you. No fucking way.

I decided it would be a good day to plough under all the weeds and other shit in the garden. That would save me a lot of time in the spring. So I put on a pair of rubber boots and gloves, picked up a ratty old pitchfork Mr. Bedner had hanging on the basement wall, and started to dig away.

I'd done about a third of the garden and, thinking it was time to take a lunch break, had stuck the pitchfork in the ground. As I turned back towards the house, I thought I saw something—a shadow or something—through what passed for our kitchen window. Slowly, I yanked the pitchfork out of the ground and, holding the business end in front of me, advanced towards the basement door. When I looked in, I could see that the door to our flat was open.

This is it, I said to myself. It's Mr. Bedner and he's gone completely bonkers. He's waiting for me with a kitchen knife and he's going to chop me up.

I thought for a second of slipping out the back gate and maybe going to a neighbour's house where I could phone the cops. But, before I could act, Mr. Bedner came back out of our flat and saw me standing at the door, pitchfork held high.

"Nicole," he said, laughing. "What you do there?"

"Mr. Bedner," I said, looking to see if he had a knife in his hand. He didn't. "What you do—I mean, what are you doing in our flat?"

"Sorry, sorry," he said. "I come to say I have good news for you. Good good news."

"Oh yes," I said, still not putting down the pitchfork. "And what good news might that be?"

"Come, come," he said. "I show you."

He indicated that I should follow him to the far end of the basement. I made sure to stay between him and the nearest door—and to keep the pitchfork handy between us.

"See," he said.

I jumped back slightly as he turned towards me, holding a dead mouse by the tail. I could see a drop of blood at the side of its mouth.

"Regular trap no work," Mr. Bedner said. "Mouse too smart. No get killed. Need trap with poison. That kill."

He walked towards me. I backed away to one side.

"You smell something?" he asked. "Something in walls, maybe?"

"No, I haven't," I said, finding it hard to keep my eyes off the mouse. "But my husband has."

"Ah," he said, touching the side of his nose, "Giulio have fine smell. You see, poison take time. Mice sneak back into walls."

"And ... and that's where they ... "

I shuddered.

"Yes. They go to die in walls." He smiled as he dumped the mouse into a garbage can. "But you no need worry. Soon, I come to take plaster down. Clean walls. Fix toilet ceiling. Okay?"

"Okay," I said, half expecting the mouse to come crawling back up the side of the can.

"Good, good," he said. "I go now. Goodbye."

"Goodbye."

He started to walk slowly up the stairs, then stopped halfway and leaned back down so I could see his face.

"Maybe you, Giulio come up for supper," he said. "Yes?"

"Sure, Mr. Bedner. That would be very nice."

"Good, good," he said. "When wife come back, we make big big feast. Invite everybody. Dance, sing, drink. And don't worry. I fix smell. Promise."

He waved at me and disappeared up the stairs. Dance, sing, drink. Sure, sure. I hurriedly put the pitchfork against the wall and stepped back into the flat, making sure not to turn around. Once inside, I locked the door and then put a chair up against the handle for good measure.

When Giulio came home that night, he seemed annoyed at me for the chair.

"I don't know why you're getting scared," he said. "We don't have anything to worry about."

"Oh yeah?" I said. "You weren't here today when that guy just traipsed into our flat."

"But he's the landlord. And he was only coming in to check the bathroom ceiling. Isn't that what he said?"

"That's right. That's what he said. But who's to stop him from going berserk when I'm here all alone?"

"Nicole," he said. "Be reasonable. If he's out to get anyone, it's not us. It's Torp. And as long as Torp isn't here, I don't think we're in danger."

"You don't think so?" Now I was getting pissed off. "*You* don't think so? That should make me feel real safe.

That should make me breathe a whole lot easier. So why isn't it?" He shrugged. "I'll tell you why. Because I was here today—not you. I saw the look on his face when he held up that stupid mouse."

"Look," Giulio said, holding my arms, "I'm not saying he's not dangerous. And I'm not saying you shouldn't be careful. But let's not get paranoid about it. After all, Mr. Bedner has never done anything to you. He's never even raised his voice in anger. Right?"

I had to agree. He'd always been the perfect gentleman in my presence. In fact, he reminded me of my own grandfather.

"I suppose you're right," I said, sitting down. "But, from now on, that chair stays right where it is. I don't want any more sudden entrances."

"Fine, fine."

Mr. Bedner was true to his word. The following afternoon, he and two men who looked almost identical came in carrying sheets of drywall and all kinds of power tools. They rushed in so quickly, they barely gave me time to pull the chair away from the kitchen door. I didn't want to make it look like I didn't trust Mr. Bedner.

"We here, my brothers and me," he said, a huge grin on his face. "We make everything beautiful."

They began to rip away at our bedroom wall, the one facing the basement. The old drywall peeled off easily—especially in the bathroom where it was all mouldy and soaked through.

"Aha," I heard Mr. Bedner say from where I was sitting in the kitchen reading the paper, "you bad boys." He came in. "Nicole, come see. Big mystery solved."

I wasn't really sure I wanted to see. But Mr. Bedner insisted. Nestled neatly against the central crossbeam were the rotting bodies of several mice, all bunched and twisted together where the poison had finally got to them.

"See," Mr. Bedner said. "No escape. All die. Mice, rats—all rodents, all die."

As he reached to pick them up with a small scoop, he accidentally turned their bodies over.

"There smell," he said, pointing to a mass of squirming, struggling maggots. "Flies get in wall. Lay eggs on dead mice. Everything rot and everything smell."

I could feel myself turning white and my stomach lurched like I wanted to vomit. But I wasn't about to give Mr. Bedner and his brothers the pleasure of seeing a woman become squeamish. That had probably been the reason he'd asked me to come see in the first place.

"Ah," Mr. Bedner said, wrapping the mice in newspaper and dropping them into a garbage bag, "that make smell. Now gone."

One of the brothers sprayed the area with disinfectant. Several maggots, left behind in the confusion, writhed as the spray hit them. Mr. Bedner scooped them up and flushed them down the toilet.

"You leave now," Mr. Bedner said. "We tear down ceiling. Dust come down."

Damn right I left. I wasn't going to stay around to see

what would come tumbling down from there. In fact, I wasn't even planning on staying in the house while they worked. Instead, I went outside and finished ploughing up the rest of the garden.

After about an hour, Mr. Bedner stuck his head out the back door and called for me to come in and have a look. I could hardly believe it was the same room.

"That's fantastic," I said, looking at perfectly white walls and ceiling. "Amazing."

"All clean," Mr. Bedner said, pointing up. "No more black. Tomorrow, you paint."

"Tomorrow I paint," I said.

"Good," he said. "Now, we go finish other side. So no more hole in wall and no more mice in wall."

"Why don't you just get yourself a cat?" I said. "That would get rid of the mice."

"Cat?" he said—and crossed himself. His brothers did the same. "No cat. No. Cat evil. In old country, cat for witch. Irena, she never allow cat in house."

"Mr. Bedner," I said. "A cat is just another animal. You don't believe in that kind of stuff, you do? Superstitions?"

"Superstitions?" he said. "I no understand word."

"Never mind," I said. "Now that you've got rid of the mice, maybe there's something you can do about the spiders. They're all over the place."

"Ah, spiders different," Mr. Bedner said. "No easy to trap like mice. Fast. You kill and kill but more there. Always."

"Spiders lost souls," one of the brothers said. "They

wait for judging. You kill, then God decide: heaven—"
he pointed up "or hell—" he pointed down.

"But I fix door bottom. Yes?" the landlord said. "Just
for you. Because I like you."

"Yes," I said. "That would be very nice."

I sat down to finish reading the paper. I don't really
know why I did. Things were getting fucking crazy all
over. The bombing was now happening across the city.
Every day, something or other was blown sky high. And,
in Quebec ... well, they couldn't find the kidnappers, and
the government was threatening to send in troops. I didn't
know what the hell was going on, really. Anyway, I had
more important things to do, like look for a job. I turned
to the Want ads. There were several secretarial positions
available. I made a note so that I could type up a resume. I
was just pulling out Giulio's portable Smith Corona when
Mr. Bedner knocked on the open door.

"Nicole," he said. "Excuse me. I forget to ask. Your
friend—ach, I forget name—"

"Torp," I said, suddenly feeling a chill go down my
spine. Here it comes, I thought.

"Yes, Torp," he said, smiling. "I no see him here. He
sick or something."

Don't you wish, I said to myself.

"No, he's not sick," I said. "He's just busy these days.
Doesn't have time to come around much anymore."

"Ah, I see," he said, turning sideways to make sure his
brothers were doing a good job putting up the drywall.
"What he do?"

"I don't really know," I said. "Why do you ask?"

"I—how do you say it?—curious." He yelled at his brothers: "No, no. Keep straight." Then he turned back to me. "This Torp fellow, he live in strange place, no?"

"I'm sorry," I said. "I don't know what you mean. I thought he lived on the beach."

"No. No more," Mr. Bedner said. "He live in warehouse, yes? Near—how do you call it?—False Creek."

"Mr. Bedner," I said. "You know more than I do."

"Oh I know," he said with a smile. "I know because I follow him there."

"You what?" I said, trying to keep the tremor out of my voice.

"I follow one night when he leave here. I want to know where he live—in case."

"In case what?"

"In case I need to speak to him," he said. "But I tell you honest I glad he not here. Too too glad. Neighbours they no like him. Say he drug addict."

"That's ridiculous," I said. "He's never taken drugs while he was here. Not once."

"Not me talking," he said. "Neighbours. They see him. Long hair and dirty clothes. They say: 'What he do here? He come to sell drugs to children.' So, better he stay away. Better for everyone. For me, for you, for everyone."

"You're right, Mr. Bedner," I said. Now, just get out of my face. I've got a resume to send out.

That night, Giulio and I had the first big fight of our married life. I could tell from the moment he came in that he wasn't in a good mood. Nothing new there. He hadn't been in a good mood all week. And I'd pretty much left him alone. But now I'd had enough. When I tried to get him to talk to me, to tell me what was bugging him, he just said I didn't understand. That's when I got pissed off.

"Screw you!" I said. "How do you expect me to understand when you don't tell me what the fuck the problem is?" He shrugged and sat down at the kitchen table, pretending to read the paper. "Is it something at school?" He shook his head. "Is it me? Have I done something to upset you?" He shook his head again. "Well, then, what the fuck is it? What the fuck's gotten into you?"

He didn't answer. That, I found out, was the worst part about fighting with Giulio. And it was something that never changed throughout all our time together. He would just stand there and take your punches without retaliating, until you tired yourself out.

"You know," I said, really starting to build up steam, "I'd rather fight with my mother. At least the old bitch lets me know what the problem is, even if it's the stupidest thing in the world."

I slammed a few things around—pans, cupboards, drawers. But it wasn't helping. I ripped the paper from under his nose and threw it to the floor.

"Stop it," he said at last, kneeling down to pick up the paper.

"Geez," I said. "It speaks. The zombie speaks. So if it's

nothing in particular, I guess that means it's everything. Isn't that the way it works? Come on. You're supposed to be the logical one. Isn't that what it fucking means?"

"Well," he said. "Not necessarily. You're making the kind of logical error many laymen—"

"Fuck you!" I screamed. "Fuck you—and your fucking logical errors! I don't need a lecture. I don't have time for that shit. What I want from you are some straight answers. Save that fucking bullshit for those students of yours. Not me. Do you understand? I'm your wife—not some prof with a fucking pipe up his arse. If you want to have an argument with me, have it on my terms. Do you understand?"

I didn't realize how loud I'd been shouting until I stopped to catch my breath. Giulio sat there with his elbows on the table and his hands holding up his head.

"Ah, fuck it!" I said. "Why should I waste my time arguing with you? You're not worth it."

I rushed by him and went into the bathroom where I sat on the toilet bowl. I had to get out of the kitchen. Otherwise, I might have conked him on the head with a frying pan. A few moments later, there was a knock on the door.

"Nicole," he said, "what are you doing?"

"What the fuck do you think I'm doing?"

"Come on out. I'll try to be in a better mood."

"You'll try to be in a better mood," I said. "Isn't that just wonderful? You'll *try* to be in a better mood. Well, that makes me feel so much better myself. Asshole!"

"Nicole, I don't want to fight anymore."

"That's nice."

"Tell you what," he said. "I'll go for a walk. It'll clear my head. And I promise to be in a better mood when I come back."

"You do that," I said "Go for a long fucking walk. And you'd better be in a good mood when you get back. Otherwise, just keep right on going into the fucking ocean for all I care."

I waited for the front door to close before I came out of the bathroom. I could see Giulio through the window. He was walking with his head down and all slouched over. It didn't look as if his mood was about to change. But, by then, I'd calmed down a bit. So, while waiting for Giulio to return, I sat down and went over my resume. Not much there other than my time as a receptionist with Raf. I'd done a couple of waitressing stints before we moved to Montreal, but I didn't think those would help me land a secretarial job.

Giulio kept his promise to be in a better mood. But I could tell he was forcing himself. He hinted at problems at school and about the fact his conferences weren't going too well. Some of the students were getting upset with him and didn't like the way he conducted the classes. I told him he had to learn how to deal with people instead of just trying to argue so-called logically with them.

"You're right," he said. "I just can't get inside of people. I can't discover what they really want. Or even what they really mean when they say they want something."

"But that's exactly the problem," I said. "Maybe, they don't mean anything more by it. Maybe if they say they don't like your classes, that's all there is to it."

It wasn't until that Friday night that Giulio's gloom lifted—and mine, too. It all started with a knock on the door as we were cleaning up after dinner.

"Oh shit," I said. "Now what does that busybody upstairs want?"

I threw open the door, ready to be really direct and curt with Mr. Bedner. To give him a good piece of my mind. And who was there before me but Torp.

"Torp!" I yelled.

"The one and only," he said, as Giulio came into the room.

"Well, well," Giulio said. "Look who's come out of the woodwork. We thought we'd lost you for sure."

"Can't get rid of me that easily," Torp said.

"Come in," I said, taking him by the arm and pulling him into the flat.

As I shut the door behind him, I glanced up and saw Mr. Bedner standing at his window.

"Oh, oh," I said. "Now, we're going to hear about it. Mr. Nosy upstairs saw you come in."

"Listen," Torp said, "I don't want to cause any trouble. If that guy doesn't want me around, maybe I should leave."

"Forget it," Giulio said. "He doesn't have the right to tell us who we can have in our flat."

"Yeah, fucking right," I said. "And if he doesn't like it, he can kiss my arse."

"Sit down," Giulio said.

Torp gave us a big grin and plonked himself down at the kitchen table.

"Shit," he said, "it's great to see you guys again." He took both my hand and Giulio's and squeezed them. "I thought about both of you a lot while I was hacking away on that magazine. And now—it's done. Ta-dum!"

He pulled a magazine out of his coat pocket and slapped it on the table.

"Ladies and gentlemen," he said, "I give you *Get Real!*, Vol. 1, No. 1."

I picked it up. It didn't look like much—a few type-written pages stapled together. On the cover was a drawing of what looked like a bunch of soldiers firing at women and children.

"I guess congratulations are in order," Giulio said. "You managed to pull it off."

"Yep," Torp said. "By Monday morning, this little baby will be all over the streets of Vancouver—all two thousand copies."

I turned to the first page. It was an article on what to do if the police came knocking at your door. There was another article about all the horrible things American troops were supposed to have done in Vietnam—and how the trial of William Calley was a sham. I handed the magazine to Giulio.

"You're really taking a chance, aren't you?" Giulio

said. "Trudeau's going to invoke the War Measures Act any day now. And you know what will happen then to anyone trying to pass these out on the streets."

"I'm not worried," Torp said. "Besides, what are they going to do? Toss us in jail for a few days? At least, it'll be warm in there—and we'll get some good food."

"You sound like you've been in jail before," I said.

"If you live on the streets," he said, "chances are you've been hauled in at some point or other. I mean, if a cop wants, he can arrest you for just standing around."

"Shit, that's depressing," I said.

"And who the hell feels like being depressed tonight, right?" Torp said.

"Right," Giulio said. "Tonight, we're going to celebrate. After all, it is the return of the prodigal son. Or the prodigal something!"

"And how do we celebrate?" I said. "We have a few drinks first—and then a movie. Right?"

"Right," Giulio said.

I took Torp by the arm and we headed out the door. As we went by Mr. Bedner's window, I had the urge to stop and stick my tongue out at him. Look at us now, Mr. Bedner, I felt like saying. What have you got to say about this? But the curtains were drawn and everything was dark.

"Looks like our Mr. Bedner has gone to bed for the night," Giulio said.

"That's too bad," I said giggling. "I'd love to see his face if I were to give Torp a great big, slurpy kiss."

"Hey," Giulio said. "There'll be none of that. I don't trust this guy to stop at a kiss."

"Giulio, my man," Torp said, putting his arm around him, "you might just be right there."

We stopped for drinks at a bar on Hastings near Nanaimo. It was a really dark place, and the three of us were squeezed into a booth that didn't give us much room to breathe. Giulio couldn't get the attention of the waitress, so he went up to the bar to get drinks for us.

"So," Torp said, "how are things going with you and Giulio?"

"Oh, alright," I said. "But he's been acting kind of strange all week. Like he's pissed off at something."

"Or someone."

"Or someone. But we'll work things out."

"I hope so," Torp said. "I really like you guys. You're my favourite couple."

"Here we are," Giulio said, putting down three beers and sitting on the other side of me. "To the success of the magazine."

"To us," I said.

We clinked bottles and then started to argue about which movie we'd see. Giulio and I had never been able to agree. I liked something where you could enjoy yourself and have a good laugh. Giulio was always going for the foreign intellectual stuff. Torp said he didn't want to get involved—he'd lost too many girlfriends fighting over movies. Ingrid-vs-Ingmar, as he put it. We ended up staying at the bar and, by the time the bartender said he had to close up, all three of us were pretty far gone.

"You guys," Torp said, leaning on us as we walked down the deserted street. "You guys are beautiful."

"Beautiful losers," Giulio said. "That's us."

"We need a cab," I said. "Where are the fucking cabs around here? How come there aren't any cabs?"

"This is Vancouver, dear," Giulio said. "You can't just whistle for a cab, you know."

"You can't?" I said. "So, what are you supposed to do? Pull down your pants or something?"

"Hey," Torp said, staggering as he tried to snap his fingers. He had to do it several times before they actually made a sound. "Hey. I got an idea."

"You know how to hail a cab," I said.

"No, no," he said, leaning against the nearest wall. "I want you guys to come with me. To the warehouse, I mean. It's not that far from here." Giulio and I looked at one another. "Yeah, come on. I want to show you all the shit we've done."

"Torp," Giulio said, "it's"—he looked at his watch—"two o'clock in the morning. And you're drunk as a skunk."

"No, no," he said, stumbling back before righting himself. "It's now or never." He stopped in front of us, still swaying slightly. "You're my friends, right?"

"Yeah, sure," I said. "Palsy-walsies."

"Then, we do it!"

"What the fuck!" I said. "We do it!"

"We do it!" Giulio said.

"That's more like it," Torp said. "This way."

Torp wasn't the only one not too steady on his feet. Supporting each other, we weaved towards an overpass that connected the two parts of the city cut in half by False Creek. When we got near the top, Torp suddenly leaned over the side.

"Hey!" Giulio shouted as the two of us grabbed him and pulled him back. "Don't do that."

"Don't you worry," Torp said. "Don't you worry." He waggled his finger at us. "I know this area like the back of my hand."

"Wow," I said, looking down. "Look at all the pretty lights."

"That's the creek," Giulio said. "Those pretty lights are the reflections from the oil patches floating on top of it from all the pollution."

"Ah," I said. "You're a spoilsport."

"Am not," he said.

"You've always been a spoilsport," I said. "A tight-assed spoilsport."

"Am not," he said again. "Torp, tell her I'm not a tight-assed spoilsport."

"He's not a tight-assed spoilsport," Torp said, stumbling down the other side of the overpass.

"So there," Giulio said, sticking his tongue out at me.

"Are we there yet?" I asked.

"Soon, soon," Torp said. "Fear not."

We turned down an unlit street with rundown buildings on either side. The windows had all been smashed and replaced by plywood sheets. There was garbage all over the place—boxes, tires, pieces of metal. And there was an awful smell.

"What the fuck is that smell?" I asked.

"Don't ask," Giulio said. "If you pronounce its name, it'll rise out of the creek and follow you home."

"Speaking of which, here we are," Torp said. "Home, sweet home."

I suddenly heard some scurrying sounds close to my feet and almost jumped straight in the air.

"Fuck!" I said.

"That's okay," Torp said, giggling. "They're just some of the other guests." He took my hand. "Come along."

He led us to the side of the building and through a small opening covered by a piece of plywood.

"Let there be light," he said, replacing the plywood.

One dim bulb came on in a far corner. Beneath it, I could see a stack of magazines, a couple of sleeping bags and several cartons of beer. Behind them was one of those plug-in baseboard heaters.

"This is wild," Giulio said. "You actually live here."

"Hey," Torp said, as he sat down against the wall, "what more could you ask for? I got light; I got heat; I got privacy."

"Until they turn off the electricity and slam a fucking wrecking ball against the side of the building," I said.

"Hey," Torp said with a shrug. "Life is short. You get your licks in—and then it gets its licks in. Right?"

He started handing out beers. They were warm,

but by then I didn't give much of a shit.

"So," Giulio said, sliding down to the floor, "what do you hope to accomplish with this magazine?"

"Sssh," Torp said, holding a finger to his nose. "If you're nice and promise not to tell anyone, I'll let you in on a little secret."

"Oooh!" I said. "I love secrets. Especially naughty ones."

Torp leaned closer to the two of us. Then he made as if to look around.

"It's a cover," he said. "A front."

"Let me guess," Giulio said. "You're actually a CEO for a multinational investment bank, and you're researching the market for mutual funds among the homeless."

"No, silly," I said. "He's a ... an angel ... that's it. An angel come down to earth."

"Quick!" Giulio said. "Get a pin! Let's see if he can dance."

"I," Torp said, standing up and beating his chest, "am a mad bomber!" He jumped up onto one of the metal shelves that lined the side of the warehouse. "I am going to blow this whole city to kingdom come." He started climbing. "I will create a new nation built on the principles of nihilism and anarchy."

He was now on the top shelf about twenty feet up—and could touch the warehouse ceiling.

"Torp," I said, standing beneath him. "Get down before you fall and hurt yourself."

"He can't hurt himself," Giulio said. "He's an angel—

an avenging angel."

"Come on," I said, getting nervous as he pretended several times to fly. "Get down."

"I'll get down," he said as he opened up his arms. "I'll get down if you take off your clothes."

"What!" I said. "Are you nuts? It's freezing in here."

"Then," Torp said, "my death will be on your conscience. Look out. Here I come."

He made as if to swan dive off the shelving.

"No!" I shouted. Torp pulled back. I looked at Giulio. He shrugged and took another gulp of beer.

"I'm waiting," Torp said. "But you'd better hurry because I won't wait long. These wings are itching to spread themselves. They want to fly!"

"Alright, alright," I said.

I sat down on the sleeping bag and pulled my blouse out of my jeans. Then, I unbuttoned it and slipped it off. I looked over at Giulio to see if he'd make some objection. But he just kept sucking on his beer. So I unzipped my jeans and wiggled out of them.

"There," I said, hugging myself. "Now, come on down."

"Hey," Torp said. "You haven't finished."

"That's as far as I go—until you come down. Right, Giulio?"

"Right," he said.

"Your turn, Giulio," Torp said. "Strip!"

"*Jawohl, mein Kommandant!*"

Giulio didn't stop at his underwear. By the time he'd

finished taking off his shorts, Torp had come down from the shelving and was squatting beside me. He reached behind my back and undid my bra. Both Giulio and I helped him out of his clothes. I had never felt like being fucked as bad as I did at that moment. Torp first licked my nipples and then worked his way down to my panties. Without taking them off, he pushed his tongue into me and moved it up and down.

"Oh God," I said as I fell back, my legs wide open. "What are we doing? We shouldn't—Oh, God—"

Giulio was kneeling just above my head, massaging my breasts. I reached up and started stroking him. And then I felt the panties sliding down my legs, felt them jamming themselves against my ankles. And Torp was on top of me, positioning himself to slip inside me. I arched up to make it easier for him. He hesitated.

"No condoms," he said, hovering above me. "Didn't come prepared."

"Don't need them," I said. "Fuck me."

He slapped against my belly with a groan and, as I looked up, I saw his hand take hold of Giulio. And the two of them kissed, a hard deep kiss. And Torp came inside me. That's when I started to moan like a crazy woman and felt the rush of an orgasm that left me shivering in my own sweat, the smell of sex all around me. As I lay there, Giulio and Torp continued making out beside me, at one point sixty-nining each other. I stroked Torp's buttocks, which were in the air near my face—and used the other hand to orgasm a second time, just as Torp and Giulio were coming themselves.

"No condoms?" Torp said, his head on my stomach. "Aren't you afraid—"

"Mandrake trees," Giulio said.

"What?" Torp said.

"Can't have babies," I said. "Doctor's orders."

"That's definite?" Torp said.

"Far as I know," I said.

"Oh well," Torp said, "who needs babies anyway? The three of us can be a family, right?"

"Fucking, eh!" I said.

"One big happy family," Giulio said.

I shut my eyes—and suddenly my head started to spin. And my stomach lurched.

"Oh fuck," I said, scrambling to my feet. "I think I'm gonna. Oh shit!"

"If you're going to puke," Torp said, moving away from me, "there's a bathroom on the other side."

But then it went away as I stood up and I motioned that I was alright.

"Giulio," I said, starting to gather my clothes. "I think we should go home."

"But, it's—"

"I want to go home! Now!"

"Alright, alright," Giulio said, pulling up his pants. "Anything you say."

Torp watched without saying a word as the two of us dressed.

"See you," Giulio said.

"Hey, yeah," Torp said. "It's been real."

"You bet," I said. "Too fucking real."

"Listen, guys," Torp said, as we were about to pull back the opening. "There's supposed to be a big to-do tonight on the beach. A celebration for the launch of the magazine. You're invited."

"Thanks," Giulio said.

We stepped outside and slid the plywood piece back into place. There was a cab stand on the other side of the overpass, and we made it home just as it was getting light out. Without a word, we pulled out the sofa and went to bed.

"You bastard!" I said at last when I realized Giulio wasn't about to speak. "Why didn't you tell me?"

"Tell you what?" Giulio said. "What are you talking about?"

"Why didn't you tell me about you and Torp?" Giulio didn't say anything. "That wasn't the first time the two of you have had sex, was it?"

"No, you're right, it wasn't," Giulio said. "It happened while you were in Montreal. I wanted to tell you. Really, I did. But I could never find the right time."

"And that's the real reason you've been pissed off all this time, isn't it? You were worried you'd never see your precious Torp again, didn't you?"

"Get some sleep," Giulio said. "We can continue this after we've had some rest—when we're not so drunk."

I lay still for a few moments, staring out the window. What was it I wanted to say?

"You want to know something?" I finally said. "You want to know what's really upsetting me? I enjoyed watching the two of you make it. Isn't that sick?"

But Giulio didn't answer. He just turned and went to sleep—like he was now an old pro at this kind of stuff. And this was the same guy who had been afraid to fart in a public bathroom in case someone heard him. The same guy who kept looking for ways to keep the bedsprings quiet—jamming them with pieces of wood and foam and God knows what the fuck else for fear his mother would hear us. But there was something else I had to admit— and that was that I'd been wanting to get fucked by Torp ever since I first saw him. Even now, the thought of him slipping inside me made me twitch all over. So why had I held back all this time? Why hadn't I made the first move? I guess because I was the one who was afraid. I was the one who didn't know what fucking Torp would do to things. And here, all this time, Giulio had already taken care of that. I guess what I was really feeling wasn't anger. I wasn't so much pissed off as I was jealous.

I slept a good part of that Saturday, hoping maybe I'd wake up and discover it had all been a drunken dream. When I finally got out of bed, it was early afternoon, and Giulio was sitting at the table, doing the crossword puzzle.

"Well," he said, "if it isn't Miss Sleepy Head. There's some coffee left in the pot."

"I've thought it over," I said.

"You've thought what over?"

"I don't ever want you fucking Torp again," I said, poking him in the chest. "Not unless I'm there, too."

"It's a deal," he said, a big grin on his face.

I spent what was left of the afternoon out in the backyard. It was a rare sunny day—the good old weathermen had got it wrong for once, calling for rain all day long. I got myself into a real routine with the ploughing and digging up of weeds. Through the kitchen window, I could see Giulio correcting papers. Every once in a while I'd go back to the night before. The feelings were so intense it was almost as if I was there again, with Torp just about to pull down my panties. And then I'd plough even harder to get my mind off the horniness that kept building up. When I finished the garden, I suddenly heard clapping behind me. It was Mr. Bedner, standing on his back porch.

"Bravo, Nicole," he said. "The garden will be too, too beautiful."

"Thank you, Mr. Bedner. I'm looking forward to planting some flowers. You get lots of sunshine back here."

"Yes, yes," he said. "Irena and I, we have big garden once. But we let it go."

"It's a lot of hard work," I said.

"Too too hard. Now, I just cut lawn."

Giulio must have noticed we were talking. He put down his pen and came out.

"Ah," Mr. Bedner said. "The other half—is that how you say here in Canada?"

"Mr. Bedner," Giulio said. "You seem in fine spirits."

"And why not? Beautiful day; beautiful woman; beautiful world."

"Yes, it is," Giulio said, looking at me. "But I thought you might be upset over Torp's visit last night."

Whoa, I said to myself. What are you doing? Don't get him going now.

"Oh no," Mr. Bedner said, laughing. "That all fixed. All straightened out. No more trouble."

"Good," Giulio said. "I'm glad to hear it."

I said goodbye to Mr. Bedner and went inside to clean up. I wanted to take a hot shower and then get ready for the beach party Torp and his friends were throwing. A few minutes later Giulio came into the bathroom.

"What a strange bird," he said, sitting on the toilet. "First, he's making all kinds of threats and warning us we're playing footsies with the devil. Now, all of a sudden, everything's alright. It's like he doesn't care anymore."

"Maybe he's going senile," I said, rinsing the soap out of my hair.

"Senile?" Giulio said. "I don't think so. More likely, he's found another way of setting his plan in action."

"What plan?" I said as I stepped out of the shower and wrapped a towel around myself. "Here, dry my back."

"Shit, I don't know," Giulio said, rubbing me down. "Don't all these crazy guys have plans? On the other hand, he may have just come to his senses."

Giulio reached around and clutched my breasts—at the same time pressing himself against my buttocks.

"Not now," I said, shaking loose. "Go wash up. We've got a party to go to."

While Giulio showered, I searched through my clothes for something appropriate to wear. There wasn't much there aside from a few jeans and some miniskirts I hadn't put on in ages. And then I saw it—just the thing. My one and only flower child skirt. I tried it on—and looked at myself in the mirror.

"Hm," I said, laughing, "looks good—at least when I wear it topless."

I took a deep breath and my breasts popped up. I started to rub my nipples, admiring how large the aureoles were. At least I'd gotten one good thing out of my mother. It was only then that I noticed a shadow across the bedroom window. I stepped back out of the light. Mr. Bedner was in the front, pushing the lawnmower. Shit, all I needed was for him to see me playing with myself. I grabbed a bra and fastened it, then put on a blouse.

Mr. Bedner tried to start the mower several times before he went back inside. That gave me a chance to button up. He came out a few moments later carrying a can of gasoline. He opened the mower tank and tipped the can into it. At the same time, Giulio came out of the shower, naked. I pointed to Mr. Bedner standing just outside our window—with a clear view of a good part of the bedroom. Giulio wrapped the towel around his waist.

"We gotta do something about that curtain," I said.

"Yeah," Giulio said. "Especially if we plan on having Torp stay overnight."

It was still light when Giulio and I stepped out of the house. The lawnmower remained in the middle of the lawn, and Mr. Bedner was sitting on his front stairs.

"Mr. Bedner," I said, "what's the problem? Tired?"

"No more gas," he said, shaking the can. "Need more."

He stood up and joined us as we walked down the street towards the bus stop.

"You too too pretty tonight," he said. "You wear something like peasant dress, no?"

"Why, thank you, Mr. Bedner. Yeah, I guess you could call it that."

"You make me think of Irena," he said, stopping in front of the gas station. "She wear dress like that when she young." Then, he winked. "You lucky man, Giulio. If she not already married, I ask for hand in marriage."

"Hey, stop it," Giulio said. "I might start getting worried about leaving you two alone all day long."

Mr. Bedner laughed and waved to us as he walked towards the gas pump. On the bus, I took Giulio's hand in mine. We looked at each other—then he leaned over and kissed me.

"Wow," I said. "This is a first. Giulio di Orio actually kissing his wife in front of strangers."

"Get used to it," he said, rubbing his leg against mine.

"Hey, hey," I said. "You can kiss me in public—but that's as far as it goes."

I looked out the window. We were passing through the downtown area, close to where we'd been the night before. In fact, there was the bar where we'd spent the evening. And soon we were climbing the overpass again. I tried to pick out the warehouse, but all I could see was False Creek and a pile of buildings that all looked alike.

"Jesus," Giulio said suddenly.

"What? What is it?"

Everyone on the bus was leaning over and looking on the other side of the street. Giulio and I stood up to see what was going on. Someone had put a bomb near the front of a department store. Where the front door should have been was a fucking huge hole. Part of the store's awning had fallen, and the plate glass had shattered. And there were several mannequins lying in pieces on the street. It was the first time I'd seen anything like it—except for some pictures in the paper.

"Who the hell would do something like that?" I said. "Seems kind of stupid to me."

"People are angry," Giulio said. "They don't think logically when they're angry. They think they can solve their problems by blowing things up. Sometimes, I almost see their point."

"Well, I don't. Shit, if they want to blow anything up, why don't they strap the bombs to themselves? I'd help them do that. I'd even shove a couple right up their assholes."

"Oooh," Giulio said. "That's would make for a real messy bang, wouldn't it?"

"I'm serious," I said. "Just like those idiots back in Quebec. All they do is go around kidnapping and killing innocent people."

"Ah," Giulio said. "But what exactly is an innocent person?"

"Don't start with that," I said. "I'm an innocent person—and you're an innocent person."

"Even after last night?"

I looked at him. He was grinning. So I leaned over and kissed him hard, giving a couple of old bags a full view of my tongue slipping into his mouth.

"Jeez Nicole," he said, straightening the bulge in his pants, "if we keep this up, I won't be able to walk straight."

By the time we got to Stanley Park, the sun had gone down. But it wasn't all that dark where we were walking. There were lights hidden in the trees so we could see the path in front of us. But I still wouldn't want to walk through here alone. Every second bench, it seemed, had some ragged-looking guy sleeping on it. They were covered in newspapers or ripped, oily overcoats you could smell quite a ways off.

"This way," Giulio said.

I took his hand, and we headed up a path that had these giant trees on both sides. Giulio stopped near what looked like a marsh with cattails and stuff around it. Then I saw the lake—or lagoon, as Giulio called it. He explained how deep it was and how something tossed into it would never be found. Looking at it gave me the shivers. Especially as it seemed so calm and perfectly flat. I could see the moon and trees reflected in it. It was kind of hypnotic—almost made you feel like jumping in, just to see what was at the bottom after all. I had always been a good diver and I wondered if I could make it all the way down.

"Hear that?" Giulio said.

"What?"

"Listen."

I listened. All I could hear was what sounded like a low roar. The ocean, of course. We were near the ocean.

"Come on," he said.

We started to run. All around us, the night creatures were making their little noises. Chirping and tweeting and croaking. The trees got smaller—from Douglas firs to regular pine trees to scrub bushes. Soon we were in a field where the grass was very sparse, and I could feel the sand beneath my feet. And then we were out into the open and on the beach. About a hundred yards away, someone had put up a huge tent and something was glowing inside it—a lantern, I guessed. The lantern reflected huge shadows against the walls. And outside the tent, I could make out a group of people. They were sitting around what looked like a baby whale or something. But it was actually a piece of driftwood. There was music, too. Guitars and drums and a flute.

"That must be them," Giulio said. "Take off your shoes. It's easier to walk that way."

"My Giulio," I said. "All of a sudden he's an expert on what to do on the beach. The same guy who not long ago wouldn't dare be caught dead in a bathing suit."

"Change is always for the good," he said. "Some famous philosopher said that. Or should have said it anyway."

He gave me a friendly shove and then ran off ahead of me. I was about to take off after him, but then decided I'd rather walk. Giulio reached the edge of the group and someone greeted him with a hug. Torp, of course. Then Giulio pointed at me and Torp started to walk towards me. I felt a familiar tingle as he got closer and closer.

"I missed you," he said as he stood in front of me.

"Me too," I said.

He reached over and put his arms around me, drawing me to him. I didn't have to be told what to do next. I kissed him so hard I almost hurt my teeth.

"Love your skirt," he said as we started to walk arm in arm towards the others.

"I've got nothing underneath it," I said.

"Nothing?"

His hand slipped down my back to my buttocks. He let out a low growl.

"I make it a policy never to lie about things like that," I said.

When we reached the others, Torp introduced me and then said he wouldn't bother with names because I wouldn't remember them anyway. Giulio had already found a seat near the driftwood pile and was busy talking to a woman lying beside him.

"Okay, everyone," one of Torp's friends said. "Time for the ceremony."

One of the people squatted near the driftwood and stuffed some newspapers and twigs underneath it. Then he struck a match and the whole thing lit, sending up sparks and flames.

"Hail," a woman standing next to Giulio said, as she raised her arms to the sky. "The God commanded, 'Let there be light,' and there was."

"Hear me," the person who had started the fire continued. "'The likeness of them is as the likeness of those who kindled a fire, and when it lit all about them the God took away their light, and left them in darkness unseeing.'"

"Boo, God," everyone started singing. "Hiss. Down with the all-mighty meanie. Down with the all-knowing weenie."

"No," the woman said. "Hear me:

> *Neither is it asserted*
> *That all the Elements are unreal,*
> *Nor are they all realities;*
> *Because there is existence,*
> *And also non-existence,*
> *And (again) existence:*
> *This is the Middle Path!"*

"Hurray," they all said, waving one hand in the air as if they were trying to clap. "Hurray."

I sat down on the other side of Giulio. He introduced me to Linda, the woman who had recited.

"That was pretty," I said. "Sounded kind of religious."

"Zen," she said. Then she turned back to Giulio. "You don't understand. 'The great Tao flows everywhere, to the left and to the right. All things depend upon it to exist, and it does not abandon them. To its accomplishments it lays no claim. It loves and nourishes all things, but does not lord it over them.'"

"That's all very well," Giulio said, "but you're not taking into consideration—"

I stood up and walked away towards the beach. I hadn't understood a single word of what Linda had said, and I certainly wasn't going to understand whatever it was Giulio was going to say. And, as much as I like to believe I didn't give a shit about not understanding that kind of crap, I did feel kind of inadequate right then. These guys might be bullshitting but it seemed to be on a higher level than most of the stuff I'd heard.

"Hey," Torp said, reaching around me. "Not letting that crowd scare you off, are you?"

He kissed my neck and all my hairs stood on end. I wanted to take him on the spot, to lift my skirt over his head and let him do whatever he wanted to me.

"Why are you hanging around with me?" I asked. "I barely finished high school."

"Hey," he said, "since when does schooling have anything to do with what I plan on doing with you? Besides, going to school doesn't make you smart."

"You can say that again," I said.

"Come on," he said, "let's go sit near the fire. It's getting fucking cold out here."

"Okay," I said, "but first tell me this: who do you like better: Giulio or me?"

"If you think I'm going to answer that question ...."
He looked at me. "Let's just say the two of you together complete my yin and yang."

"Your what?"

"Never mind."

He took me by the hand and led me back to the fire. Everyone was sitting around it now, listening while some musicians played. A girl with a beautiful clear voice sang the title song from what was then Simon & Garfunkel's latest album—*Bridge Over Troubled Water*. I'd never heard the song before but, by the time she'd finished, I was wiping away the tears. I would hear that song hundreds of times in the years to come, but it never affected me in the same way again.

Someone passed a joint. I took a hit and handed it to Giulio beside me. I don't think he'd ever tried grass before. On the first puff, he started coughing.

"First time, eh?" Linda said.

"Yeah," he said. "Guess I've led a sheltered child-hood."

The joint came around again. This time I really took a puff and held it in for as long as I could. When I passed it on to Torp, I felt a strange tingling, the sign I was starting to get high. And it brought back memories of my teen years—some good, some bad.

"Does smoking get you horny?" Torp asked, his head on my shoulder.

"Shit," I said nodding. "As if I need to get any more fucking horny right now."

The musicians started to play "*El Condor Pasa*," beginning with a solo flute. I wanted to float away with the sounds, to release my body and let it go wherever it wanted.

"Music," Giulio was saying, his words slurred and slow. "That's the true opiate of the masses."

"Spoken like a true neck-up man," Linda said. "If it's something you can't analyze, then you dismiss it."

"Come on," Giulio said. "That's not fair. The moment somebody tries to make a logical point you jump in with a personal attack."

"Torp," I said, slipping my hand inside his shirt and pressing against his chest, "can we go someplace? Right now. I need a fuck."

"Your wish is my command," he said. "Come on."

We stepped inside the tent. Someone had turned off the lantern, and it was dark in there. But, all around me, I could hear the sounds of other people going at it—with one woman trying to muffle herself as she was about to orgasm. Torp found a couple of empty sleeping bags. We lay down, and before I knew it, he was under my skirt, his tongue probing between my thighs. I started to make harsh moaning sounds and pushed down hard on the back of his head. It didn't take very long for me to come. Then, Torp lowered his pants and eased himself up into me. As he pumped harder and harder, I felt the warmth spreading out, heard his grunt, and prepared to come again as he shot his load inside me.

"Time to get back to the party," Torp said, as he rolled

162

away.

We had just stepped out of the tent when someone came running down the beach. He was shouting something. He stopped in front of Torp and fell down, trying to catch his breath. Everyone else had gathered around.

"Lennie," Torp said. "Easy, man. What's happened?"

"Fire!" he said. "The fucking warehouse is on fire. It's burning down."

"Shit!" Torp said. "Shit, shit, shit!"

"I was sleeping inside, you know," Lennie said. "And then all of a sudden there was this explosion and these 30-foot flames. It was fucking scary. If it wasn't for that opening on the side, I wouldn't have made it out alive. The front was a fucking wall of flame. There was no way I'd have made it out."

Torp said he had to go see if he could save anything. One of his friends agreed to drive him and so four of us— the driver, Torp, Giulio and me—piled into the car. But, when we got there, they wouldn't let us get any closer than the overpass. The fire department had already closed off the street, and no one was going to get near the place. We could still see some flames, but there wasn't much left of the building.

"Fuck," Torp said, sitting down on the edge of the sidewalk, head between his hands. "The thing's burnt to the ground."

A man who said he was an investigator for the fire department approached the crowd and asked if anyone had seen anything. I was expecting Torp to step forward and tell them about Lennie. But, when he didn't, I realized he didn't want the police to know they'd been using the place. They might be accused of setting the fire themselves. Suddenly, a car pulled up with *Vancouver Daily News* written on its side. A reporter came running out, holding a notepad.

"Excuse me," she said, pushing her way through us to get to the investigator. "Hello, Fred." He nodded at her. "Have you any idea how it started?"

"All we know," he said, "is that there was some sort of explosion."

"So you're saying it was deliberate?"

"We won't know that until we've finished our investigation," he said. "But chances are pretty good."

"Was there anything inside?" she asked. "Anything of value, I mean?"

"No, not that we know of," he said. "It was an abandoned warehouse. That's why we concentrated on protecting the other buildings around it and just let it burn."

"Do you think there's any connection between this and the PFRG explosions?"

"Your guess is as good as mine," the investigator said before turning away.

"Fred," she called out, "why would anyone want to burn down an abandoned warehouse?"

"Who knows?" the investigator said, without looking back. "Maybe that's how he gets his kicks."

Giulio and I convinced Torp to come back to our place. And his friend agreed to drop the three of us off in front of our flat. We sat in the kitchen for several minutes without saying anything. What the hell could we say? It was a little late for moaning—or giving Torp our condolences.

"This is a real fucking bummer," Torp said at last. "Two thousand magazines—all bound, stapled and ready to go. Two thousand magazines now just ashes and muddy water."

"I just can't imagine who—," I began to say.

And then I looked at Giulio and he looked at me—and we got it at the same time.

"No," I said, shaking my head. "That can't be. No way. He wouldn't do that."

"Who?" Torp said.

"No, I guess you're right," Giulio said. "He's not that crazy. At least, I don't think so."

"What the fuck are you guys talking about?" Torp asked.

"Mr. Bedner," Giulio said. "Who else?"

"What? You mean, the old fucker upstairs?" Torp laughed. "That's nuts. Why would he—?"

"Wait a minute," I said. "It's not so nuts. He's as good a suspect as any. Better actually."

"And he's let it be known far and wide that he doesn't like you very much," Giulio said.

"Come on," Torp said. "He's a harmless old coot. So he spouts off a bit. Big deal."

"Oh yeah," I said. "So how come he followed you to the warehouse one night? Answer me that?"

"He what? How do you know that?"

"Because he told me," I said. "He told me he knew where you lived. And he also told me he and the neighbours didn't want to see you around here any more. He didn't say: 'Or else'—but that's what he meant."

"Okay, okay," Torp said. "So he knew where I lived. But that doesn't mean he set fire to the warehouse."

"You don't know the half of it," Giulio said. "After his wife died—"

Giulio told Torp the story of how Mr. Bedner believed his wife was going to come back to life one of these days and how he was preparing for her return. He also told him about the coffin and the hints that only Torp's death would make it a sure thing that his wife would come back.

"This is too fucking wild," Torp said. "But, like I said, the guy may be a fruitcake, but that doesn't mean he could actually go through with something like this."

"You can't say that for sure," I said. "How far would you go if you believed you could bring the one you loved back to life?"

"It's still too crazy," Torp said.

"How do the police put it?" Giulio said. "He had the motive and the opportunity. All we have to do now is to place him at the scene of the crime."

"No," Torp said, shaking his head. "Much as I'd like to believe you, you guys are wrong about this. If that fire was set deliberately, it had to be someone who didn't want the magazines to get out. The RCMP, maybe. They don't like the citizens to know their rights."

"The RCMP *is* a possibility," Giulio said. "But, if we're talking probabilities here instead of possibilities— then Mr. Bedner is the most probable."

I stood up and stretched.

"We're not going to get anything done tonight by just sitting here and talking about it," I said. "I'm going to bed. You guys coming?"

Before Giulio pulled open the sofa, I cut out a piece of cardboard and fit it snugly in the bedroom window. I wasn't going to have Mr. Bedner peering in on the three of us. No fucking way. Torp and Giulio snuggled up on either side of me. The sofa was kind of cramped, but I didn't mind. For a while, I couldn't sleep and so I just lay there, listening to their breathing and staring up at the ceiling. This is crazy, I said to myself. Here I was with two men in bed with me for the second night in a row. What would my mother think now? Shit, she'd probably tell me about the time she had three lumberjacks at one time in the back of a pickup truck or something like that. Or giving some guy a blow job right under the counter where he was eating his fried eggs. You know what, she told me once. You kids today think about sex too much. Think about it, mind you. It's like you got sex on the brain. Maybe if you got fucked more often, you might loosen up about it—and realize that it's just a cock stick-ing it to a cunt. You go in-out for a while and he shoots his wad and you get to come, too, if you're one of the lucky ones. Otherwise, it's the old finger job. And it's got absolutely fucking nothing to do with love. Let me tell

you that right now. And she'd jab her finger at my chest—
just like her father used to do to her. Well, mother, I said,
what would you say about being in *love* with two men at
once? Impossible, right. No such thing. It's nothing but
fucking lust—I should know. One thing about my mother, she didn't pull her punches. How about you, Mrs. di
Orio? Oh, my poor son. Look, look at the kind of woman
he finds. She open her legs to every man who whistle.
Puttana! And then she'd get down and scrub a few more
stairs—or light a few more candles for her poor, poor son.

But what was I supposed to do? There was no way I
was going to let Torp go again. And there was no way
other people were going to allow me to hang onto both
men at once. They'd want me to make a choice. They'd
want me to make up my mind. Not want me to—force
me to! I could see the judge right now—with Torp and
Giulio standing naked on either side of me, hands covering their privates, waiting for the decision. Waiting for
one of them to be cast into the hell of never seeing me
again. Oh boy. Talk about being fucking melodramatic. I
placed one hand on Torp and the other on Giulio. Like I
was trying to weigh them or something. And that's when
I knew that, if it came down to it, if it really came right
down to that, I would choose Torp. It was the tingling in
my fingers that did it. Starting right on the tips of my fingers as I passed them over his flesh—and then spreading
over the rest of me until I wanted to swallow him whole.
But I wasn't going to make that choice until they actually
forced me. No fucking way. I was going to stall for as

long as I could.

"No fucking way," I whispered—and curled up against Giulio.

The next morning, the three of us had sex again—slow, unhurried, as if we had all the time in the world. And then we took turns showering. As I waited my turn, I lay in bed watching Giulio towel himself off.

"Giulio," I said. "Now that he doesn't have a place to live, we should ask Torp to move in with us."

He sat by the side of the bed and pulled on his shorts. My hand went up and down his spine. I could feel the bumps of his vertebrae as he bent down to put on his socks.

"What do you think?"

"I think," he said, "it's a great idea." He leaned over to kiss me. "There's just one little problem." He pointed upwards.

"Fuck him," I said, returning his kiss. "He's not going to tell us what to do."

"Hey, you two," Torp said as he came out of the bathroom, towel wrapped around his waist. "Time out."

I held out my hand for Torp and drew him onto the bed with us. He lay with his head on my chest. I could feel the long, wet strands of his hair across my breasts.

"We were just discussing your future," Giulio said.

"My future?" Torp said, his finger poking my belly button. "Now there's a risky subject. I never knew I had one—especially after what happened last night."

"Temporary setback," Giulio said. "Nothing some

hard work and a Gestetner machine won't fix."

"Yeah," I said, pushing Torp's hand down and knowing we were going to have sex for the second time that morning. "Besides, I'm not letting you get away again. No fucking way. You're stuck with us—until the end of time."

"Or we get tired of you," Giulio said.

"Whichever comes first," I said.

"And that'll probably be the end of time," Giulio said.

The three of us spent the rest of the day just lounging around the flat. Giulio and Torp talked a bit about the magazine and how to get it back on its feet. But no one was in the mood for any serious discussions. I kept hoping Mr. Bedner would show his face—just to see his reaction when he spotted Torp. But there was no sign of him. Once I thought I heard a noise on the other side of the basement. But, when Giulio went to look, there was no one there. He did, however, come back with a gasoline container in his hand.

"Look at this," he said.

"It's Mr. Bedner's gasoline can," I said. "The one he uses for his lawnmower."

"That's right," Giulio said, shaking it. "And it's empty."

"Empty?" I said. "But he just filled it last—"

"Exactly," he said. "And he couldn't have poured it all into the lawnmower tank, now could he?"

"Guys," Torp said. "You're jumping to conclusions again. Practically everyone in this city has one of those

cans. Some dumbos even keep them in the trunk of their
cars—filled. Waiting for the sun to heat them up."

"Still," Giulio said, "I have a strange feeling about our
dear old landlord. He's playing some deep game here."

"For once," I said, "we agree on something."

"How about supper?" Giulio said. "Can we agree on
that?"

"Pasta," I said.

"Pizza," he said.

We both looked at Torp.

"Pasta pizza," he said.

And all three of us started laughing and horsing around
like kids. We took turns pinning each other down. Giulio
whispered something in Torp's ear—and the two of them
came at me from different sides, wiggling their fingers in
front of them.

"Stay away!" I shrieked. "No tickling. That's not fair."

I reached for the broom—but it was too late. Giulio
tackled me low and I fell over with Torp on top of me.
They both started tickling me and I was bucking up and
pleading for them to stop when there was a knock on the
front door.

"Now you've done it," Giulio said, whispering.
"That's Mr. Bedner—and he's got an eviction notice for
us."

"Let me up," I said. "I want to give that old goat a
piece of my mind."

But it wasn't Mr. Bedner at all. It was a couple of po-
licemen. RCMP officers.

"Excuse me, Miss," one of them said, holding up his badge. "We're looking for a Steven Palmer."

"Who?" I said. "There's no—"

"I'm Steven Palmer," Torp called out behind me. He stepped forward towards the door. "What's the problem?"

"Mr. Palmer," the officer said, "we have a warrant for your arrest—"

"What?" both Giulio and I said at the same time.

"On what charge?" Torp asked.

"We don't need to charge you," the other officer said.

"What are you talking about?" Torp said. "I know my rights. You can't arrest me without charging me first."

"You're absolutely right, Mr. Palmer," the first officer said. "Except under the War Measures Act."

"The what?"

"That's right," the second officer said, a big grin on his face. "Don't you guys have a television? Or even a radio? Earlier today, the Prime Minister declared a state of emergency under the War Measures Act."

"But that's for Quebec, isn't it?" Giulio said. "The FLQ kidnappings?"

"That's where you're wrong," the first officer said. "The Act takes effect across Canada. We can't let those Pepsis think they're privileged." He turned to Torp. "Now, will you come with us, please? We don't want to make this more difficult than it has to be."

"I guess I don't have much choice, now do I?"

The officer shook his head.

"I want to know one thing," I said. "Who told you

Torp—I mean, Steven—was here?"

"That's confidential information," the officer said. "You can understand why we can't give it out."

"Was it that bastard over there?" I yelled, pointing at Mr. Bedner who was standing at his window.

"Miss," the second officer said, stepping up towards me. "I'd calm down if I were you. We can always arrange it so you share a cell with your boyfriend."

"Nicole," Giulio said, "do what the officer says."

I took a deep breath—and then another.

"Hey, guys," Torp said, as they led him away towards the police car, "don't sweat it. As the bad smell said to the sock: 'I'll be back.'"

Then he waved and lowered himself into the back seat of the car. I leaned on Giulio as we went back into the flat. I hadn't felt this bad since the day I saw my father walk out of the house, two battered suitcases in his hands, and my mother was standing in the kitchen, throwing whatever she could get her hands on after him.

"Ah," Giulio said, "what can they do? Hold him for a couple of days. It's not like they're going to link him to the FLQ or something like that. They're just using this as an excuse to pick up anyone who's ever been arrested before."

"I guess you're right," I said. "I hope you're right."

But that didn't make the really cold feeling in my stomach go away. And all I could think of was Mr. Bedner up in his living room, gloating.

"It had to be him," I said. "Who else knew Torp was

here? None of his friends would have turned him in, would they?"

"I don't know," Giulio said. "No. I don't think so. What the hell would they have to gain?"

"The only way we're going to find out for sure," I said, "is to confront him."

"You mean now?"

"That's right," I said, getting up my courage. "Right now. Come on. We're going to strike while the iron's hot."

There was no answer to our first knock. I rapped more loudly.

"He must have gone out," Giulio said, about to turn back.

"No," I said. I placed my ear to the door. "I can hear something inside—running water."

I knocked a third time, even more loudly, and the water stopped.

"Coming, coming," Mr. Bedner said.

The door opened and we were greeted by Mr. Bedner in a bathrobe.

"Come in, come in," he said. "I just finish shower. I like shower. Scrub-a-dub fun."

Cute, I said to myself. But you're not going to pull the wool over our eyes this time. Not with all the fucking scrub-a-dubbing in the world.

"Mr. Bedner," I said. "Do you know the police just arrested our friend Torp?"

"Yes, I see," he said. "Through window. But I tell

you long time ago he bad man. You no listen. He do bad things."

"No, Mr. Bedner," Giulio said. "He wasn't arrested for anything he did."

"I no understand," he said, looking at each of us in turn. "You do bad, you arrested."

"The War Measures Act," Giulio said.

"Ah, yes. I hear on radio. Like martial law, yes? Big emergency in Quebec."

"You wouldn't have had anything to do with his arrest, now would you, Mr. Bedner?" I said.

"Me?" he said, raising his eyebrows. "Why I do that?" Then he laughed. "Oh, I see. Because I no like him. Hmmm. That good idea. Why I no think of that before."

"And I suppose you deny setting fire to the warehouse, too?" I said.

"Fire? Where fire?" he said.

"The fire you set with gasoline you bought the other night," I said. "Remember? We were there."

"I tell you I no start fire," he said, raising his voice. "You think I crazy or something?"

"So why was the can empty this morning?" I asked, feeling like a prosecution lawyer.

"Gasoline can? Empty?" I nodded. "Sure it empty. Because I only buy enough to put in mower. No need for winter."

"Mr. Bedner," Giulio said. "Do you deny saying your wife was coming back to life? Do you deny that?"

Mr. Bedner looked at us—and then suddenly sat down

on the living room sofa.

"Ah, now I understand," he said. "I sorry. I very sorry. This my fault. When wife die, I go a bit cuckoo. You know." He made the crazy sign with his hand against his head. "I say silly things. Too too silly. But I know wife no come back. Wife deep in ground." He wiped his eyes. "And soon, I go there too."

"And the coffin," I said. "I suppose you're going to deny ordering that, too."

"Coffin?" Mr. Bedner seemed really confused. He looked from Giulio to me and then back again. "You make joke, yes? Coffin?"

"No," Giulio said, "she's not joking. She's talking about the coffin I saw your brothers bring to your house a couple of weeks back."

"My brothers? Coffin?" he said again, this time slapping his bare thigh and laughing loudly. "That no coffin. That my place for taking shower. You want to see? Come on. I show you." He stood up. "Come, come."

He led us to the washroom. Sure enough, he had a brand new shower stall.

"Beautiful, no?" he said, passing his hand over the wood. "Brothers too too good carpenters."

Giulio and I looked at one another. I don't know about Giulio, but I was feeling pretty fucking foolish.

"Mr. Bedner," I said. "We're sorry—"

"No, no," he said. "You right to suspect. I go cuckoo there. Real cuckoo. I no see straight. I say crazy things."

"We'd better get going," Giulio said. "We've taken up

enough of your time."

"No, no," he said. "You stay, okay. Have drink with me. I no like to stay alone. Make me happy. Come in living room."

"Alright, Mr. Bedner," Giulio said, looking at me for approval. I nodded. "I guess we can stay for one."

He led us back into the living room and then took out a bottle of his plum brandy.

"I think maybe I move," he said. "Too much remind me of wife. In bedroom, in kitchen, in living room. Here, she sew and sew and sew. She sew everything. Everything. Even curtain, beautiful curtain."

"Where would you go?" I asked.

"Move in with brothers maybe," he said. He laughed. "Then, we talk about when we young and crazy. Here, I show you."

"Really," Giulio said, "we've got to get going now."

"Just this," he said. "Make old man happy."

He pulled an old photo album from a shelf over the fireplace and wiped the dust off it.

"Real name Bednescu," he said, as he opened up the album. "I change; brothers change. Bednescu too much like spy, yes." He laughed. "You think I make fire; government think I spy."

The photos in the album, all in black and white, were mostly of Mr. Bedner and his wife when they were young. In one picture, which took up a whole page, the two of them were standing near the fireplace of a gigantic room, with a huge chandelier and twin sets of stairs.

"Honeymoon hotel," he said, his voice cracking.

"It looks like a beautiful place," Giulio said, looking at me and indicating we should leave.

Suddenly, Mr. Bedner broke down and started to sob, the tears streaming down his face. Then, as quickly as he'd started, he stopped and wiped the tears away.

"Look at me," he said, shutting the album and gently replacing it. "Once, I freedom fighter. I fight filthy Nazis. Then I fight filthy reds. Now, I like baby again. Like baby, I must learn many things for myself. Things I forget how to do. Wash clothes. Making bed. Cooking. Cleaning."

He sighed. We stood up.

"But you," he said. "You young and healthy. You have full life to go. No waste, okay."

"We'll try not to, Mr. Bedner," Giulio said.

"Good, good." He took my hand for a moment. "And we have coffee again, okay? Just like before."

"Sure, Mr. Bedner," I said. "We'll do that."

Giulio and I sat in the kitchen for several minutes before either of us said anything.

"Well," Giulio said at last, "we certainly showed him who's boss, didn't we? Christ, he almost had me crying, too."

"Is he that good a liar?"

"Who knows? All I know is that the warehouse burnt down, Torp has been hauled off to jail—and we've got no proof Bedner's the one responsible for any of it."

It didn't take long for Giulio to go into another one of his shells. For several days, I'd asked him to find out where Torp was being held. Maybe we could do something about getting him out. Or at least getting him a lawyer. But Giulio just shrugged his shoulders and said that the police were being very secretive about the whole thing—especially after the body of that kidnapped Quebec minister was found in the trunk of a car.

"That's stupid," I said. "What does that have to do with arresting people in Vancouver?"

"Our beloved mayor decided it would be a good time to clean up the streets. He's arrested everyone with long hair. Or that doesn't have a permanent address. Last night, while the RCMP was taking Torp in, whole squads of riot police swooped down on Wreck Beach."

Giulio had told me that on Monday evening. On Tuesday, I managed to get out of him that most of the people who'd been arrested had already been released.

"So where's Torp?" I asked. "Why hasn't he been let out?"

Giulio said he didn't know and then, without eating any supper, he excused himself and went into the bedroom, saying he had a conference to prepare. He also mumbled something about applying for another job. But I didn't really hear what he said and I didn't bother asking him to repeat himself. To tell the truth, I didn't give a flying fuck at that moment.

Wednesday was the same—just a lot of waiting around. I had stayed in bed until past noon. I was hoping that would make the day go by faster. Each time some person walked by the front of the house, I looked up, fingers crossed—and then my heart sank again as the person continued past. Giulio came in all excited and I thought, at first, he had some news about Torp being released. But all he could talk about was some silly class he'd had and how successful it had been. As if I could give a fuck about his stupid classes. Where's Torp, I wanted to scream. I want my Torp back—and I fucking want him right now. If he were here, I'd let him screw me on the kitchen floor and I wouldn't give two shits about being on the rag either.

By Thursday, I was reaching the end of my rope. And it didn't help that Mr. Bedner came snooping around during the day. He pretended he was there to staple a piece of weatherstripping to the bottom of our kitchen door. But I knew the real reason.

"There," he said, opening and closing the door several times after he'd finished the job. "No more spiders. And smell?" He sniffed. "Smell all gone?"

"Yes," I said. "All gone. And no, Torp hasn't been here. In case you were about to ask."

"Good, good," he said, looking around. "I mean about smell."

I could tell he wanted to stay a while and maybe talk some more. But I wasn't in the mood and so didn't offer him any coffee. He took the hint after a few moments.

I spent the rest of the afternoon seething. I was angry and pissed off and ready to explode. When Giulio came home, I barely gave him a chance to sit down at the table before I confronted him and ordered him to tell me the truth.

"What do you want to know?" he said, his head down over his soup plate.

"I want to know—why you're lying to me?"

"What are you talking about?" he said, still not looking up. "Why should I lie to you?"

"Well then," I said, standing in front of him. "If you're not lying to me, look me in the eyes."

He tried—but couldn't.

"Come on," I said. "I'm not a baby, you know. You can tell me what's going on."

"Torp was released on Monday afternoon," he said at last, sighing. "He was only held overnight."

"What!" I slammed the soup ladle down. It hopped up and fell to the floor. "And you've known this all along?" He nodded. "Son of a bitch! Why the fuck didn't you tell me earlier?"

"I didn't want to hurt you."

"You bastard," I screamed. "You didn't want to hurt me. Sure. You mean you wanted to keep him for yourself, don't you?"

"Nicole," he said. "What are you saying? Listen to yourself."

"So, why didn't you let me know right away then? Why did you wait almost four days before you told me. And … and you probably wouldn't have said anything tonight either—if I hadn't pried it out of you."

"I didn't tell you before," he said, "because I haven't

seen him since Sunday evening either."

"Wait a minute," I said. "Wait just a minute. You expect me to believe that. He gets out of jail on Monday—and you're trying to tell me you haven't seen him yet."

"It's the truth," he said. "And you should know that you're not the only one hurt. How do you think I feel?"

It was only then I noticed he was trembling. He was trembling so hard he couldn't bring the soup spoon to his lips.

"What's happening to us?" I said, sitting down and biting my lip. "Just what the fuck is happening here?"

But it was a silly question on my part. I already knew what was happening.

"We've got to find him," I said.

"And then what?" Giulio said. "What if he doesn't want to be found?"

I hadn't thought of that. All along I'd assumed he was in jail, being kept from us against his will.

"We'll convince him to come back," I said. "We'll find some way to convince him."

FOUR

GIULIO

*There is a difference between the act of injustice
and what is unjust,
and between the act of justice
and what is just.*

—Nicomachean Ethics,
Book 5, Chapter 7

I couldn't sleep the night of Torp's arrest. The next morning, without waking Nicole, I stuffed some papers and Torp's *Get Real!* magazine into my briefcase and headed for the university. Lightheaded from lack of sleep, I kept floating in and out, feeling as if I was skipping parts of the reality around me. The only thought that kept stirring in the centre of my brain was Torp. I wanted Torp. I wanted Torp more than I'd ever wanted anything in the world. Nicole faded away without Torp beside her. And, no doubt, the same thing was happening to me in her eyes.

When I arrived at the philosophy department office, Reginald Worthington III was waiting for me.

"You had better be prepared, old boy," he said, straightening his bowtie and then wagging a finger at me. "There seems to be a general revolt afoot."

"What are you talking about?" I asked, barely looking at him.

"You'll see. You'll see."

What I found was a conference class in a state of chaos, with students milling about in small groups and refusing to sit down when I requested they do so.

"What's going on?" I said, trying to put as authoritative an edge on my voice as possible.

A chorus of students all started to speak at once,

each one trying to shout above the other.

"Could we please have one person do this," I said. I spotted a girl who served as the vice-president for the undergraduate philosophy society. "Liz, why don't you tell us what's going on?"

"We feel we're not getting the best possible use out of our conferences," she said.

"Yeah," a voice shouted from the back, "we're getting shafted. And that's putting it mildly."

"It's nothing personal," Liz said, pushing back a stray hair. "Just that we feel you're not providing the leadership necessary to make the class come together."

"I still don't understand," I said, scratching my head. "What am I not doing that needs to be done?"

"Well," she said, "we seem to have two different views of philosophy. We're here to experience it, to make it part of our lives. For example, we want to know the implications of the War Measures Act and the morality of a government willing to throw people into jail without presumption of innocence. You seem to feel philosophy is something that comes straight out of a book, like we should be happy to quote authorities. Almost like a religion." There was a chorus of 'yeahs' and 'right ons'. "As I said, this is nothing personal. Just that you seem to come from a different space and it's not fitting in with ours."

She sat down, her face flushed, sweat marks showing through under the arms of her blouse.

"I see," I said—and truly I did. Or think I did. "Hm. What can I say? I'm sorry you feel that way. I would suggest that you lodge a formal complaint with the department."

"But we don't want to do that," Liz said. "We like you. We don't want to see anything happen to you."

"That's very kind of you," I said, dawdling on my notes. "I must warn you, however, that, as much as I'd like to help you, it's a little late for me to change the direction of this conference. I am bound, after all, to follow what your professor lectures on."

"Aw shit," someone yelled out. "This is fucking ridiculous. I'm not putting up with this jerk anymore."

And they began to file out, leaving in the end but three students in the conference, none of whom had ever said a word in any of the conferences. Act normal, I told myself. Don't let them rattle you.

"Okay," I said smiling, "so last time, following Professor Lebekyer's lecture, we were discussing Book III, Chapter 5 of Aristotle's *Metaphysics*, weren't we? And I think we left off at the point where he analyzes the various senses in which a thing may be said to 'be': 'A question connected with these is whether numbers and bodies and planes and points are substances of a kind, or not. If they are not, it baffles us to say what being is and what the substances of things are.' Any questions about that?" I looked around. Just as I had expected, all heads down. I told the three students there was little point hanging around—and we'd meet again in two days' time.

I didn't feel like going back to the philosophy department—especially with Reginald Worthington waiting there with a smirk on his face. Instead, I went to the library. It had always been one of the few places I'd felt at ease. The library was probably the reason I had been attracted to philosophy in the first place—the knowledge seemed all put away already, all lined up and inviolable. There weren't the upheavals of modern genetics, for instance, when a six-month-old paper was obsolete, where new discoveries made headlines every second day. Just when was the last time somebody came up with a new definition of morality? Or logic, for that matter? But now I was no longer so sure. I looked out the tinted glass, amazed at all the various groups defying the ban against demonstrations under the War Measures Act. In one corner of the campus, radicals were protesting higher tuition fees, a huge effigy of the university chancellor leading the way. Across from them, as if in defiance, Students for a Christian Society distributed pamphlets on the evils of abortion and free love. Further down, the Marxist-Leninist Anarchist Faction, masked and in combat fatigues, preached all-out war against the instruments of our society. In front of them, blocking off any escape, was a line of riot police. Everything was in a state of turmoil. And, I realized, things weren't much different for me. I had wanted to tell those students back in the conference that I sympathized with them—but I just wasn't sure how to go about it. Besides, I had my own concerns right at that moment.

Tuesday morning, there was a sealed envelope with "Personal and Confidential" stamped across the top waiting for me on my desk. It was a note from Professor Lebekyer:

My Dear Giulio di Orio,

I find this quite distasteful but I must inform you that I was visited by a delegation of students yesterday afternoon. They had strong complaints about the way you are handling the conferences, as well as your general comportment in the classroom and level of interest in the subject matter.

Now, normally I would dismiss—and have done so in the past—these lamentations from students as my basic teaching philosophy is that the teacher knows best how to teach and the student how to learn. The democratic form has to be preserved for obvious reasons during these troubled times, but on no occasion should we be seen as bowing to the half-formed, ill-grounded demands of radicals.

Having said that, I must remind you that a teacher's strongest asset is his rapport with the students, his ability to excite them and stimulate their urge to learn. With that in mind, I took the liberty to ask several of your colleagues for their opinion of your abilities and character.

On the whole, these opinions were

favourable. However, most seem to have noticed a steady decline in interest on your part.

Please note that, for the present, this is simply a casual letter, a heads up as it were. This letter will not be included as part of your record here and the only other copy will be in my personal file. Let's call it nipping a bad habit in the bud. However, you must realize that, as a non-tenured assistant lecturer under my purview, my recommendation at assessment time carries some weight. I expect you to take this as a challenge."

"A little love note from a member of the upper echelons, eh wot?" Worthington said as I looked up and rubbed my eyes.

"Quite so," I said.

And I decided on the spot that I *would* take the warning as a challenge—and as a way to show Reginald Worthington that I, too, could compete. The first thing I did was to fill out the application and type up a CV for the job in New Zealand. And I wrote to my old thesis advisor back in Montreal for a reference, which I asked him to send directly to the University of Auckland philosophy department. Then, after sending both special delivery, I went to the library and prepared myself for the next day's conference. I would go in with a completely new approach, determined to win over the students. The next morning, I walked into the conference class with my head high and a big smile on my face.

"I believe," I said to the half-dozen or so who'd bothered to show up, "that your latest lecture was on Aristotle's *Nicomachean Ethics*. Am I correct? Today, then, we'll discuss the opening lines of the *Ethics*—and how they impact on the so-called ongoing police action."

"Excuse me," the student who had been so belligerent two days before said. "Did I hear right? Are we actually going to talk about the war in Vietnam?"

"I believe that's what I said. And at the next conference I'd like to get into Book VI, Chapter 8 of the *Ethics*—political and practical wisdom—and how it relates to the War Measures Act. If that's okay with you, of course."

After the conference, which had turned into a lively debate on whether or not collective rights superseded those of the individual in time of war, I stopped one of the students I recognized from the beach and asked if he'd seen Torp. He said he hadn't seen him since the night of the fire. I asked if there was anywhere else Torp might go, but he couldn't answer me—and suggested I speak to Linda. And where might I find her? I asked. On the beach, of course. So I spent the afternoon walking around the beach area. I wasn't surprised not to find anyone there. The kids were either still in jail or they'd been scattered and probably warned to stay away.

That evening, I found Nicole in even worse shape than the night before. I tried to cheer her up by telling her what had happened at school during the day. But she wasn't interested, not even when I related the latest gossip of a hot romance between Pamela and the head of the department. My heart wasn't in it either. I wanted to know about Torp's whereabouts just as badly as Nicole did. We spent the night staring at walls and avoiding each other—which was pretty tough to do in our place. At one point, I even suggested she go see a movie or something. But she just looked at me—almost as if I weren't there.

And I was glad to leave the flat Thursday morning, glad to be away from the tension that was building up between the two of us. A tension that neither of us could dissipate. Worthington was waiting for me in the office, *The Manchester Guardian Weekly*, the "only civilized paper in the colonies," propped up prominently in front of him.

"I say," he said, peering up so that his granny glasses slid down his nose. "Heard you had a spot of trouble during your conference."

"No," I said. "Not that I know of."

"Come, come, now," he said. "We're among friends here. I understand the class walked out on you. En masse, as they say across the Channel."

"Oh that," I said. Across the channel? Oh, that channel. "A misunderstanding. Besides, everything was straightened out for yesterday's class."

"Yes, I heard about that, too," he said, neatly folding the paper. "A mistake, my friend. A mistake. No kid gloves. Never use kid gloves. Threaten them with failure. That's the only thing the buggers understand. Tell them their academic careers will come to an abrupt end if they don't toe the line." He leaned over. "I don't normally offer my teaching secrets to potential adversaries on the job market. But I like you."

"That's very kind of you," I said, suddenly realizing what I wanted to do, what I had an uncontrollable urge to do. "How about a cup of tea, then?"

"That would be grand," he said. "Absolutely splendid. Two sugars please. Splash of cream. Ten percent, mind you. None of this skim milk rubbish for me."

In the philosophy lounge, I lowered a tea bag into a styrofoam cup and filled it with hot water. Then, I detoured to the toilets. There—to the image of Nicole, Torp and me having topsy-turvy sex—I masturbated into the tea and then added the cream.

"Here you go," I said, stirring the mixture with a plastic spoon before handing it to Worthington.

"Ah," he said. "There's nothing better than a good hot cuppa on a chilly day, eh wot?" I watched him take a sip and smack his lips. "Just the way I like it. Thick and creamy."

"Think nothing of it," I said. Just watch out for the mandrake trees, old boy.

On the way home that evening, I marvelled at what I had done. It was crazy. Wild. I'd never done anything of the sort before, not even as a child. I felt a little nervous about the whole thing. After all, what if Worthington had noticed something fishy—or at least lumpy? But I also felt exhilarated by it.

That mood stayed with me all the way to the flat—

until Nicole greeted me at the door and demanded to know what had happened to Torp. I told her the truth, all except for having searched the beach the day before. At first, she accused me of all sorts of things—not the least being that I really wanted Torp all to myself.

In some ways, that was true. If I had to choose between Nicole and Torp, I would have taken Torp. But, after her bout of shouting, she calmed down and said we had to find him. She didn't say that without him our relationship no longer existed. Or that in some way he'd redirected through himself whatever feelings Nicole and I had had for each other. She didn't say that—and neither did I. But, as we lay beside each other in bed that night, I not quite touching her and she not quite touching me, I knew it was true. And not just true—but the truest thing in the world. I understand, I said to myself, what must be done.

I passed most of the night in wild, untamed dreams, flying off into space. Nicole and I were lying in a field too perfect to be true. She was curled up naked, with her back to me. My thumb, a huge prehensile thumb, slid along the curve of her spine, feeling the bony ridges from the knob on her neck to the coccyx nestled neatly between two mounds of flesh. My thumb continued down to a larger-than-life anus, brown-edged, rayed-inwards. And then there were suddenly three of us again, under a vast canopy, under what looked like rocks with holes in them through which the stars could shine. Or perhaps one huge Swiss-cheese rock. Nicole was in the middle, on her side, flubbing back and forth. I was upside down, against her back, my face between her buttocks. On the other side I could hear heavy breathing and the lapping of a tongue against flesh. I worked my way down, parting her legs from behind. And there our eyes met, Torp and I. And we kissed. And took turns stimulating Nicole from both sides. And Nicole, sounds muffled by the bobbing motion of what must have been a mouth filled with Torp, shuddered in a series of spasmic orgasms. And I awoke pumping semen into my pyjama bottoms.

Oh shit, I said, as I lay awake at 3 a.m. and felt the liquid sliding down the side of my thigh. The magic was all in a dream, the ache at the root of the penis, the intensity of imagined physical contact, the realization of perfect love. Nothing I could do was going to duplicate it. Nothing in this life anyway. I wanted desperately to get back to that dream, to return to that point where our eyes had met between her splayed legs. Instead, the rest of the night was spent in fragmented worlds and galaxies where I kept flying off into space and never once returning to the same spot, as if the universe turned out to have even more dimensions than string theory had predicted, where a point became a line that turned into a surface that sphered around to meet itself—and yet was still only a point. It was a universe where Torps moulted, burst their skins to become landlords; where a wife turned into a mother in the middle of sexual intercourse; where the visages of friends, relatives, neighbours, acquaintances floated detached like balloon-masks or sat immobile in a deadly parody of classroom behaviour.

And yet, in the morning, I felt calm and not at all perturbed, watching the first rays of the sun inch their way across the lawn and into the bedroom, making the dust suddenly visible in the air. I slipped a hand into my pyjamas. The semen was dry now, leaving my pubic hair matted and glued together. I stroked my testicles, enjoying and not enjoying the way they receded at my touch; slid up the back of my penis, where it felt almost sutured together; touched the highly-sensitive lip; pulled back the foreskin to expose the smooth eyehole and the milky-white liquid that would congeal like untended lard if given enough time. Then, I moved to my navel, circling there, waiting for something to happen; and finally up to the nipples that quickly hardened to my touch, the nipples that were the first to sound the alarm. It was a body, I thought, that I'd hardly noticed before, that I wore like a shell without actually feeling it was an integral part of me.

I passed my fingers over my face, tracing my nose, my mouth, my cheek bones, the line of my forehead, the back of my ears, the protuberance of the skull over my eyes, the carotid artery with its slow pulsing, the throb of the vein on my left temple. Oh, I'd thought about the body before but always as an imprisoning form, as "that lowly flesh" which keeps us from achieving our highest dreams, as a kind of distraction, especially when it came to philosophy. After all, what could this collection of nerve endings, probes, sneeze holes, feeding cavities, excretion facilities and reproductive organs teach us about substance, essence, the nature of the universe, God? It's what's inside that counts, isn't it?

Nicole stirred, let out a small moan and rubbed her eyes. Then, she rolled towards me, her hot morning breath against my face. Suddenly, we were holding one another tightly, making sure every possible part of our bodies touched.

"I dreamed about Torp last night," she said, yawning. "We were shopping and getting these incredible bargains, just filling up cart after cart. And when we went to pay, the cashier told us we'd bought so much that the store owed us money. Isn't that silly? And then Torp and I had wild sex, right there in the middle of the supermarket aisle. It was crazy wild. There was food flying all over the fucking place."

"Was I there?" I asked.

"I don't know," she said. "I couldn't tell. You know how dreams are?"

"I guess," I said. "But *you* were in my dream."

That afternoon, after another rowdy class that had the War Measures Act as its focus and the students hurling insults at one other, I was summoned into Professor Lebekyer's office. I thought for sure the old geezer was going to give me another reprimand and was preparing the way to ease me out at the end of the term. And I was already planning some appropriate revenge, along the lines of the Worthington tea party. Instead, he told me a number of the students had been back to see him and now they felt I was the greatest thing since ... since ... St. Anselm's proof that God exists, I prompted, knowing his fondness for the Medievals. Yes, exactly! He said he wanted to tell me right away because he felt praise should be given as quickly as blame. And, if I kept it up, he foresaw no problems providing a sound recommendation for the department to extend my contract into the following year. I thanked him and let him know I'd put in an application for the New Zealand job. He thought that was an excellent idea. Showed ambition. Strength of character. He leaned towards me and whispered: "Balls."

"Every young man should put out across the unknown seas when given the chance," he said. "Look at me—over the perilous Atlantic to the New World. And, if you should need a word in the right ear, let me know. I happen to be great chums with the chairman of the department. As a matter of fact, why don't I scribble something right now? Yes, why don't I do that?"

I sat there while he wrote out a letter on my behalf—and then stamped it across the top and handed it to me with a flourish.

"How's that then?" he said. "Will that do?"

I read the letter. It said I was very competent as an assistant lecturer and had tremendous potential for higher scholarship. I thanked him for it.

"I'll have my secretary mail it off then," he said. "Without fail. They should have it in a week or so."

I thanked him again and left. For once, everything seemed to be going according to plan. Now, I had the weekend ahead of me and only one task to perform.

Only one very important task. And that was to find Torp. To bring Torp home. To put things back in their proper order. To make things right between Nicole and me.

With that in mind, I spent the rest of the afternoon sitting on a park bench on the edge of Wreck Beach, huddled up against the wind. Just the thought of having to spend a night on that sand made me shiver. At first, there was no one else there, except for a man tossing a stick down the beach for his dog to fetch. Then, slowly people came straggling in—one by one, looking around warily. I watched as each grabbed a piece of driftwood and dragged it to the fire pit. They worked in complete silence—with none of the excitement or joy we'd experienced the previous weekend. It was as if a law had come down condemning happiness—or at least expressions thereof. After about half a dozen or so had gathered, I stood up and approached them. They immediately ceased what they were doing and stared at me. One of them swung a small club in his hand, a smooth piece of wood that seemed to have been worn down to its essence. I didn't recognize any of them—but that may have been because I'd only seen them in the dark.

"Hi," I said, smiling and waving vaguely at no one in particular. "Remember me?"

"No," the man with the club said, his tone menacing. "What do you want?"

"I'm looking for someone," I said.

"Oh you are, eh?"

I smiled and nodded.

"He's a pig," one of the women said. "He's been snooping around here. I saw him hanging around the other day. He's a pig, I tell you."

"What!" I said, genuinely upset at the accusation. "I'm not a policeman. I'm—"

"Look, friend," the man with the club said. "I don't give a sweet fuck who you are. Just beat it, okay?"

I was turning to walk away when I spotted Lennie coming down the beach. Warehouse Lennie.

"Lennie!" I said. "Am I ever glad to see you." He looked at me as if he didn't recognize me. "Giulio. Last Saturday. I was there when you told Torp about the warehouse fire."

"Oh yeah, right." He walked past me. "What brings you here?"

"I'm looking for him. Torp, I mean."

"Haven't seen him, man," he said, dragging his own piece of driftwood towards the pit. Must be some sort of ritual, I said to myself. Some due-paying ritual. "Not since the pigs let him out. But I'll tell him you're looking for him—the next time he shows up. Okay?"

"You wouldn't happen to know where he is, would you? I have to talk to him."

"Nope," he said, and emphasized it by shaking his head. "All I know is that he's lying low right now. And, when Torp lies low, forget about it, man. He could be anywhere from here to Timbuktu. Know what I mean? On the other hand, he could show up again just like that."

He snapped his fingers.

"Could I leave something for him then?" I asked. "Just in case he shows up here first."

"Hey, no skin off my nose."

I took Torp's magazine out of my school briefcase and wrote a note on the inside cover: "I presume this is the last copy of *Get Real!*. Thought you might like it back. Nicole and I are very much looking forward to seeing you again." Then I put the magazine in a brown envelope, sealed the envelope and handed it to Lennie.

"Thanks a lot," I said. "Appreciate it."

I stopped at the liquor store on the way home and picked up a couple of bottles of wine. Then an all-dressed pizza at the corner greasy spoon. I had a strange urge to celebrate. Almost as if I could sense Torp's imminent return. Besides, it had been exactly one week since our warehouse get together. In fact, I felt so confident about it I told Nicole that Torp would definitely show up later that night. It wasn't the truth exactly, but it could have been.

"We'll eat in the bedroom," she said. "That way we won't have to move when he comes in."

"I like the way your mind works," I said. "And the rest of you, too."

We moved the sofa aside and brought the card table from the kitchen. Nicole threw a folded white bedsheet over it and even found a pair of candles. Then, before sitting down, she took out some of Mr. Bedner's finer cutlery and set the table for three. I poured wine into three glasses.

"Here's to me and you and our absent friend," I said. "And to a time when we'll no longer be apart."

We looked at each other across the table, then clinked and downed the first glass in one shot.

"Let's eat," Nicole said. "I'm starving—"

"—for love!" we both said at once.

We burst out laughing as I refilled the glasses.

"Here you go, my dear," I said, handing Nicole a slice of pizza. "A fine example of the art of gourmet cooking."

It took only a few minutes to finish off half the pizza and the first bottle of wine. I was just about to open the second when Nicole let out a low whistle.

"Holy fuck," she said, standing up and going to the window. "You gotta see this. Mr. Bedner's all duded up."

I looked out. It was dark but I could just make out Mr. Bedner under the porch light. Hair slicked and parted down the middle, shoes polished, dressed in a striped suit and holding an assortment of flowers, he headed off down the street.

"The old bugger's got a girlfriend," I said.

"Come on," Nicole said, giggling. "Let's follow him. Let's see where he goes."

"But—"

"Come on," she said. "Don't be such a fuddy-duddy."

She grabbed the other bottle of wine and headed out the door. I hesitated for a moment, then took off after her. At the end of the street, we spotted Mr. Bedner. He had turned in the direction opposite the downtown area and was walking slowly up a long hill.

"I know where he's going," I said as we slowed to assume the same pace as him. "He's going to visit his wife." I stopped and took Nicole's arm. "Let's go back and finish supper."

"No fucking way," she said, taking a swig of the wine before passing it to me. "I want to see this."

When we reached the cemetery gates, Mr. Bedner was walking down the path towards his wife's grave. The path was lined with poplars so that it was easy to keep hidden simply by walking along the edge. But that didn't take away the sense of unease I felt. Nicole, on the other hand, seemed exhilarated. Her eyes glittered brightly and she kept urging us to get closer. She wanted to hear what Mr. Bedner would say to his wife.

"What makes you think he'll say anything?" I whispered.

"Oh, he will," she said. "You just wait and see. I know about these things."

And she was right. By this time, we were behind a poplar barely thirty feet away from where Mr. Bedner was standing motionless in front of his wife's grave, holding the flowers out towards it like some sort of offering. A coloured spotlight between his feet lit both the tombstone and his face, giving it an unnaturally blue glow.

"Irena, Irena," he said, kneeling down to place the flowers on the grave. "Why you go? I miss you. Why you no come back? Everything ready. Irena, please. Speak."

He bowed his head. Suddenly, Nicole darted away from the tree to the nearest tombstone. I had no idea what she was up to—and I was afraid to call out in case Mr. Bedner heard me. I tried signalling instead for Nicole to get back behind the tree. But she simply took another swig of the wine and circled closer to Mr. Bedner, going from tombstone to tombstone.

"I love you," Mr. Bedner was saying. "I never say when alive. Only now. What you say to that? I love you. I need you. Come back. Please."

Nicole was now only one grave over from where Mr. Bedner's wife was buried. Because the spotlight was so bright against Mr. Bedner, Nicole was practically invisible. All I could see was a part of her shadow where she leaned up against the headstone. And I suddenly realized what she was going to do. Oh Jesus, I said to myself. We're going to get caught for sure. How was I going to explain my way out of this?

"Goodbye, Irena," Mr. Bedner said as he stood up and brushed the dirt off his knees. "I come to visit again. Soon." Then, he turned slowly, shoulders hunched, and started to walk away towards the path.

"I come, my love," Nicole said, making her voice as deep as possible.

Mr. Bedner stopped and, for what felt like an hour but was probably closer to ten seconds, didn't move. It was as if he'd been frozen on the spot. I wanted to step out from behind that tree and snap him out of it. An early Halloween trick, Mr. Bedner. That's all. Nothing to get upset about. But then he snapped out of it all by himself and swung back.

"Irena," he said, making the sign of the cross before kneeling once again in front of the grave. "Irena. You speak. To me, you speak."

He laughed. Then he started to hug and kiss the ground hysterically. Any moment, I expected him to collapse for good, to lay sprawled there, dead on his wife's grave. His heart giving out. Instead, he took several deep breaths and managed to calm himself down.

"I get rid devil," he said, gently, delicately brushing the earth with his fingers. "Devil gone. Now, you back. Yes?"

He looked at the tombstone, obviously expecting an answer. Luckily, Nicole didn't say anything more—and barely kept herself from bursting into loud laughter.

"No matter, no matter," Mr. Bedner said. "I hear the first time. I hear. Now I go home. I get ready. I prepare everything for you. Yes? Soon, soon."

He went back down the path and out the gate. The moment he was out of sight, I rushed over to where Nicole was sitting, trying hard to contain her laughter.

"That was a crazy thing to do," I said, my heart still pounding as I slid down beside her. "You could have frightened him to death."

"Ah," she said, waving the bottle. "That fucking old coot. You don't think he's that easy to kill off, do you?"

"Come on," I said, looking around. "Let's get out of here before the caretaker shows up."

"I like it here," Nicole said. "I think I'll stay right here for the night." She took another swig. "Yeah, I think I'll do just that."

"Nicole!" I said. "You're drunk."

"Oh yeah?" she said. "Is that so?" She stood up but had to hang onto the headstone. "Whee! I guess you're right. But who the fuck cares? Right?"

She finished the second bottle of wine and then, before I could stop her, threw it up in the air. It shattered on one of the tombstones.

"Holy shit!" she said. "Let's get the fuck out of here."

She started running down the path and almost fell several times before I caught up to her. I managed to hold her up.

"That was fun," she said, leaning against me. "I haven't had that much fun since ... since. Shit, I've never had that much fun with you before. We've got to do it again." Then she laughed and slapped her side. "That poor old bastard really thinks his wife's coming back to life, doesn't he?"

"Looks that way."

"Well, then," she said, beginning to slur her words, "we've got to do our part, don't we? It's our duty."

"Nicole, what are you talking about?"

"I mean, we can't leave the guy hanging like that. We've got to see it through. That's what my grandfather used to say: Don't start anything you can't finish. Right?"

She was weaving back and forth in front of me, several times almost falling before she managed to clutch onto something. I took her hand and led her to a nearby bench.

"Nicole," I said, sitting her down. "You're drunk."

She shook her head. "You've got to stop this right now."

"Why?" she screamed. "Oops! Sorry." She giggled, covered her mouth and looked around. "Kinda loud, eh?"

"Somebody's going to get hurt," I said.

"Somebody's already been hurt," Nicole said. "You heard the fucker talking to his dead wife. You heard what he said. He said he got rid of the devil. What do you suppose that means?"

"It means he's cracking up," I said. "It means he can't tell the difference between what's real and what's not."

"And we're going to teach him," Nicole said. "Aren't we?" She jabbed a finger at me. "We're going to fucking well teach him. Right?"

She stood up and raced off down the street. I let her go, not bothering to chase after her. In some sense, I felt the same way Nicole did—only she had the courage to say it out loud. Or maybe it was just the booze talking. No matter how many times Mr. Bedner denied it, there was no escaping the suspicion that he had been in some way responsible for Torp's imprisonment and consequent disappearance. Not to mention the warehouse fire. And, if that was the case, then he—like all criminals—had to be punished. And, if the police wouldn't do it for lack of evidence, then ... it was up to Nicole and me. Well, wasn't it? Maybe, if I said it often enough, I might convince myself of it. But I certainly didn't have to convince Nicole. When I got home, I found her in the bedroom, sitting at the table. She had re-lit the candles and was busy eating the rest of the pizza. Our bottle of brandy was also on the table and she was using it to wash the pizza down.

"Torp's not here," she said, leaning her head on the table. "I knew he wasn't coming tonight. I knew you were only trying to make me feel better when you said he'd show up tonight."

"No," I said, helping myself to some brandy, just so there would be less for Nicole. "I really thought he'd be here."

"He's not coming around again," she said. "Not while that busybody upstairs is here."

"We could always move," I said.

"Right," she said, taking the bottle out of my hands and swallowing a large gulp before she gave it back to me. "And how do you expect Torp to find us then? With a ouija board?" She shook her head for emphasis. "No, we've got to get rid of him." She pointed up. "He's gotta go. He's gotta fucking go."

"Nicole," I said, starting to feel the effects of the alcohol. "How do you propose to do that? Kill him and stuff him in a bag?"

"Don't be silly," she said, hiccuping. "Remember last week he mentioned something about moving in with his brothers. Well then, we'll just speed things up a little bit. We'll just push him along a little bit faster than he wants."

"Push him along?"

"That's right." She stumbled once as she got up, then took me by the hand. "Come on. Before he goes to bed."

Maybe it was the alcohol—or the wishful thinking. But, at that moment, Nicole's idea didn't seem half-bad.

All we had to do was to scare Mr. Bedner into moving out. Then, Torp would return and everything would be back to normal. Ta-da.

Humming to herself, Nicole knocked on Mr. Bedner's door. Mr. Bedner was still in his pinstriped suit when he answered.

"Ah, my children," he said. "Come in, come in. I have good news. Too, too good news."

"So do we," Nicole said, patting him on the chest and then putting her face right up against his. "So do we."

Mr. Bedner looked at me. I motioned with my hand that Nicole had been drinking.

"Ah," Mr. Bedner said. "Some fun. Young have fun."

"You betcha," Nicole said, plunking herself down.

"So, Mr. Bedner," I said. "What's the good news?"

"Tonight, I get message," he said, still looking at Nicole as he sat on the sofa. "Message from beyond."

"Message from beyond?" Nicole said, glancing at me and then turning away so Mr. Bedner couldn't see her attempts to stifle a giggle.

"Yes." His eyes glowed. "From Irena."

"From Irena?" Nicole said, making as if really surprised.

"Yes, yes."

"Come, come, Mr. Bedner," I said. "Are you sure? You haven't been dipping into the plum brandy yourself, now have you?"

"No, no!" he said, standing up and starting to pace. "I, sober."

He held up his hand as if he were swearing an oath. Nicole imitated him.

"Sober, sober," she said.

"She spoke, yes," Mr. Bedner said. "To me. Now, I know I not crazy. Now, I hope again. Feel like young man."

He stopped pacing and looked at us, a huge grin on his face. I was beginning to feel sorry for him.

"That's won ... wonnerful," Nicole said, having trouble with "wonderful."

"And you?" Mr. Bedner said, looking back and forth between Nicole and me. "You say you have news, too."

"Yes," Nicole said, leaning back and shutting her eyes. "Torp." She looked sideways at Mr. Bedner. "You remember Torp, don't you? Our good friend Torp?"

Mr. Bedner nodded warily.

"Well," Nicole said, clapping her hands, "he's coming back, too! Wee! Just like your wife! And this time, he's staying for good."

"Nicole," I said. "What—"

"Shut the fuck up!" she yelled.

I shrugged. Mr. Bedner turned completely white. Then glowed red. He started shaking his head and his knees buckled.

"No!" he said as he fell onto the sofa.

"But yes," Nicole said, nodding over and over. "He's going to move in with us. Won't that be won ... wonnerful? Eh, Harold. What do you think about that?"

"Not true, right?" Mr. Bedner said, turning to me for

help. Hoping I would negate what Nicole was saying.

I shrugged again and then nodded.

"I'm afraid Nicole is right," I said, deciding to get into the act. "This weekend, in fact."

And suddenly, Mr. Bedner went berserk. He started screaming for us to get out, for us to vacate the flat.

"Harold, Harold, Harold," Nicole said, the voice of reasonableness. "I don't see where shouting will get us. You can't force us to leave. We have a lease."

"Get out!" Mr. Bedner continued to shout. "Get out! Or I call police."

"Is that right, eh?" Nicole said, suddenly concentrating on a piece of lint. "Just like you called the police on Torp?"

"I no call police," Mr. Bedner said, calming down. "But he dirt. He scum."

"Now, now, Mr. Bedner," I said. "Careful what you say. That's a friend of ours you're talking about."

"Scum!" he said. "Not friend. Friend no fuck wife."

"I beg your pardon," I said. "What did you just say?"

"I see," he said, pointing to his eyes. "Have good eyes. I see him fuck her."

He thrust a finger towards Nicole who was practically asleep on the sofa.

"Fuck me?" she said. "Fucking right! And did you also have good enough eyes to see Torp fuck my husband?"

"What?" he said. "What you say?"

"You heard her, Mr. Bedner," I said. "Or isn't your hearing as good as your eyesight?"

"Sick!" Mr. Bedner said, holding his head. "Sick! You all sick. World sick!"

"Well, then," Nicole said, "maybe it's about time you leave. Maybe it's about time you get the fuck out—and leave the rest of us sickos in peace."

"I no leave," he said. "This my house. I wait for my Irena. She tell me what to do. She tell me devil downstairs. She tell me how to get rid of devil again."

Nicole burst out laughing. I followed her example. Soon, both of us were laughing as loudly as possible.

"Why you laugh?" Mr. Bedner said. "No laughing matter. Irena soon here. Then, you sorry. She tell me herself."

"Oh, she did, eh?" Nicole said. Mr. Bedner nodded. "I guess you're talking about the wife from the beyond who said: 'I come, my love'." She leaned up really close to him. "Harold. Is that who you're talking about, hmm?"

"Yes, I—"

Mr. Bedner stopped in his tracks.

"How you know that?" he said. "How you know words? I no tell words to you." He looked first at Nicole and then at me. Both of us were grinning. I was doing my best to stand still; Nicole was weaving back and forth on the sofa.

"No! No! Not true! You—"

"Yep, Mr. Bedner," Nicole said. "The one and only."

Mr. Bedner clutched the edge of the sofa for a moment. He reached out towards us, his legs giving out from under him. I managed to hold him up just before he collapsed to the floor.

"Devils," he said weakly, as I lowered him onto the sofa beside Nicole who was practically asleep by now. "Devils follow me from old country. Everywhere devils. Irena! Help me, please. Irena." He shook his head. "Wife dead. Dead. Dead. She no come back. Soon, I dead too." He looked up at me. "You call brothers, yes? Please?" He took a card out of his pocket and tried to hand it to me. "You no bad people. I know. Devil put curse on you. You call brothers. Tell them. They come for me."

"Yes, yes, Harold," Nicole said, patting his hand. "We'll call your brothers. But, first, we want the truth."

"Nicole," I said. "Are you sure—"

"I told you to shut the fuck up!" she yelled. She turned back to Mr. Bedner. "Do you hear what I'm saying? I want the truth. Do you understand?" Mr. Bedner nodded. "You set the warehouse fire, didn't you?"

"Yes," Mr. Bedner said, breathing heavily and clutching his chest.

"You sneaked over there," Nicole said, relentless, "and used the gasoline from the lawnmower to set the fire."

"Yes," he said, growing ever weaker.

"And you had Torp arrested, right?" she said.

"Yes," Mr. Bedner said, now barely audible.

"You called the police," she said, "after hearing about the War Measures Act on the radio."

Mr. Bedner didn't answer.

"Didn't you?" she shouted.

"Yes. Yes. Yes."

"That's all I wanted to hear," Nicole said.

"Now you call brothers?" Mr. Bedner said, pleading. "You call?"

"Sure, Harold," she said. "We'll call your brothers. No problem."

"Thank you, thank you," he said, leaning his head back on the sofa. "You nice people. Too too nice. Like children. Like children I no have."

He was smiling again and prattling on and on—just like the first time we'd met him—and as if what had just happened had left no mark on him at all. I wasn't sure we should phone his brothers. After all, what if Mr. Bedner should start screaming again that he wanted us out? Or that we were devils? Wouldn't the brothers get suspicious? But Nicole insisted.

"It doesn't matter what he says," she said, waving her arm in the air. "They're gonna think he's gone over the edge. And they're gonna take him away. You watch."

And she was absolutely right, although she wasn't there to see it. Right after my phone call, she excused herself and lurched out of the house. The two brothers pulled up in their van about half an hour later. Mr. Bedner was still babbling away when they came in.

"Very kind to call," one of them said while the other sat down beside Mr. Bedner and began to talk to him in their own language.

"We should take away first time," the talking brother said. "When he first mention wife and how she come back. Mistake to wait. Terrible mistake."

"Irena," Mr. Bedner called out. "You come now. Everything fixed for you."

He looked at me and smiled. I shuddered, sweat breaking out on my forehead and scalp.

"We take him our house," the brother said. "Lots of room. Maybe we rent. Maybe we sell. But you ... you stay, yes?"

"Yes," I said, wiping my sweaty hands on the side of my trousers. "We'll stay."

"Thank you," he said, shaking my hand. "Harold tell me you good people."

The other brother had Mr. Bedner by the arm and was leading him slowly across the living room towards the front door.

"Bye, bye," Mr. Bedner said, waving.

I went outside to watch Mr. Bedner being placed in the van. He looked around one more time, almost as if sensing he might never see the place again.

"I leave key," the brother said. "For emergency. Yes? You use phone to call."

They drove away. When I entered our flat, Nicole was already lying on the bed, curled up with all her clothes on.

"They've taken him away," I said. "Poor old deluded bastard."

Nicole didn't say anything. Didn't even stir. I got up and switched off the light. Then, I undressed and lay in the dark for more than an hour until I finally fell asleep. And dreamt again. Only this one didn't need much of an interpretation.

I was back in Mr. Bedner's living room. Mr. Bedner was lying on the floor. Help me up, he said in perfect English and without a trace of an accent. I reached down to lift him up. He floated to the sofa and just hovered there, a little above the padding, a malevolent Buddha with all sorts of extravagant powers at his fingertips. Then, several of the candles went out and the room darkened, turning purplish at the edges. Mr. Bedner looked up at me. So, you're still here waiting for me to confess, he said. Well, cheer up, my little tenant, your wish is about to come true at last. This is the moment you've been waiting for, isn't it? But before I tell you anything, I want you to understand that this isn't the result of your efforts. Or those of your drunken, slatternly wife. I confess only because I want to, not because you forced me to or because I feel any need to. Does your puny mind grasp that much?

He let out a sigh. Thin strands like spiderwebs floated towards me. I brushed them aside. And then I saw a tiny halo, an aura surrounding his body. Not a supernatural halo. Not one of those. It was as if he'd acquired a surplus of energy. Yes, he continued, I killed Tramp … Trip— Steven Palmer, whatever his name was. You wouldn't listen. You paid no heed when I warned you about him. So I took matters into my own hands. Mr. Bedner paused for a moment, folding his hands. Wax had gathered in smouldering mounds on the carpet beneath the chandelier. Candles, not replaced since his wife's death, melted away, leaving only the wick to burn in pools of clear liquid. Descartes' *Meditations* came to mind: "What then do

I know so distinctly in this piece of wax?"

Mr. Bedner went on: I waited all day for my wife to return; all night lying in bed hoping she would suddenly materialize beside me, her body warm once again and yielding to my touch. But there were only mice scurrying about, heading inevitably to their traps. I realized then the second half of my plan had failed. I knew she wasn't coming back. I'm telling you all this in order for you to understand the motives for my confessing. It's not for Thump's murder that I'm being punished—no, that was only fair and just. He deserved that and more. I'm being punished for a not close enough observance of the rituals, perhaps, or an inadvertent sacrilege along the way. No matter. I accept the verdict. And I recognize there's no reason to stay alive without my wife. Can you think of one? I shook my head before realizing what I was doing. He laughed.

Now, hand me a piece of paper, he said. Quickly. I don't have much time left. I looked around for one. Couldn't find any. Finally tore a blank page from Mr. Bedner's photo album which appeared magically on the floor. Better still, he said, do it yourself. My fingers are shaking too much. I took back the paper and tested my pen to see that it worked by making a little circle at the top of the sheet. An 'O' with a glass, I thought. Everything comes full circle. Are you ready? he asked. I nodded. Remember I'm doing this only to please you, only to save you from yourself. Because I care for you as I care for a child. In my haste, I'd already copied half this sentence before realizing it was still part of his preamble and had nothing to do with the confession per se. I made a line through it and started a little lower on the page.

The landlord held his breath and then dictated: "I, Harold Bedner, born Karola Bednescu, age sixty-four, of extremely sound mind and reasonably sound body, do here confess to the pre-meditated murder of one Steven 'Torp' Palmer, having clubbed him to death on the night of October twenty-three (23) nineteen-seventy (1970). This murder was committed neither viciously nor without purpose but as the only means of recovering my previously deceased wife—who died out of excessive fear of what the world was coming to."

Mr. Bedner stopped and looked up at me. Will that do? I said yes. All it needed was his signature. Of course, he said laughing, it must be authentic. I handed the paper over to him to sign. After he scrawled his name across the bottom, I snatched it quickly out of his hands for fear he might have a change of heart.

And that's when I awoke, my hand still fisted as if clutching something. I looked at the alarm clock's luminous dial. It was 4 a.m. Nicole hadn't moved, curled up at the far side of the bed. The dream had felt so real I had to make a conscious effort to keep from sneaking upstairs to make sure Mr. Bedner hadn't returned. To make sure he wasn't waiting for me, floating just above the sofa. I also had to remind myself that, contrary to what I'd taken for granted in the dream, Torp wasn't dead—as far as I knew.

But when I went back to sleep, something took place that had never happened before: I found myself in the continuation of the same dream. Mr. Bedner was now prone on the sofa ... obviously dead ... and I was celebrating, waving the confession in the air and dancing recklessly about the room. Then, without warning, I was crawling along the straw floor of a foul and putrid dungeon, unable to get up, the only light a shaft of sun from an immensely high window. The dungeon door flew open with a clang and two men came in. Hooded, they were dressed in identical velvet wasp-waisted black and red cloaks that shimmered like carapaces in the ray of sunlight. They removed their hoods. Mr. Bedner .... Torp, I shouted. Boy, am I glad to see you.

Without a word, they stood on either side of me and lifted me up by the arms. I was being led away, being dragged away backwards, the heels of my shoes leaving two trails in the mud and shit. To what? My freedom? No, Mr. Bedner said, as if reading my thoughts, to the place of your everlasting perdition. For some reason, I felt a sense of relief. This feeling continued as I was dragged to an immense fireplace, the flames roaring within. And then, with a choir singing, "For He's a Jolly Good Fellow," I was tossed into the flames.

And found myself back in the living room. From the sofa, Mr. Bedner fell to the floor with a thud. I could hear creaking at the back of the house. The last candles went out. I was having trouble breathing. There were damp, mouldy things coming towards me, things just out of the ground, things bearing a grudge. And I was fixed to the spot, the carpet fibres weaving themselves into me, holding me down like some type of Gulliver. I struggled to free myself, to reach the curtains. I knew for a certainty I'd be fine if only I could open the curtains. If only I could let some natural light in. I stretched to reach them, my feet cemented to the floor. Whatever was coming had made it part-way down the corridor, shuffling along. It was about to turn the corner. It was about to enter the living room. I kept shaking my head, trying to will it back. I tried not looking, tried keeping my eyes closed. But it forced them open. Irena, I said. I know it's you. Go away. Go away. I come, my love, it said, I come. And I looked up to see Nicole—

I sprang up in bed. The sheets around me were soaked, and I couldn't keep myself from shivering. Nicole moaned in her sleep, said a few words I couldn't make out, and then curled up into an even tighter ball. It was barely seven, barely light out, but there was no way I'd go back to sleep. Maybe, I could get some schoolwork done instead. I pulled on a robe and, as quietly as possible, made my way to the bathroom. There, I brushed my teeth to get rid of the taste of rancid alcohol in my mouth. I needed a cup of coffee—but I didn't want to risk waking Nicole. So I dressed and, carrying my briefcase with me, walked down to the local greasy spoon.

Isn't it strange? I said to myself. We've been here two months now; I've bought pizza here half a dozen times— and I still don't know the name of the restaurant. I guess it was because the place was so typically greasy spoon: some worn-out stools along the central counter and three booths whose leather—Naugahyde, more likely—was held together with duct tape. This time, I made it a point to look up at the sign as I walked in: Luigi's Home Cooking. Like Mamma Makes It. Of course, I said, what else could it be?

The only customers at the counter, a pair of old men with the blue tinge of recently-shaven faces, turned towards me briefly as I entered. Then they went back to their coffee and conversation. I recognized the language they were speaking: an Italian dialect—Sicilian, it sounded like. Luigi, behind the counter, joined in when not busy preparing pizza or stirring the tomato sauce. I sat at one of the booths and opened the briefcase, pulling out a pen, some paper and a copy of Aristotle's *Politics*. In keeping with my new approach, I wanted to prepare for my next conference—a discussion of Book V of the *Politics* in conjunction with the Pro-Form Radicals for the Good: the causes of and various approaches to revolution. It would be a real bombshell. I loved my choice of words. A sleepy-faced young woman, no doubt Luigi's daughter, came to wipe the table and take my order.

"Hi. Some coffee and toast," I said. "And no butter on the toast, please."

A few moments later, Luigi himself brought me the order. At first, I thought it was because he didn't trust me with his daughter or something like that. But I soon realized he just wanted to talk.

"Hello," he said. "How are you?"

"Fine," I said. "Just fine."

"Beautiful morning, isn't it?"

"Yes, the mountains are really spectacular this morning," I said, making sure I mentioned them before he did. "Quite a view."

"You're Mr. Bedner's tenant, no?"

"Yes, that's right."

"So," he said, sitting down across from me, "what happened? Mr. Antonelli over there"—pointing to one of the men at the counter—"he only lives a few houses down from you. He tells me they took Mr. Bedner away last night."

Jeez, I said to myself. News sure travels fast around here.

"He had a bit of a breakdown," I said, trying to keep my hand from shaking as I dunked my toast in the coffee. "Nothing serious. But his brothers thought it would be best if he stayed with them for a while. At least until he gets better."

"You think he'll get better?" Luigi asked.

"Truthfully, no," I said, not knowing how much to tell him. "He has this ... this ...."

"He thinks his wife will come back from the dead, is that not so?" Luigi said. "Mr. Wazchuk, the milkman, told me."

"That's right," I said. So who in the neighbourhood didn't know?

"Sad, eh," Luigi said, shaking his head. "Big, strong, healthy man like that. Worked hard to get where he is. Loses his wife and it's all over. But that's life, eh?"

"Sure is," I said.

Luigi stood up, still shaking his head, and went back to the counter. He leaned down and whispered to the two old men. They both turned towards me. I gave them a smile and then opened up Aristotle:

> *In considering how dissensions and political revolutions arise, we must first of all ascertain the beginnings and causes of them which affect constitutions generally. They may be said to be three in number; and we have now to give an outline of each. We want to know (1) what is the feeling? (2) what are the motives of those who make them? (3) whence arise political disturbances and quarrels?*

This was going to be fun, and I could see the arguments flying already. When I looked up again, two hours had gone by—and Luigi's was filling up. I put everything back in my briefcase and rose to leave. But before doing so I ordered some take-out coffee and a bag of dough-nuts—both freshly-made. Nicole was sure to appreciate the gesture.

Nicole, however, was in no mood for appreciating gestures of any kind. She was suffering from a vicious hangover and the smell of the coffee made her rush to the bathroom. When she came back out, wiping her mouth with a wet rag, she promptly plopped herself back onto the bed.

"I had the weirdest dream," she said after a few minutes. "The weirdest fucking dream." She opened her eyes for a moment—and then shut them tight again. "I dreamed we got Mr. Bedner to admit he'd called the cops on Torp. Isn't that too too wild?"

"That was no dream," I said. "You just don't remember. Too drunk and out of it, I guess."

"What!" she said. "What the fuck are you talking about?"

I explained it all to her.

"Oh my God," she said, holding her head. "What have we done? Is he going to be okay? Shit … shit … shit."

"I don't know," I said. "We'll have to wait and see."

"I still can't believe it wasn't a dream," she said.

"Go and see for yourself," I said.

Nicole went upstairs. When she came back down, she just headed straight back to bed, swearing under her breath. I brought the table into the kitchen and continued working on the conference. There was only so much I could do, however, without some newspaper clippings on the activities of the PFRG. So I decided to head down to the university library to see what I could find. As I was going out the door, Nicole jumped out of bed and, without even looking around, rushed into the kitchen.

"I think I'll turn over the earth again," she said, pulling on her rubber boots.

The microfiche newspaper files at the university had every single story ever done on the PFRG—both in the daily press and in some of the more radical student journals. A magazine called *The Georgia Straight* even published the group's manifesto, a long rambling attempt to justify the use of violence as the only sure way of achieving social change. The manifesto ended with: "Of all the good stuff, this is the stuff. Stuff several pounds of this sublime stuff into an inch pipe (gas or water pipe), plug up both ends, insert a cap with a fuse attached, place this in the immediate neighbourhood of a lot of rich loafers who live by the sweat of other people's brows, and light the fuse. A most cheerful and gratifying result will follow ... From thought to action is not far, and when the worker has seen the chains, he need but look a little closer to find near at hand the sledge, with which to shatter every link. The sledge is dynamite (T. Lizius, Feb. 1885)." I photocopied the material and then took the bus back to the flat.

Nicole was still in the backyard, ploughing away. She'd made a bunch of neat little rows. Now, she was sifting through the earth, breaking up the clods and removing the rocks. These she piled up along the sides. Watching her like that, I thought she'd missed her calling. She should have been born an Italian peasant woman. Right! An Italian peasant woman who liked to have sex with two men at once. I wonder how long she would have lasted before the priest and the other upstanding citizens conspired to drive her out. Along with her perverted *cornuto* of a husband who not only enjoyed watching his wife fuck another man—but got into the act himself, screwing first one and then the other. I thought of all the sayings and truisms I'd heard as a child when the relatives visited: "Too much knowledge is a dangerous thing"; "Science is the ruination of man"; "The trouble with the young of today is that they have too much time on their hands—give them some knitting to do." But it was all a bunch of bull. No wise saying could replace the taste of a body beside you about to come. And, if one body, why not two?

"There," Nicole said as she came back in, suddenly perky and bubbly. "All I have to is to send away for the seeds." She looked around. "Now, what else can I do?" I shrugged. "I know. I'll tidy up Mr. Bedner's place. Don't you think that's a good idea?"

"No, I don't," I said. "It gives me the creeps."

"Well," she said, kicking off her rubber boots, "it doesn't bother me. Not in the least."

And that's where she spent the rest of the afternoon. While I compiled correlation after correlation between Aristotle and the PFRG, the vacuum whirled around above me. Then I caught the strong whiff of bathroom cleanser and I imagined Nicole on her knees, scrubbing away. New Zealand, I said to myself. Can't get away soon enough.

When Nicole finally came down from Mr. Bedner's place, she seemed in even better spirits. She put her arms around me from behind and hugged me.

"You know," she said, "that's a real nice place up there. Sure beats living down here. It's got two bedrooms and a real stove in the kitchen."

"Nicole, what are you getting at?"

I knew what she was getting at. I just wanted to hear her say it.

"Well," she said, in a little-girl voice. "It's a real shame to keep it empty that way, don't you think?"

"Mr. Bedner's brother says they'll rent it out as soon as they get the chance."

"So why don't we take it?" She was pushing her breasts against the back of my head.

"Because we wouldn't be able to afford it."

"I'm sure if we call them," she said, unbuttoning the top of my shirt, "they'll let us have it for the same rent we're paying now—just to have someone taking care of it."

"No."

"Here's an idea," she said. "I'll get a job."

"If you want to get a job, that's fine. But we're not moving upstairs."

"Oh, come on."

Her hands were now inside my shirt, searching for my nipples. I could feel myself getting hard.

"Tell you what," she said, her hands sliding down below my belt buckle. "Let's try it for tonight. Okay? If you don't like it, we'll just forget about it."

She didn't give me a chance to respond before turning and sitting herself on my lap, facing me.

"Ooooh," she said, rubbing herself against me. "Something wants to do something naughty."

She stood up and started to undress. As she took off her clothes, she moved towards the kitchen door, dropping them one at a time.

"Come on," she said, undoing her bra and snapping it at me. "Come on."

Giggling and wearing nothing but her panties, she went out the door to the other side of the basement. I sat for a moment, not sure what to do. When she called out again, I decided to go out after her. I couldn't resist, really. She was on the edge of the stairs, massaging her breasts. Then, crooking her finger at me, she dashed up into Mr. Bedner's place.

"Nicole," I called out when I couldn't find her in the living room.

"I'm in here, lover boy," she said, her voice coming from the other side of the house.

I found her in what must have been the master bedroom, lying on a bed that looked as if it had been made from one piece of wood. The walls were covered with weird paintings of what looked like Virgin Marys. But not quite the ones I was used to. These had much colder eyes and their gold-speckled halos radiated out even beyond the picture frames.

"Isn't this something?" Nicolé said, bouncing up and down. "Come on. Try it."

"I don't think we should be here," I said.

"Don't be such a fuddy-duddy," she said, reaching up and pulling me down. "Enjoy it while you can." She pushed my face against her breasts. "Lick me. Come on. Suck. Come on. I've left my panties on on purpose. Rip them off with your teeth."

But suddenly nothing worked. I'd gone limp. Nicole tried everything to get me hard again. She rubbed her panties across my face; she licked and sucked me; she even suggested anal sex, offering to smear Vaseline all over my penis. I tried to shut everything else out, to concentrate on becoming horny again. But it was no use. All I could see were images of those Virgin Marys superimposed on images of Mr. Bedner superimposed on his wife superimposed on my mother. I rolled off the bed and hit the floor with a thud.

"What the fuck are you doing?" Nicole said.

"I can't," I said. "I can't help it."

"Jesus fucking Christ," she said, falling back on the pillow. "What an asshole!"

I felt like I couldn't catch my breath. I dressed and hurried out of the room, leaning against the kitchen wall. It smelled as if it had been recently scrubbed clean.

"Torp would have done it!" Nicole shouted after me. "He wouldn't have been such an asshole! Asshole! Asshole! Asshole!"

I stumbled back down the stairs and into our flat, picking up Nicole's clothing along the way. Nicole didn't come down. Later in the evening, I heard the sound of frying. She was making herself supper. Once in a while, I'd catch snatches of songs and loud whistling. Whenever one of the songs mentioned a name, she'd substitute Torp. Then she settled on: "When Torp comes marching home again, hurrah, hurrah! When Torp comes marching home again, hurrah! We'll fuck and we'll fuck till we fuck out our brains. We'll fuck and we'll fuck till we both go insane. When Torp comes marching home."

It turned into a battle of wills. I promised myself I wouldn't go back up those stairs; Nicole obviously felt she'd be capitulating if she came down. And so it was that, one of the rare times since our marriage, we slept apart. I tossed and turned most of the night, sleeping only fitfully, listening for the slightest noise in the belief it would be Nicole finally relenting, finally joining me.

To top it all off, a second dream remembered in as many nights. In this one, I'm sitting on a train, squeezed between Raf and Nicole. I'm hunched up, looking from one to the other, trying to carry on a conversation. But the conversations die away and we move forward in spurts: towards a colder world, the mountains with their unfathomable tunnels, the snow-covered bridges spanning empty space (they remind me of Chinese watercolours), the occasional deer or thick-furred goat scampering away. Then come the frozen flatlands. This is distance, I tell myself. This is escape. Torp is being left far behind; the landlord, still drawing air, is rotting in a grave beside his wife.

Would you buy me a pipe? I suddenly ask Nicole—or the person in my dream who represents Nicole. A what? she says, looking up from her magazine. A pipe. All professors smoke pipes. You want a pipe, Raf says, she'll get you a pipe. Right? Nicole nods. Ah, this truly is distance. Especially after we cross into the lower tundra and down into the rock-face. Can time run backwards? I ask. Nicole shrugs; Raf pretends not to hear. I mean, is time asymmetrical like everyone says? Or could there be a thin rubber band somewhere like one of those worms that hooks itself in your intestines and you have to try to pull it out a bit at a time, stretching it ever so carefully around a pencil or ballpoint pen for fear it doesn't snap in half? A thin rubber band that at any moment can pull you back to the beginning?

I look expectantly at one, then the other. I can tell it isn't the sort of thing that normally preoccupies them—for which they are to consider themselves lucky. Have you ever had someone suck you off? I ask Raf. What! Keep it down, will you? The other passengers will hear. You know, I continue, a blow job? Give you head? Lick your lollipop? Stop it, Nicole says. Fucking stop it right this moment. I can see she's angry—her face and neck are a crimson colour—so I decide for her sake to change the topic. What do you think of New Zealand? Supposed to be a nice place, Raf says. At least, that's what I heard. Yeah, me too. Do you think it's good for philosophy though? You've got me there, he says. Yeah, I suppose I do, I say.

Then, we're pulling into Montreal just like that. And I'm walking up the familiar street into the familiar house. My mother hugs me and says I've lost weight; my father says I'll never change. I'm a little upset by this attitude. After all, don't they know something is eating me up inside? Don't they know I'm wasting away from the burden I'm carrying, that I'm almost lighter than air? But no. They're making jokes about Nicole being pregnant. News to me, I say—and everyone laughs and laughs and laughs.

All right, who was it? my father asks. The milkman? No, Dad, Raf says, it was the travelling Fuller Semen salesman. And then it's night again and Nicole and I sleep in the first room we'd shared together. As if we've never left: the claustrophobia of having barely enough space to sit up on the side of the bed, the squeaking bed itself, the slow-motion shifting about, the ears listening in, ears stuck to the walls.

In the morning, I stay in the room, unwilling to come out for some reason. Out the window I can see the first flakes of snow collecting on the balcony and several birds puffed up against the wind. In my dream, I dream. I'm sitting on a huge throne with rays fanning out in all directions. As I sit there, my subjects are lined up before me, waiting to come up to see me. They are all grotesque, warped little creatures and each has a piece of paper to hand me. I read these papers and throw them on to a stack behind me. Then they file past and disappear behind multiple doors, millions of multiple doors, which close with a solid click. As they close, my personal guard—more grotesque little creatures, but this time in uniforms—bolt them from the inside and I inspect the locks one by one.

Someone just beyond the moat is calling out my name, but there's no way to unbolt all the doors in time, even if I wanted to. And the voice gets louder and louder until I snap up out of bed, startled at the darkness, with Nicole rattling the door. Quickly, I tear the sheets from my bed into thin strips and tie them together. Then I secure open the door of the balcony by wedging a book beneath it—Kierkegaard's *Concluding Unscientific Postscript*,

I distinctly remember. Look, I say. Look at the snow coming in through the open door and the light of the moon, the bright, almost brilliant light of the moon.

One by one, I remove my clothes, fold them neatly on the bed, then strap on the pack sack. I'm on the ground now, the wind whistling around me. I can feel my balls shrivel up into my body, tuck themselves in like a pair of pampered princes avoiding the world's horror. I look back up towards the house. The entire family is standing on the balcony. They're looking for me. They're following my progress in the snow, my tracks in the pristine whiteness. But they don't really believe it's me. No son, husband, brother of theirs would voluntarily run naked through the snow. Yet I am running naked through the snow. Mr. Bedner and Torp are vying to be my guides. I know him well, the landlord says. I know his secrets. I know him and his wife well, Torp retorts. He has no secrets. While they're fighting, I run right through them. When I look back to say goodbye, they're gone. I miss a step. There are no more steps. There are no more stairs. How foolish of me to believe that stairs must lead somewhere. I let out a scream that echoes through the chambers, growing louder and louder till it's about to burst my eardrums. Luckily, I awoke.

The next day, Nicole came down and I thought I'd won. But she was merely there to pick up some of her clothing.

"I've called the brothers," she said. "They think it's a great idea."

"That's because they don't know."

"Don't know what? That you're an asshole?"

Without giving me a chance to respond, she turned and headed back up.

I suddenly felt drained of all energy. I had hoped to pay another visit to Wreck Beach, to confront Torp's friends once and for all about his whereabouts. I was positive they knew where he was—and I was going to force it out of them. But I just couldn't arouse myself to do it. I had fallen back to the days when it was an effort just going out of the house, when meeting someone new was like a death sentence, when the only safe spot was the corner of the library late at night, a soft light illuminating just me and the book I was reading. A hermit monk in the grand old style of St. Jerome or my old favourite, St. Simeon Stylites. So I stayed in the flat, going out only when hunger pangs drove me to Luigi's. I returned and went straight to bed, the lethargy so powerful I could feel the air being squeezed out of my lungs. But I didn't want to sleep. Or perhaps a new type of sleep might help. I searched through the medicine cabinet until I found Nicole's stash of sleeping pills. I swallowed a couple—and then a third. Maybe, they'd knock me out so badly I wouldn't even have the strength to dream.

No such luck. No sooner had I fallen asleep than I was back into it. I'm shivering and frozen in a park; I'm in the centre of a park with no clothes on; I'm a statue in a park and snow falls on the tips of my fingers, melting imperceptibly from the tiny heat still pulsing there. No one can imagine the force needed just to move one of those fingers a tenth of a millimetre. It's the bronze—the form that shapes the matter. And the next time, the same force will only move it one twentieth of a millimetre. Zeno's inexorable laws. I presume there must have been a time when I moved so fast no one could see me.

Below me—at the base of a pedestal splattered with yellow and brown markings—several people kneel and talk to me. As if I could answer. How silly can they be? Or do they pray to me? A saint in the middle of a park. They're waiting for an answer. But it takes me hours to pronounce one letter. All they hear is an elongated howl that resembles the bending of the trees, the swirling of the snow, the clapping of gigantic bird wings. After a while, they hurl rotten fruit at me, shake their fists and leave. When night comes, two men—I can't recognize them because they're wearing masks but somehow I feel I should know them—tie ropes around my neck and secure them to the back fender of their junk heap car. Then they drive away, pulling my head off. It rolls to a stop before the rest of me, facing the statue. I read the inscription:

FOR TRANSFORMATIONS
ABOVE AND BEYOND
THE CALL OF DUTY
TOWARDS THE SOLUTION OF THE MURDER
OF STEVEN 'TORP' PALMER BY HAROLD BEDNER

Everything goes dark. I can hear voices. A flurry of

voices. Oh my God! Why is the bed all ripped up? Where is he? Shit, aren't those his clothes? He's out in the snow without any clothes. He's tied the sheets to the balcony. Jesus. Call the police! Call the police before he freezes to death. Close the door, will you? That poor bastard. He won't last long. Ssh! Not so loud. Mom will hear you. Besides, they'll find him. How far could he get anyway? A car with bald wheels has skidded sideways down the icy street, coming to a halt a few inches before a telephone pole; there's the head of a statue in the back seat; the car straightens itself out and slithers on. Listen to this, the voices in the dark say. This is real juicy stuff. Listen to this: "I, Harold Bedner, born Karola Bednescu, age sixty-four, of extremely sound mind and reasonably sound body, do hereby confess to the premeditated murder of one Steven 'Torp' Palmer." Son, if you don't care about what I say, at least think of your mother. She cares for you. A lot. Can't you see that? And your wife and brother, too. He was sick, wasn't he? Who else would go around writing notes like that? What happened? He always seemed so happy with me, especially towards the end. Fears of inadequacy probably. Jealousy.

I'm standing, tasting the snowflakes. What do they taste like? Like snowflakes. I'm counting the stars: and a billion and two and a billion and three and a billion and … I grow tired of counting. Suffice it to say they are countless. No, not countless. For the universe is bounded. Bounded? By what? Ah, can you hear the music of the spheres. I'm running in the snow, turning blue in the snow. I'm running in the middle of a blue field. Ahead of me a forest in deeper blue. The line between field and forest is like a blade. I fall across it, feeling the gritty powder underneath me, sticking to my flesh, preserving me, causing the molecules within me to slow their motion, to eat their own energy for warmth, to retreat literally into themselves. And the spaces between them grow immensely large—till they can no longer make contact. The voices are calling to me: Giulio, Giulio. The time. Look at the time. Hands reach in to grab me. I fight them off. No, no, no.

"Hey," Nicole said, shaking me. "You want to lose your job? It's ten o'clock. You're going to be late for your classes."

"Huh? What?"

I came out of my drugged sleep and looked around. Nicole had already turned away and left the room, was already climbing back up. I rushed to the bathroom, showered as fast as I could, dressed and ran towards the bus stop. But I knew that, no matter how fast I moved, I wasn't going to make the 11 o'clock conference—not unless I took a taxi. I arrived in front of the philosophy department with five minutes to go. The conference was waiting for me, practically a full house, including some students I'd never seen before. In fact, the only people missing seemed to be Torp and his crowd. Too bad, I said to myself, they would have probably enjoyed this. I started off by reading the PFRG manifesto and juxtaposing it with Aristotle's causes and reasons for revolutions. I didn't have to say much more than that. Within minutes, the students were shouting back and forth at each other. It got so loud at one point that Worthington, teaching a class next to mine, came in and asked us to tone it down. But, when he did so, I was glad to note that several of his students took the opportunity to sneak into my conference. At the end of the two hours, I had trouble breaking up the class. Small groups were still arguing with one another. I had to intervene to prevent two students from coming to blows.

"Okay," I said, "listen up. For our next conference, we'll be discussing the enigmatic Unmoved Mover. Thesis: The world is like a crime. Someone must have committed it. If we take substance to be the fact of that crime, the proof of it, then someone must have put it there. You can take it back as far as you want, trace the matter to its origins, work the murder from the body lying there, i.e., the universe, to the murderer. The uncaused cause, the actuality that has no potentiality, the substratum underlying all. Antithesis: Of course, we might not believe that today because the last time we looked, Bishop Berkeley had proved that material objects don't exist. This effectively removes both the crime and the criminal. Everything becomes your word against mine. Or rather, it becomes a choice of interpretations. So the next time someone asks you: what is the matter?, you can truthfully say: nothing."

After spending another fifteen minutes in the corridor answering questions from students about the conference, I managed to slip away to my office. Worthington was already there, sipping tea.

"A couple of chaps asking for you," he said. "Unsavoury looking, to say the least."

As he said this, two men knocked on the door: one older with greying hair; the other young and brushcut. I recognized them as two of the new people sitting in on my conference.

"Giulio di Orio?" the older one asked. "Professor di Orio?"

"Giulio di Orio, yes. But not professor. Just a simple assistant lecturer."

"Okay, not professor then," he said, looking at Worthington. "Is there someplace we can talk?"

"I'm leaving," Worthington said. "Just give us a shout if they're beating you up or something."

He shut the door behind him.

"Who's the wiseguy?" the brushcut asked.

"No," I said, "the question is: Who are you?"

"Sorry," the first one said, taking out his wallet and flashing a badge at me. "Inspector Lisgaard, RCMP. And this is Sgt. Anscombe."

"RCMP?" I said, feeling my heart beat a little faster. "What can I do for you?"

"Do you usually give lectures on radical terrorist groups who go around blowing up things?" Anscombe asked.

"I beg your pardon?"

"That class today—you talked about the PFRG."

"I did. Is that a crime?"

"No," Lisgaard said, smiling. "Not yet. Do you know a Steven Palmer?"

"Yes," I said. They looked at each other. "Inspector, what's this all about?" Suddenly, I panicked. "Something hasn't happened to him, has it? He hasn't been ..."

"What's your relationship with him?" Lisgaard asked.

"Relationship?" Oh shit, the vice squad. They know about our little three-way get-togethers. Mr. Bedner's last service before his brothers took him away.

"Yeah," Anscombe said. "You know? Are you buddies with him—or what?"

"I know him a little," I said warily. "He used to attend my Aristotle conference. And we've met a couple of times socially."

"Do you know anything about this?" Lisgaard said. He took out a familiar brown envelope and plopped it on the desk.

"Where did you—?"

"Let us ask the questions, if you don't mind," Anscombe said brusquely.

Lisgaard opened the package and read out the note I'd left for Torp.

"Sounds like there's a little more here than just a couple of casual meetings," he said.

"My wife and I felt sorry for him," I said. "We invited him over for dinner once or twice."

"Well, ain't that just neighbourly of you," Anscombe said.

"It's a tight community around here," I said, regretting

the words the moment they came out. "But ... but I haven't seen him in ... in a couple of weeks. Ever since ..."

"Ever since the locals picked him up, right?"

I nodded, not wanting to say more than I had to.

"Do you expect him back?" Lisgaard asked.

"Now, look," I said, standing up. "I'm not answering any more questions until I know what this is all about."

"I'll tell you what it's all about, my friend," Anscombe said, pushing his face forward. "Either you co-operate— or we haul you in under the War Measures Act."

"Haul me in for what?"

"We don't need a reason, buddy."

"Professor di Orio," Lisgaard said calmly, obviously in the role of the good cop. "My friend here gets a little overwrought at times. As a respected member of the academic community, we have no intention of hauling you in. It's Steven Palmer we want—Torp, as you call him."

"Torp? What for?"

"Well, let's start with conspiracy to commit criminal acts, sedition, endangering lives, destroying public and private property, unlawful possession of explosives. That's just off the top of my head. I'm sure the prosecutors will come up with a few more."

"That's ridiculous," I said. "Are you saying that Torp is a member of the PFRG?"

"No," Anscombe said, gritting his teeth as if spitting the words out. "He's not a member—he's the fucking leader, the fucking snakehead of the SOBs."

"I don't believe this," I said, shaking my head. "You must have the wrong guy. The Torp I know doesn't have a violent bone in his body."

"Oh no," Lisgaard said, "there's no mistake. We have the right guy."

"How can you be so sure?"

"We have our sources, Professor di Orio. And you must appreciate the fact we're not at liberty to disclose those sources."

"Especially not to PFRG sympathizers," Anscombe said.

"You will let us know if Torp contacts you, won't you?" Lisgaard said, standing up. "We've received information he may still be in town."

"But you had him in jail already. Why did you release him?"

"Along with several hundred other shit disturbers," Anscombe said, clenching his fists. "Those fuck-up locals let him—"

"A slight miscalculation," Lisgaard said, "that we're not about to repeat." He tossed the envelope with Torp's magazine on my desk. "Here. You might want this as a memento. We've got several hundred down at the station."

"Is it true no one's ever been hurt in a PFRG bombing?" I asked, as they were about to go out the door.

"What's it to you?" Anscombe said.

"Just curious, that's all. Wondering if we've been fantastically lucky or if they've intentionally avoided hurting anyone."

"A bombing is a bombing, Professor di Orio," Lisgaard said. "Damage to property is a crime. And the danger to innocent people is always there. So let us do the investigating—and we'll leave the hair-splitting to you. Is that a deal?"

After they left, I sat stunned at the desk, still unable to believe what I'd just heard. But I also knew the police were seldom wrong about such things—and wouldn't come out until they were certain they had the right man. In my dreams, I'd had Torp killed off by a demon-crazed landlord—and then had earned myself a statue and plaque for solving the crime, for extorting a confession out of the dangerous criminal who played at being an old man. Now, Torp was a wanted terrorist. Would I be given a commendation if I turned him in? If I lured him into a well-laid trap, caught naked and in flagrante between Nicole and me? If I sacrificed my body—and soul—to capture him? Worthington stepped back into the office, dying to know what it was all about. I could see several other people behind him.

"The entire office is abuzz," he said. "Some have gone so far as to place bets. Income tax problems? A metaphysical crime or two? Come, come, di Orio, don't keep us in the dark. Let us in on this little mystery of yours. Those two chaps didn't come here to discuss the view."

"Reginald, old chap," I said, patting him on the shoulder. "Just heading to the lounge. Care to have that tea refreshed?"

FIVE

GIULIO & NICOLE

What is the use of philosophic and of practical wisdom?
Philosophic wisdom is the formal cause of happiness;
practical wisdom is what ensures
the taking of proper means to the proper ends
desired by moral virtue.

—*Nicomachean Ethics,*
Book 6, Chapter 12

Why? Why did I go home that evening and tell Nicole that Torp was dead? Was it to make a clean break? To have Nicole believe there was no hope of ever seeing Torp again, thus putting an end to the cruel expectations? I guess I felt that was less messy than having to explain Torp's possible involvement in illegal activities and the fact he might still be prowling around out there, ready to appear when least expected. Understandable maybe. I needed a story about how he died ... how he was killed.

But Nicole, who was still staying upstairs and awaiting good news, didn't give me a chance to elaborate. The moment I announced Torp's death, she collapsed with a thud onto Mr. Bedner's living room floor, saved from serious injury thanks to the plush carpet. I had to lift her and drag her to the sofa. When she came to, she insisted I tell her what had happened.

"I ... I ..." What to tell her?

"A mugger," I said, making it up as I went along. "The police ... they came to see me ... they think he was killed by a mugger. One of the bums that hang around the park. Beaten around the head with a piece of wood." Nicole sat there staring straight ahead. "The police had me go down to the morgue to identify the body."

I sat down beside her. After some thirty seconds,

she finally turned and looked at me. I prepared to hold her … to comfort her.

"Get out of my sight," she screamed, throwing punches against my chest. "You disgust me. You make me want to fucking puke every time I look at you. You're scum. Where's the devil when you need him? If I could, I would trade you right now for Torp. What good are you? What fucking good? You stood around and he's dead. Fucking dead. Motherfucker."

I had no idea what to do. I tried to touch her, maybe calm her down. But she pushed me away. Violently.

"Get the fuck out," she yelled, standing up and suddenly clutching her stomach as if in pain.

"What's the matter?" I asked, leaning over her. "Is something wrong?"

"You're what's wrong," she said, falling back on the sofa. "You make me want to vomit. So get the fuck out. And don't come back unless Torp's with you."

"You're not making sense," I said.

"Make sense?" she said, tears streaming down her face. "Is that what I'm supposed to do? You fucking make sense! Bring Torp home!"

"He's dead," I said.

"I don't give a fuck," she said. "Bring Torp home—or I'm out of here! Do you understand?"

I turned and headed down into the basement.

"I don't need you any more," she shouted. "I'm going to get a job. You hear me? And you and your philosophy can go fuck yourselves."

I could hear laughter behind me. It wasn't the kind of laughter that makes you want to laugh along.

And then I started thinking about what I'd told her. What if Torp should suddenly show up? What if Nicole decided she wanted to attend his funeral? What if the police paid me a second visit—this time at home? What if there was a news bulletin announcing either that Torp was wanted or that he'd been arrested? After all, the two officers did say he was the ringleader. Stupid, I told myself. I should have told Nicole that Torp was a wanted fugitive, a desperado, a freedom fighter who was willing to put his life on the line for his principles. That would have made her proud, if not happy. But was that really the case? And why hadn't he let us in on his secret when he had the chance? I guess we were good enough to fuck but not to trust.

Who was this Torp anyway? I took out the *Get Real!* magazine and searched through it for clues to Torp's real identity. But there didn't seem to be any. Everything had been written in an analytic, impersonal style—as if the author had planned it that way. Of course, it would have been the smart thing to do, considering the police would sooner or later get their hands on a copy. The articles talked about intimidation, about the rights of the people on the street, about what to do in case the SS (a.k.a. the RCMP Special Service) started to hassle you. But there was no impassioned plea to burn down buildings, steal explosives, violently resist. So it couldn't have been from this magazine that the police had put together their profile of the man they considered the PFRG leader. Their evidence must have come from other sources.

But from whom? Lennie, perhaps. From Lennie yes, who was even now ingratiating himself with Torp's friends so he could get more clues to his whereabouts. Of course. It made sense. All along I'd assumed that the police had confiscated the magazine from Lennie. But what if he'd handed it over voluntarily? And what if he'd been the one to set fire to the warehouse that night—to keep what he and the police considered subversive material off the street? Lisgaard had mentioned that they had several hundred copies of the magazine down at the station. How had they obtained them if they were supposedly all burned in the fire? Lennie must have taken several boxes out before setting fire to the place. It followed he was working for the police—and that Torp was in danger. And that the only person who could save him was me. Then, perhaps Nicole would once again wish me alive.

I started crying again after Giulio left. I asked myself why I had reacted as if he was to blame for Torp's death. I knew it made no sense. But I didn't care. I was hurting all over, and I had to take it out on somebody. At one point, I lurched into the bathroom and threw up. Christ, that's all I needed—to get sick. I stared at myself in the bathroom mirror. Jesus. I looked like fucking death warmed over. Whatever that means. Hollow eyes, hair plastered against my skin, whatever make-up I'd managed to put on running down my face. And I ached, especially my head and back. Had trouble catching my breath. What the fuck was happening to me? Maybe I could sleep it off. Forget the whole fucking world.

But there was no way. I slept on and off, waking every half hour or so. Mr. Bedner's bedroom was suddenly stuffy and hot. I felt like I was suffocating, the way the bed sank towards the middle and threatened to swallow me. I threw off the heavy quilt. That didn't help. I took off the rest of my clothes. But, even lying naked on the bed wasn't any use. Fuck, I said to myself. Then I started to hear noises: hardwood floors creaking; water dripping in the sink; the refrigerator starting up; a loose screen being rattled by the wind. It was as if I was back in my grandparents' house, the one that had been built a bit at a time and gave me the creeps. I felt like it was always shifting, always changing shape.

I knew then I'd never get back to sleep. I looked at the oversized alarm clock Mr. Bedner kept in the bedroom. Just past three. What the fuck. Might as well get up. I threw on a robe and went to stand by the living room window. The moon was moving in and out of the clouds; every once in a while, a star would get through, twinkle for a bit and then vanish again. There were shadows everywhere, being whipped around by the wind. One flitted right across Mr. Bedner's lawn. I jumped before realizing it was nothing but a stray newspaper sheet. A light came on a few houses down: Mr. Antonelli getting up for a glass of water or a trip to the bathroom. I shuddered, clutched at my aching stomach.

Fuck it, I said out loud. I don't need this shit. I pulled the robe more tightly around me and made my way downstairs. But not before switching on every light I could find along the way. I had no intention of tripping over a party of mice at work or at play. Or a new spiderweb laid across at exactly face level. Still, there were places on that side of the basement where only a direct flashlight beam would penetrate—and even then I wasn't so sure. Without meaning to, I turned to look into just such a corner, spotting a shapeless figure. Only a mound of clothes, I kept telling myself. Only a fucking mound of clothes. No need to panic. I repeated this as I closed the door behind me and locked it for good measure. Then I tiptoed towards the bedroom, not wanting to wake Giulio up. I realized I'd have to apologize eventually for all the nasty things I'd said—but I sure as hell didn't feel like doing it right then. Plenty of time for that later. All I wanted to do was get a good night's sleep, hope the pain and cramps went away, and start over in the morning. That's all I wanted. Was that too much to ask?

Giulio's Journal

Oct. 27: *I awake in the middle of the night to find myself lying naked on the kitchen floor, gasping for air and making swimming motions on the cold linoleum. A spider wanders in beneath the basement door, somehow finding a hole despite Mr. Bedner's every effort. It isn't an ordinary grey house spider, the kind that invites brooms and folded newspapers. This is a spider with the vividness of a dream, a multicoloured exotic creature with red stripes and black crescents, with ringed black-and-white legs, with a long white abdomen that pulses in step with its breathing. It stops several inches before my face, then twitches its ... its—I didn't know what to call them then—its fangs. It twitches its fangs in a gesture of prayer or pleading. As I breathe more and more quickly, so does the pulsing of its abdomen. No other part of its body moves. Are you waiting for me? I whisper. It seems to nod—or at least bob.*

Shaking all over, I hold out my arm in front of it. The spider turns to spurt away. I block its path, surround it on all sides, forcing it to make its escape over my arm. It hesitates as we would at the base of a cliff, then advances. The sensation of its eight legs moving in rapid succession over my hair is exquisite, sexual, the delicate touch of unknown worlds. I shudder. The spider climbs over and across, slips away under the door, looking suddenly less exotic and colourful, as if having left a part of itself behind.

I stand up and go back into the bedroom where I take out the canvas backpack stored in the bottom drawer of the dresser. It smells musty, but that doesn't matter right now. I stuff it with whatever I can find: underwear, T-shirts, a pair of jeans, sunglasses. For a moment, I look over and see Nicole. She's talking in her sleep, smiling, reaching out, no doubt full of love and tenderness, full of the need to be human. For a moment, I feel the urge to fit myself against her. And then she vanishes, leaving only the crumpled sheets. I could have sworn she was there, I say, smoothing out the sheets. I could have sworn. No, it's not possible, a voice calls out. Who's that? I ask. It's me. Here. Out the window. I look up. The curtains are gone; the front lawn is gone; the street is gone; the houses are gone. Time to get going; time to save myself.

I shake myself free and stand up quickly, feeling the blood rush to my head. In the kitchen, I take out my wallet and empty it on the table. In it are ID cards ranging all the way back to high school, Medicare cards, citizenship cards, library privilege cards. Plus a little over $200. I take half of that and leave everything else scattered on the table. The bank savings are in joint accounts, I say to myself. So I needn't worry about that. And the month's rent has been paid. I put Torp's magazine into the backpack. Then I dress and, throwing on a raincoat, walk out of the house and down the dark street. It doesn't surprise me in the least to find both the landlord and his wife—half-hidden behind him—standing in their window. They wave at me. I wave back, blink, and they too are gone.

It was dark in the bedroom and, at first, I couldn't make out Giulio. But then I saw him. No, I don't care what anyone says—I saw him. I'll swear to it—to this day. He was at the far edge of the bed and all curled up under the blankets. Trust him to keep to his side even when he was the only one there. And trust him not to fight back after I'd insulted him, called him every name under the sun and had even wished him dead. Like punching a bag full of fucking Jello. I remember thinking how unprotected he seemed right then. Like I could crush him with my bare hands. Or beat him to a pulp. That got me thinking about Torp. Of course, there was no reason for me not to believe Giulio. Several other people had already been killed in that area—so why not Torp?

Without meaning to, I started to imagine what he must have looked like in the morgue, all battered and stiff. I couldn't really. Torp kept opening his eyes and yelling: "Surprise! Fooled ya, didn't I! You didn't think I'd stay dead, did you? Hey, that's not like me. You know that. Irena isn't the only one who can pull off that trick!" And the two of us fell into one another's arms, right there on the morgue slab. You're not dead! I found myself yelling as I felt his warm body pressed up against mine. You're not dead! Fucking right, I'm not. And then it all vanished again and all I could see was scrunched-up Giulio. Poor old scrunched-up Giulio. It would be nearly twenty years before I discovered the truth about Torp—and then it was too late. And it wouldn't have made any difference anyway. That was the saddest part of all, wasn't it? It wouldn't have made the least fucking difference.

Giulio's Journal

I'm walking in the middle of the night, walking down Hastings St. towards the downtown core. Why am I walking? Because there aren't any buses at this time of night. All the buses are tucked away safe and sound in their garages. And you can't hail cabs in Vancouver—they won't stop for you. So I'm walking, looking for a taxi stand. And then I'm crouching in the wooded area just off Wreck Beach, listening to the ocean. I'm in luck. The tent is back up, and there are definitely people on the beach. Torp, perhaps? No, I doubt that very much. I doubt he would come back to this spot. He wouldn't take that kind of chance. In fact, I'm willing to bet there are police around at this very moment. I chuckle. Probably disguised as trees and sand dunes. But then I realize that's not very funny—that's exactly the sort of thing they might resort to. Or maybe set up a watching post way up in one of the evergreens, dressed up as a squirrel. Pay RCMP constables thousands of dollars in overtime to make sure Torp is spotted if he ever returns. I'm sitting beneath just such a tree. I look above me, trying to see through the thick branches. There's nothing there—and there's nothing I can do until it's light enough for me to make out who these people on the beach are. So I snuggle down, using the backpack as a pillow and the raincoat as a groundsheet.

Still dark, the tent comes suddenly alive, its walls crawling with menacing and ritualistic shapes. They're performing undecipherable gestures beneath a yellowish glow. One prone shadow in particular is rising from and falling on to another, moving faster and faster, occasionally blotting out the light from the lantern. Then, they start to emerge, one by one. The dead embers of the fire burst into flame, shooting sparks straight into the air. I can see their faces now. Torp! One of them is Torp! He's standing nonchalantly next to Linda, laughing as if this is the safest spot in the entire world. Torp! I yell. Get out of there! The police are all around you! Get out while you can! But he doesn't seem to hear me.

I fight my way through the tree branches, rush out towards the beach. I'm nearly out on the sand when I'm right back behind the tree again, right back where I started from. Torp! I yell again. Don't do this to us! Nicole is waiting for you. She's waiting for you with open arms. Ready to give you all her charms. And mine, too. We'll set up a secret rendezvous somewhere. We'll join the underground. We'll follow you wherever you go. And then Torp is walking away from his friends, walking away from the fire. Towards me.

That's it, I say. Get into the woods. Now! You'll be harder to spot. You'll be harder to follow.

Back on the beach, Linda is chanting and dancing around the fire, lifting her legs high into the air. Then she does a quick somersault and walks on her hands. Slowly, the others join her, each one performing his or her own special trick: one hops about on one leg; another stands on her head and twirls in the sand; a third and a fourth form a wheelbarrow and scurry back and forth. I can hear the ocean rolling with more force against the sand and rocks. Hard gusts of wind bend the treetops inland, send sprays of water into my face.

Torp is walking down the path now to one side of me. He passes by, passes right by me—without seeing me. Or he pretends not to see me. I call his name. He turns for a moment. Stares right at me. And then he's gone again. I look back. Linda and her friends are still performing their contortions in complete silence. Now, they are taking turns leaping across the fire, double and triple jumps, flips, more somersaults. One of them gets too close and goes up in flames. The others clap as she rushes headlong towards the ocean, a human torch. I'm watching in awe when I hear a heavy muffled thud from the pathway in front of me. Then another. And I'm standing over Torp's body, wiping tears from my eyes. He is lying face down, the back of his head caved in by a thick piece of driftwood.

I lean down and struggle to turn the body over. His shirt collar and shoulders are covered with blood; his eyes are half-opened; his lips slightly parted. I brush away the hair from his forehead and, leaning over, kiss him on the lips, tasting the blood that has gathered there. As I pull back, the body decomposes beneath me, attacked by millions of insects, reduced to gleaming bone in the moonlight.

I half waken with something sticking in my ear, something soft and hard at the same time, probing, brushing my cheeks. And I bite hard, the bitter taste of twig juice in my mouth. The leaves around me seem to be tapping each other or trying to get each other's attention. Like Morse code. A drop twists its way through my hair and settles on my forehead. It is raining lightly. I open my eyes as wide as possible and can see nothing but the leaves all around me, leaves before my eyes, leaves and branches above me. For a moment, I am totally lost. This is a forest. A dark forest? What am I doing all alone in a thick dark forest at this time of night? And where's Torp? Didn't I just leave Torp's decomposed body?

Something is crawling along the inside of my leg. I rub my fist against it. It continues to crawl, oblivious. I crush it again, then try to shake it free. There's nothing there. Just my own skin crawling on itself. God, I think, this forest is all around me. Neverending. Now it's trying to edge its way back to recover what I've carved out of it, the niche I've hacked out of it. I shiver. There's a noise behind me, like the growl of some wild beast, only more rhythmic, more constant. The purring of a sated animal perhaps. Or water rushing along a shoreline. That's it! I spin quickly and, one part at a time, come to full consciousness.

The forest doesn't continue behind me. There's a beach and a tent. And a glow in the sky to the east. Dawn. The rain has stopped, the slow drips merely a residue. I'm shivering on the damp ground, unable to stop myself from shaking. I have a sudden craving for coffee. Boiling hot coffee. Scalding coffee. Luigi's cappuccino, milk frothing across the top. Cinnamon slowly melting into it. As the weak sun reaches across the bottom of the tent, those inside start to stir. Really stir this time. Several rise up and stretch. Then, one by one, they emerge, poking their heads out from the tent.

I recognize a few of the people from the other day—the same people who, irony of ironies, thought I was a police informer. One of them heads my way, unzipping his fly. I pull back a little deeper into my camouflaged observation post. He stops about ten metres away and releases a stream of urine into the nearby bushes. Then he shakes himself, zips back up and turns back towards the others. The last one to come out of the tent is Lennie. There's your police informer, I want to

shout. But who would believe me? Whose word
would they take? Satisfied that Torp isn't there,
I slip away down the path towards the bus stop.
Along the way, I pass several drunks lying asleep
on the park benches, their faces covered with news-
papers—but no body. No gleaming bones. No
bloodied piece of driftwood. And, for that, I'm not
sure whether to be grateful or not.

I didn't get much sleep that night. Several times, after
jumbled dreams, I awoke with my arms stretched out.
Like I was trying to hold someone. Clutch at someone.
Torp and Giulio. Giulio and Torp. But they kept changing places, kept going in and out of focus. I remember
calling out their names. Remember saying over and over:
"Torp, where are you? Torp. Giulio. Answer me. Come
out, come out. Don't fuck around. Stop playing games."
And I jerked up in bed and looked around in the dark.
Stupid me. Torp had never been there, of course. Even
I knew that. And Giulio, whom I'd felt beside me earlier
in the night, was no longer there either. Must be in the
kitchen, I said to myself, throwing off the covers. Trying to avoid me by pretending he had work to do. Papers to mark or some fucking thing like that. I'd better
get it over with. Unlike Giulio, I didn't believe in beating
around the fucking bush. Straightforward and upfront.
What was wrong with that? If I had a problem, if there
was something to hash out, I wanted to confront it right
away. Get it over with. But I needed someone else to do

that. Couldn't do it on my own. And that wasn't going to happen that night.

Right then, my stomach lurched. I barely made it to the toilet before vomiting. There was nothing to vomit but this green scummy stuff. What's wrong with me? I wiped my mouth on a towel and looked out into the kitchen, all set to have it out once and for all. But Giulio was nowhere to be found. Fuck, I said. The SOB has sneaked off already. Didn't have the nerve to face me. Just like he always does at the first sign of conflict. Scurrying off into the closest hole he could find. Torp would never do anything like that. No sir. Torp was like me. Someone who faced up to things instead of pretending they didn't exist or would just go away by themselves. No problem, Giulio, I said. You can't hide forever. I'll just wait for you to come home tonight. Probably better that way. More time to calm down. But I didn't want to calm down. I wanted to punch something. I wanted to stay mad. So stay mad, I told myself. What's stopping you?

But right then, I needed something to get rid of the dull ache I was feeling all over. I needed something to perk me up, bring up my energy levels. I needed a hot shower. I dropped my robe and walked into the bathroom. I was about to turn on the water when I noticed that the green scum was back. All along the edges of the shower stall. I looked up. Holy fuck! The ceiling was splotchy and sagging again. It looked as if all of Mr. Bedner's work had been for nothing. Shit, I said, the moment Giulio comes back tonight, I'm gonna point this out to him. I'm gonna rub his nose in it once and for all. If he doesn't want to move upstairs, then we're going to get out of this place. We're going to find some other fucking place to live.

But that wasn't the biggest surprise that morning. When I finally went into the kitchen to have some breakfast, Giulio's identity cards and a bunch of money were spread out all over the table. And, on one of the chairs, was his briefcase, with the papers and books I figured he would have needed for his classes.

I had no idea what to make of it. Maybe, he'd just forgotten the briefcase. I'd probably pissed him off quite a bit, and he might not have been thinking too straight. But what the hell were all his ID and other cards doing all over the kitchen table? And that hundred dollars? It didn't make any sense. Unless, of course, he'd been in such a hurry to get away they'd fallen out. That must have been it, I told myself, trying to keep my heart from jumping up into my throat. Because even then I really didn't believe that. Giulio had never done anything like that before. If anything, he was too careful, checking things two and three times before going out. No, if he left that stuff behind, it must have been on purpose.

I needed to find out what was going on. How? I tried to get some breakfast down but managed half a toast before the urge to vomit returned. After my stomach settled a bit, I went upstairs and found the university number in the phone book. I had to go through a whole load of shit—and a lot of yelling—before they finally put me through to the philosophy department. And then I got told Giulio wasn't there. I gave the secretary Mr. Bedner's number and a message for Giulio to call me the moment he arrived. And then I lay down on the living room sofa and waited for the call.

Giulio's Journal

I'm standing near the edge of False Creek, the raincoat keeping out some of the damp. But everything else is fogged in all of a sudden. As if I've descended into a deep pit where the mist keeps rising to blot out my view. All I can make out are some murky, amorphous shapes, iridescent bubbles on the water, strange angles jutting out of nowhere. Somewhere before me is Torp's warehouse, the charred pieces still dangling where they've collapsed. I grope slowly through the tall grass, careful not to trip over some half-buried steel rod or car tire. Do these things grow here? Does someone seed them? Or is it the earth spewing them up out of anger and anguish?

The smell of wet, charred wood is sharp and acrid. I come up against the brick wall, blackened and cracked in half. I touch it, feeling the rawness, a streak of black across my fingers. What am I looking for? Surely, Torp isn't in this heap of shattered dreams. I'm inside now—or what was once inside. What do they call that object with no inside? A Kline bottle. Yes. All surface.

There are beams here at head level and the shelving has pitched forward. The shelving where Torp had dangled like a monkey. I squat and run my fingers along the singed pieces of sleeping bag, hoping for some flash or charge. Nothing. Everything's been squeezed out of it. All memory; no sensation. Or am I the one without? Without what?

I'm outside again—moving forward almost blind, hands out before me—and come within inches of falling into a ditch. Warning lights flash. The road has been torn to shreds, its metal and clay guts exposed for all the world to see. I look up at shadows looming overhead. Huge insect-like machines stand waiting for their orders, pincers up and raring to go. Clackity-clack. There's a wooden crossway where the sidewalk should be. I cross it, one foot carefully in front of the other. I wouldn't want to fall in. Down below, new drainage pipes gleam like giant grubs, the dew slipping off their sides. I walk down the middle of the road, up towards higher ground and the roar of traffic. And, just as quickly as it had appeared, the fog vanishes. I stand on the overpass, looking down into the water.

For some reason, I'm reminded of identity, echoes and rebounds of identity. What does an oil-slicked and polluted creek have to do with identity? Or is it another type of identity, having nothing to do with self and everything to do with mathematical certainty? We all carry our little flags with us, I remember my adviser telling me once. And our hope is to pin that little flag on something that will identify us once and for all: a number, a variable, an equation, anything that'll make the world make sense. Torp? Does Torp qualify? He certainly made the world make sense. Or rather: it no longer made any sense when he wasn't there. Is that the same? I lean over the edge and spit into the water. Down below, I hear the sound of deep rumbling—like some slimy monster rising out of the creek, rising to wreak havoc on the city. But it's only the machines being activated, getting ready to chew up more earth and to spit it out as concrete, as metal, as asphalt. Only their reticulate limbs are visible above the fog, seem to float above the fog. Only their limbs.

Lying down wasn't helping my stomach ache. Now it was hunger pangs. I decided to go downstairs and maybe try to have something to eat. I was just about to sit down when there was a knock on the front door. Who the fuck …? Giulio! He'd left his keys behind. I opened the door, ready to give him shit. It was the postman.

"Registered mail," he said, holding up an official-looking envelope. "For a Giulio di Orio."

"For my husband?"

"Yep. Looks mighty important, too. But you can sign for it." He winked at me. "I won't tell if you don't."

I signed and took the letter inside, trying to decide whether or not to open it. When I saw the return address, I thought it was some information Giulio had asked for. Why else would he be getting a letter from the University of Auckland? Auckland? Where the fuck was that anyway? New Zealand, it said on the return address label. I tore it open. I had to read it twice to realize he was being offered a job at the university. The job was still conditional, according to the letter. They were waiting for his reference letters to arrive. But they said they were very impressed with his credentials and he was just the sort of person they were looking for—still young and enthusiastic but with the ability to do superior scholarship. And, if the references were as good as the credentials, they didn't see any problem with him starting as an assistant lecturer in January. My Giulio? Are they talking about my Giulio? What the fuck's going on around here? And then I got really pissed off. Why hadn't he mentioned anything about this before? What was going on?

I decided to check something out. I looked through the dresser. Some of Giulio's clothes were missing. Some socks, underwear, shirts. I knew because I was the one who usually put them away. The bastard! He was planning on sneaking out on me. He was planning on fucking off to New Zealand or whatever and leaving me by myself. The fucking prick! I started throwing things—whatever I could get my hands on. Plates, glasses, frying pans. Then, I sat down at the kitchen table and burst into tears. That's when I saw his ID cards in front of me again. How did he plan on going anywhere without identification? I started laughing and wiping my tears at the same time.

This was crazy. None of it made any sense anymore. If he *was* thinking of sneaking out on me, he'd have to come back for the rest of his shit. They weren't going to let him into New Zealand on his say so. Last time I'd looked, you needed some proof of citizenship and identification for that. *And* a passport. Passport! I pulled open the top drawer of the dresser. Both our passports were there, held together with a rubber band. He wasn't planning on going to New Zealand without me after all. So what did he have in mind? And where the fuck was he?

I called the university again. The secretary passed me on to some guy who talked like he had a clothespin clipped to his nose and a large pole up his arse. Giulio had told me about him: some fucking stuck-up Brit who thought he was king of the whole stinking pile. Regibald Worthlesston the Turd or some shit like that. He said they hadn't seen Giulio all morning but they were "most most definitely" expecting him at any moment. I told him to "most most definitely" have Giulio call me as soon as he got in. It was extremely urgent. Regibald suddenly wanted to know more and suggested that, if it was really important, I give him the message to pass on. Over my dead body, I said to myself. But I just told him I'd prefer to give Giulio the good news.

I gathered up some more of Mr. Bedner's dinnerware and glasses to replace those I'd smashed. But then I changed my mind. Not having any plates in the flat might help speed up the move. Instead, I cleaned up the mess I'd made and sat down to wait for Giulio to return. He was going to get a piece of my mind. One fucking awful shit-honking piece of it.

Giulio's Journal

I'm sitting in a greasy spoon, looking out the window. Across from me is one of those new glass-walled skyscrapers that reflect sky, clouds and other buildings like distorted disembodied entities floating high up its sides. The waitress comes over and I order bacon and eggs and a large glass of orange juice. The fog is all gone now and it's turning out to be a pleasant morning. I lean back in the booth, basking, breathing in and out like someone who has the right to do just that. The waitress brings my orange juice. I drink it up in one gulp and ask for a refill. On the other side of the street, a barbershop pole swirls slowly. I feel wisps of hair curling over my shoulders, look at my reflection in the window. Yes, it's definitely too long. It'll have to go. No question about it.

I eat and pay for my breakfast, leaving a handsome tip. Then, toothpick in my mouth, I walk across to the barbershop, bringing back childhood memories. I have this impression of the city's unique characters all gathered there, talking in funny accents to an anxious newspaper columnist who's jotting it all down for the day's audience, for the day's dose of nitty-gritty truth and humorous puns. But there's no one in the place—not even the barber himself. The walls are littered with pictures of boxers, their faces pounded in, their eyes swollen shut. I peer more closely. These posters are all signed: "Love, Vinny"; "A Cut Above The Rest, Sonny Boy".

Only in one corner is there something that seems personal, something that resembles a family portrait: a severe-looking young woman, her hair in a tight bun, holding two gaudily dressed children on her lap. This one isn't signed. After about thirty seconds, a wizened old man with a thick crop of white hair comes through a dirty curtain that leads to the back of the building. He doesn't notice me at first, as he has his head buried in a magazine, tongue hanging out the side of his mouth. Oh hello, he says when he finally looks up, eyes glazed. Come for a haircut? I say I have, removing my raincoat and hanging it, along with my backpack, on a wooden coat rack.

Nice, eh? he says. He thrusts the magazine towards me and sticks his tongue out so that the tip almost reaches his nose. Hot stuff. I nod. It is a two-page centrefold. In an untouched image of violently-painted buttocks, spread labia and hot probing mouths the colour of sunset, two women are performing cunnilingus on each other, intent on licking away the glistening jelly that has been lathered between their legs. He leaves the magazine open. I sit in the barber chair. You want nice style? New style? Short, I say. Cut it all off. No more hippie, he says laughing. No more hippie. Yeah, I say. A bunch of losers.

At first, he shears away with delight, the hair falling on all sides of me. But then he becomes reluctant to cut it really short and keeps stopping, holding his scissors in the air, to ask if it is enough. Each time, I indicate I want it shorter. I only register my satisfaction when the hair bristles under my fingers. You catch cold, the barber says, ringing up the cash register. No, I won't. I put on my raincoat and pull out a blue woollen cap from my pack. Ah, smart. Very smart, he says before sitting down and returning to his magazine, tongue once again hanging from the side of his mouth.

On the street, the sun is blinding as it reflects from the glass towers. And it is suddenly very hot, unseasonably hot for the end of October. I remove my raincoat and hat, slinging them across the back pack, then reach in and pull out my aviator sunglasses, the ones that had been a gift from my brother. Which way to go? Ah, it's warm and blustery; the air is sensuous; in the distance I can see the mountains, the perennial mountains, the mountains the locals can't stop talking about. There's a feeling of uncomplicated freedom, of muscles flexing and nerves uncoiling.

I whistle to myself as I walk down Main Street, heading towards the upper part of town. Manuscript, anus-cript; mountain, Montaigne; Descartes before the horse; Einstein fiddled while time warped; Pascal gives up philosophy to start a chain of hardware stores. Suddenly, I hear a muffled blast, like a puff in the distance. Or the sound made by an avalanche as it comes crashing down the side of a mountain. How do I know what an avalanche sounds like? I'd heard it on TV as a child. The wind blows a leaflet into my face, plastering it there for a moment before I have the chance to claw it off. I'm about to throw it away when I notice the words "Pro-Form Radicals for The Good (PFRG)" in large type across the top. I lean against a building and read what it says: "You may jail us. For a day. For a week. For a month. Forever for all we care. But you can't prevent us from telling the world the truth." The truth, I say to myself. Now there's an interesting word. "Until now, we've been careful to destroy only property—not lives. But no more. The War Measures Act has brought our battle to a new level. To a new and more deadly level. From now on, death to betrayers of the public trust. Death to the megamoral misfits. Death to those who hold the purse strings and abuse them for their own benefit."

I look up. There are hundreds more of the

leaflets flying about, bundles of them scattering in the wind. And one moment the street is quiet and empty, save for a dog, a mother pushing a carriage and a postman—the next, there's a tearing sound, and it's filled with police sirens and fire engines howling, and people running out of offices past me. I turn the corner to see where they all seem to be heading. At the end of the street, one of the highrise apartments is on fire. Glass showers down, followed by bits of furniture, torn books, fragments of Inuit carvings and ... and ... then a scream as someone points up. There, hanging mangled on the balcony, is a woman. Or parts of a woman. She's nude. Her leg has wedged itself between two pieces of the metal railing, preventing her from tumbling on to the street a good dozen storeys below. Her arms are pushed out in front of her as if afraid of facing the ultimate horror and the wind swings her body back and forth. You can tell the leg bones are mashed for she couldn't swing that way otherwise.

As I stand there, the police come out the building with two burnt and blackened people between them—one a man, the other a woman. I recognize them as two of Torp's friends from the beach. Hey, maybe they know where he might be hiding. Hi, I say. I know you. Would you know where Torp is? I have to find Torp. The police push me back. I notice the man and woman are handcuffed.

*You know them, a man beside me asks suspicious-
ly. I shake my head. No. Just thought I did.*

*I look up. A rescue team is trying to dislodge
the other woman's body from the balcony. They
can't stand too far out on the balcony for fear the
rest of the structure might collapse. The building
has a huge chunk knocked out of its side, as if some
monster had taken a nice healthy bite. The False
Creek monster? They won't be able to get her out
of there, the man beside me says. They're gonna
have to let her go. Wanna bet? I nod my agree-
ment. The man in charge orders everyone back out
of the area. Then the firemen place a foam-like
material on the ground below the balcony and one
of the officers signals a thumbs up to the people on
the edge of the balcony. Using a long hooked stick,
they dislodge the body, push the leg through the iron
grating. And it tumbles, flipping several times on
its way down. Heads turn away as it thwacks on
to the foam. Several photographers rush forward,
snapping pictures as they run.*

*While the police are busy driving them away,
I'm able to get close enough for a good look at the
body. She has her face turned towards me and one
torn arm stuck in a weird position behind her back.
It's Linda, the mantra woman from the beach.
She, too, had wanted to go to bed with me. I had
to explain that I was a one-woman man and she
thought that was cool. What is she thinking now?*

The ambulance arrives to take the body away, wrapped in a bright yellow bag. Serves the bastards right, the man beside me says. Terror begets terror. You sure ain't gonna solve anything that way. If they asked me, they should string the bastards up. Those who live by the sword, etc. You fuck around with dynamite, it's bound to blow up in your face one day.

I called the university a third time and still no sign of Giulio. Something was definitely up. He just wasn't the type to take off without saying anything. And he also wasn't the type to get in trouble with the law or anything like that. And then it hit me: You didn't have to be in trouble these days to get hauled in. You just had to be at the wrong place at the wrong time. Maybe he'd been picked up by mistake. But who the hell was I supposed to call to find out? Who would tell me if Giulio was in jail?

It took me several hours and several trips to the toilet to work up the nerve to call the central police station number. When I told the cop who answered that I was looking for a missing person, he asked how long he'd been missing.

"Since early this morning," I said.

"I'm sorry, madam," he said. "That's not long enough to start a search. Call back in forty-eight hours."

"Okay," I said. "That's fine. What if he's been picked up because of the War Measures Act?"

"Why, madam," the officer said, "are you saying your

husband is a subversive? Has he done anything that would warrant our arresting him?"

"No, of course not," I said. "It's just that I can't think of another reason why he would go missing. It's just not like him. Not like him at all. He's always so punctual and—"

"Sorry, madam," the officer said. "I don't know what to tell you."

"Can't you check? Just in case he has been arrested."

"I can tell you right now he isn't in jail—at least not under the War Measures Act. We've had a couple of robberies and several muggings. But no one's been brought in under the War Measures Act."

"Are you sure?"

"Yes, madam. I never make a mistake."

After I put the phone down, I started imagining all sorts of things. If he wasn't in jail and he wasn't at school, and he would have called if he had the chance, then ... then ... he could very well be ... I didn't want to say the word. I had to tell myself to calm down and not panic. Like the officer had told me, he'd only been missing for a few hours. I shouldn't be jumping to stupid conclusions. But what else could I do, really? All the tears I'd held back on the phone now came flooding out. I bawled like a little baby. What would happen to me if Giulio was found ... if he was dead? What would I do? And the other side of me kept saying: Stop it, you idiot. What the fuck's gotten into you? And then I was bawling again. First Torp. Now Giulio. No, first Mr. Bedner's wife. Mr. Bedner!

It just shows how desperate I was to believe that Mr. Bedner could help me. After all, I was the one responsible for practically driving him out of his own house.

I rushed down into the flat and searched through Giulio's cards again. There I found the phone number for Mr. Bedner's brothers. When I called and tried to explain, the brother who answered said he didn't understand.

"Giulio, my husband," I said. "He's gone."

"Gone," he said. "Moment please."

I could hear talking in the background. Then he came back on the line.

"You wait," he said. "We come. We come."

I was about to pour myself a stiff shot of brandy when I remembered the unmade bed upstairs. Shit! I raced up and straightened it out as best I could, covering it with the quilt. Then I looked around to make sure there was nothing else that might give me away. All good. I went back down to the flat and poured myself that brandy.

Giulio's Journal

I'm in the elevator on my way to Pamela's apartment. What am I doing here? I don't know really. She sounded a little surprised when I rang the front-door buzzer and she asked who I was. But then she buzzed me up. I find her in a housecoat which keeps slipping because the belt won't stay tied. Hi, I say. Mind if I come in? She has a startled look on her face. Giulio, she says.

I almost didn't recognize you with that new hair cut. Come in, come in. Thanks. I sit down on the sofa.

What brings you here? she says, looking about nervously. I tell her I'm looking for Torp. I thought maybe he might be up here. She laughs. Torp? Why would he be up here? No reason, I say. Just a hunch. Well, he isn't here. I've applied for a job in New Zealand, I say. That's wonderful. I knew you had it in you. Why, just last week the chairman was mentioning your name and saying what a fine Aristotelian you were. He's fond of Aristotelians, you know. Seems we're a scarce lot today. Jeez, look at me doing all the talking. A regular motor-mouth. She lights a cigarette, then puts it out again. Let's go to bed, I say, reaching for the belt that barely holds her housecoat in place. I beg your pardon, she says, pulling back slightly.

I hear a noise in the bedroom, like a shoe dropping. She stands up and lights another cigarette. You'd better go now, she says. That's all right, I say. We'll fuck right here if you want. Look, she says, I don't want to be rude but you can't just come into a person's apartment and demand to be fucked. Why not? I ask. Isn't that what you did last time? When I brought you up here, she says, it was a spur-of-the-moment thing. Besides, you turned me down. Yes, I say. That was a mistake. But I couldn't help myself. Now, I know better.

Well, you may know better, she says, but I have no intention of fucking you. As a matter of fact, I'm quite busy so if you don't mind …. Have you ever heard of the PFRGs? I ask. Sure I have, she says. The Pro-Form Radicals for the Good or some such nonsense. Aren't they the ones going around blowing up whole city blocks and claiming all they want to do is bring people back to their moral senses? That's them, I say. They blew away an apartment building just like this one earlier today. A few minutes ago, in fact. Well, it wasn't quite like this one. It was kind of squalid and a bit worried by the sea air—you know how bad salt can be for stucco?— and it didn't face the ocean, which is important, after all. Come to think of it, they didn't actually blow it away. It blew them away. I bet you're probably wondering what I'm getting at, aren't you?

She nods. I suddenly notice her eyes. They're like wide beacons surrounded by deep purple slashes of paint. Well, I'm not really getting at anything, I say. Just making small talk, you know. I've never been very good at making small talk. And I envy people who do. So I just wanted to get a little practice. Giulio, she says, are you alright? I think so, I say, holding a hand across my forehead. No fever or anything like that. Although I have been feeling kind of lightheaded these last few days. Like I'm not anchored very solidly to the ground. You ever get those kinds of feelings? Only when

I've had too much champagne, she says laughing. Now, if you'll excuse me, I'd like to get dressed. I've got classes later today. Oops, sorry, I say, standing up. Just inertia, I guess. Another victim of Newton's Laws. Yes, she says, I know how it is. But we've all got to overcome it. Otherwise, nothing ever gets done.

I get a sudden urge to rush to the bedroom door and fling it open. But what would that accomplish? I'm only deluding myself if I believe it's Torp behind it. Instead, I walk slowly towards the front door, concentrating on Pamela and her housecoat, the one with the tendency to open up. You sure you don't want to fuck me, I say. I've learned lots of new tricks recently. I'm positive, she says. A rain-check, maybe? Sure, a rain-check. I say goodbye and step out into the corridor. Pamela is quick to shut the door behind me. I take two steps down the corridor and then return to place my ear to the door. Just as I thought. There are several people laughing inside, several male voices. One of them mentions my name and there is more laughter.

I don't bother to knock. There on the floor I catch a glimpse of two men, lying on either side of a naked Pamela. The two men are naked as well. Well, not quite naked. One of them is wearing a polka-dot bowtie; the other an ascot. Before I can see their faces, the two men scramble, crawl, hurl themselves into the bedroom. What the fuck is

this? Pamela yells, pulling on a pair of black pant-
ies with a red target front and back. What right
have you——? Sorry, sorry, I say. I thought Torp
was up here. I bloody well told you he wasn't, she
yells. Yeah, I guess you were right, I say. Can I
have my tie back? Your what? she says. My tie.
Sure, she says, reaching into a hamper, pulling out
my still-knotted tie and tossing it at me. Now get
the fuck out of here before I call the cops. Sorry,
sorry, I say again, placing the tie around my neck
and tightening it.

Mr. Bedner's brothers were true to their word. Not half an hour after I called them, they drove up to the front of the house—and with Mr. Bedner in tow since they didn't want to leave him alone. But now that they were there, what exactly did I expect them to do? How were they supposed to find Giulio?

"You tell, you tell," Anton, the one who did all of the talking, said.

I explained as best I could what had happened, what I'd found and the shit that was missing. At the same time, I kept an eye on Mr. Bedner, who was busy passing his hand along the walls. I still feared some sort of retaliation from him, some sort of striking back for what we'd done to him that night.

"Girlfriend?" Anton said.

"No," I said, shaking my head. "At least, I don't think so."

The two brothers conferred at this point, literally putting their heads together.

"Too too nice flat," Mr. Bedner said. "Lots sunshine. Fix bathroom, okay?"

Oh God. Here I was, asking for help from a pair of eighty-year-olds and a guy who'd never recovered from the death of his wife. Just what am I doing here? What the fuck is going on? The university couldn't help me; the police gave me the brush-off. Now what were these guys going to do? Take out the ouija board? Ask Mrs. Bedner to pitch in? I watched Mr. Bedner open the kitchen door and head out to the other side of the basement. Like a fucking zombie. I called out his name a couple of times. He didn't answer me. Then I turned to the brothers but they still had their heads together. So I went out and got Mr. Bedner myself. Took him by the arm and led him back into the kitchen. That's when he started to talk to me as if I was his wife. I tried to take his arm away but he was too strong. He giggled and kept telling me about his new shower stall and how we should take our showers together from now on. Finally, I yelled for him to let go of me and the two brothers pulled him away from me.

"Sorry," Anton said. "Mean no harm."

"No, I'm the one who's sorry," I said. "I'm sorry I called you over here for nothing. I mean, there's nothing you can do."

"No, no," Anton said. "Not true. We go look for Giulio together. Okay?"

"What? What are you talking about?"

"You tell us where he go. We find him."

"Are you serious?" I said. "You'd do that for me."

"We are gentlemen, yes," Anton said, tapping his chest.

His twin brother followed suit. Mr. Bedner started to wander off again. I collapsed on a chair and burst into tears.

"Why you cry?" Anton asked. His brother offered me a handkerchief.

"I'm crying because you're too good," I said, wiping my eyes with the handkerchief. "And I don't deserve it. I don't deserve any of it."

"Not true. You care for Harold. You watch for him. He tell me himself."

That brought a fresh round of tears.

"You good person," Anton said while his brother looked at me with puppy eyes. "Your husband good person."

You can't imagine how much I hated myself at that moment. I felt like all my sins were being paraded in front of me. Like I'd felt when that bastard priest back at my grandparents' place said that I'd never be good enough. That I'd never make the grade. That I was wicked and that my evil desires would get the best of me some day. That I was the spawn of the devil.

"Okay," Anton said, clapping his hands. "No more talk. We go. Now. Before dark. Dark, no good." He laughed. "Blind in dark."

Giulio's Journal

It's a trail I'm following. Definitely a trail of some kind. But what kind of trail it might be, I'm not at all sure. Right now, I'm wandering around the downtown area again. I'm wandering around, going from alley to alley to familiarize myself with them. What have I found thus far? First, the remnants of cats-long-gone and the ghosts of cats-to-be. And that makes me reflect upon the perennial philosophical question: How can a cat that isn't become a cat that is? Where is the line that snaps a potential cat into an actual cat? As the alleys become sleazier and more difficult to navigate, the cats are replaced by other creatures. Creatures with bottles of Williams Lectric Shave in their hands. Creatures that make it hard at times to tell where the garbage ends and they begin. But the question of long-gone-ness and soon-to-be-ness remains.

At the end of this sleaziest of all alleys, this slimy paradigm of all possible alleys where you stumble over the prone bodies and misshapen ideas, sits a little sun-drenched park (Pieklo Plaza, the tiny wooden sign says) with two benches and an overflowing trash can. Autumn wasps buzz around the trash can, dipping into the sweet nectar of Orange Crush dregs; men stumble in and out, throwing themselves on to the patch of grass and immediately falling into a deep sleep which can

be rescinded only with a rain of kicks to the head.
Others search brazenly through the fallen ones'
pockets or pull bottles of wine from beneath their
weary arms. I look about, wondering why I've
never seen this place before and why I'm here now.

Garbage-strewn alleys lead into it from all four
directions; the shattered backs of abandoned buildings stare down at it; somewhere a rock band prac-
tises, guitar howling, drums pounding; and the
smell is of rotting vegetables, of rendered meat flying from the back of dripping dump trucks. I squat
down at the edge of the park, holding on tightly to
my backpack, feeling the trickles of sweat and the
itch, yet chilled at the same time. Peace, man, a
voice says beside me. I jump slightly, tense up. I
can't tell if he's young or old. But there's something familiar about him. His face is all puffed up
and splotchy with patches of beard between skin
that resembles the parched earth following an ex-
tended drought. His eyeballs are streaked with red.
He wears a thick blue ski jacket, with a long tear
where the stuffing threatens to come out. Peace, he
says again, holding up two fingers in a shaky 'V'
and smiling. The teeth along the front of his mouth
are all missing. Peace, I say.

And then I recognize him. He's the guy Torp
and I met that day going through Stanley Park.
It's the blue ski jacket that identifies him. I suddenly feel safer for some reason.

282

Listen, man, he says, lowering his voice and leaning quite close. His breath smells the same as the park itself, as if he's sprung out of it in a show of spontaneous generation. Youse got any money? I been kinda sick, you know. His stomach growls horribly, bringing up a belch of even fouler air. Doc at the Sally Ann says I gotta eat sumtin, gotta put sumtin in my gut. I stand up and tell him to follow me if he wants some food. No, youse follow me, he says. I know a swell place. Youse gonna like it. I shrug and follow.

It's an eerie, unresolved area of the city, in the midst of rapid transition. Alongside the abandoned sheds and gutted firetraps rise up-and-coming boutiques with exposed brick walls and fancy neon signs. And there are as many Mercedes on the street as bicycle skeletons. He leads me to a place with a huge For Sale sign across the smashed-glass front window and men in similar ratty ski jackets waiting in a long line to get in. No, I say. I'm not going in there. I think I like the place just around the corner better. Come on. Hey man, he says. Youse crazy or sumtin. That's for the big shits. They ain't gonna let us in. Come on, I say. They'll let us in.

It's called La Cena Semplice, *a hanging-fern eatery catering to the nouveau urban gentry. I explain* La Cena Semplice *means 'The Simple Meal'. From the reception they give us,*

it's obvious they don't much appreciate our going in. But I flash them my wad of money and
threaten to make a big scene—in broken Italian—
if they don't let us in. Hide us in a corner if you
want, I say. But you can't keep us out. So they sit
us behind a huge potted plant where none of the
other customers can see us.

My friend—for he's fast becoming my
friend—sits nervously at the edge of his wicker
chair, arms folded tightly across his chest, ready to
bolt. I flick my finger to indicate that we're ready
to eat. The waiter comes over, trying to smile.
We'll have the onion soup, I say, lifting a packet
of matches and slipping them into my backpack.
Lots of cheese, if you don't mind. And then we'll
go from there. The waiter brings the first course.
How's the soup? I ask my friend, who's having
some trouble keeping the strings of cheese out of his
beard. Fine, he says, eyes shifting from side to side.
Say, I ask, do you mind if I call you Torp? I don't
give a shit what youse call me, so long youse don't
call me late for dinner. For some reason, I find that
hilariously funny and keep repeating it throughout
the entire meal—which consists of tagliatelle with
bay leaves, sautéed veal scaloppine with lemon
juice and spinach with raisins and nuts.

I keep having to tell "Torp" to slow down and
savour the food but there's no holding him back.
He scarfs it down as if it's his last meal—and it

may well be, come to think of it. With the meal,
I order several bottles of excellent wine. Then, we
settle back for an espresso and Irmana's country
ricotta cake. Towards the end, I notice there's a
waiter positioned at each of the two entrances. Ah,
who could blame them actually for being suspi-
cious? That's what capitalism has done to us, I tell
"Torp" as I slap money down on the table. Fuck-
ing right, he says and belches.

Outside, "Torp" suggests we really get into
it—with a gallon of Thunderbird from the lo-
cal liquor outlet. They all seem to know him at
the store and that makes me feel better, removing
any lingering doubts I may have had about him.
"Torp" shows me one of his tricks—how to squirt
out a huge stream of red wine some five metres
simply by curling his lip. That depletes the gal-
lon more quickly than we intend and we go back
for another. By late afternoon, we're stumbling
around behind dilapidated buildings, throwing
up on to some expressway far below us, dangling
from a window ledge legs kicking, and scrambling
to climb back in when we almost lose our balance.

After that, things flow together and break
apart, twist as if time itself were warping. There's
a room. Yes. I remember that. And a rat-faced
woman taking money. There are more brown-
bagged bottles of wine, clinking dully together; a
narrow, rickety stairway with broken linoleum

runners; "Torp" and I singing and holding each other up; insects scurrying away at the flick of the light switch. There are the two of us in a room that smells of piss and vomit. And sweat. Rancid sweat. There's him kneeling on the floor beside the bed, spitting into his hands. There's me kneeling on the bed, my pants down, bottle of wine in my hand, sluices of it down my chest, my eyes shut, feeling suddenly the hard gums sucking on me, the wet hands gripping my buttocks, and the faces going through my mind: Pamela, Mr. Bedner, Raf, Reginald Worthington, Nicole, the chairman of the department, my parents, Torp. The real Torp, rising from the dead. The never dead.

And it's Torp, the real Torp, that does it. That makes my testicles contract. That makes me grip the back of this "Torp's" head. That makes me blubber about my dreams and my nightmares and what I can't do without any longer. And then there's "Torp" grinning up at me, curling his lip, squirting into my face. And I hit him then against the side of his grinning face, hit him as hard as I can with the wine bottle. And I hit him again to make sure before collapsing head-first onto the bed. Or is it all a drunken fantasy? Yes, I do awake a few hours later to find myself splayed naked across a filthy bed in a sleazy hotel room. To look up at a single light bulb against which a moth has seared itself. That much I can see at one glance.

But I awake alone, my head not simply throbbing but pounding, hammering—and no sign of my friend "Torp".

Then, always close to the surface where I'm concerned, logic sets in again. If I'd actually hit him the way I remember, he wouldn't have gone anywhere. His head had jerked sideways from the blow and he had hit the ground with a solid thud that still reverberates in my mind. But why had I hit him? He was giving me a blow job, boasting he could make me come even after all that wine and ... and I'd hit him because he wouldn't believe me ... and he was making fun of me, was calling me a loony tune ... and ... Blood! Of course! The way I'd hit him there would've been blood everywhere. A sea of blood. I get down on my knees and search the floor. No blood. Nary a drop. Lots of other things, sticky things and lots of insects stuck to the sticky things—as if they can't resist. The lure of nascent mandrake trees. But no blood. So I've just imagined the whole thing in a drunken stupor. And I don't know if that makes me feel better—or just more of a fake. More of a poseur.

I dress slowly and, clutching my backpack, stumble down the narrow stairway, past the rat-faced woman and out into the street. The sunny day is gone. Is it even the same day? Who knows. It's drizzling and cold. I lean against a wall. There are hundreds of us leaning against these walls, each one stiff and cold and unrelenting. These were my favourite kinds of days as a child. Days spent at home sitting in front of the TV or in the kitchen where the steam from the cooking pots misted up the windows so you could write on them, spell your name on them. What a weird time to remember such a thing. What a strange time to bring it up.

I had no fucking idea where to start searching for Giulio.

"Where he go?" Anton asked as we got into the van.

"I don't know," I said. "He goes to the university. But I've tried them. He wasn't there."

"We try again!"

When we arrived on campus, a student pointed out the philosophy department building to us.

"We wait here," Anton said.

A stuck-up woman sat at the front desk typing away, pretending not to notice me. Are all secretaries so fucking self-important? No, I wouldn't be that way if I got a job. I cleared my throat.

"Yes," she said, barely looking up. "Can I help you?"

"I'm looking for Giulio," I said. "Giulio di Orio. I'm his wife."

"Oh yes. You called here this morning, didn't you?" I nodded. "Several times." I nodded again. "Well, I just got back from lunch myself so he might have come in while I was away. One moment."

The secretary picked up the phone and spoke into it.

A moment later, this guy in a silly bowtie and pipe in hand came bouncing in. Ah, Reginald Worthington the Third.

"Hullo," he said. "You must be Nicole. Giulio has told me so much about you."

"He has?"

"Oh yes, rather."

"Is he here?" I asked, looking around. "Has he come in?"

"No, I'm afraid not. A pity. We had some rather important things to discuss. A new course, you see. The latest thing really: Post-Modern Existential Hermeneutics with a parallel, less strenuous credit in Deconstructivist Kafkaesque Ontology from the English lit. department. I was hoping to get Giulio's input. You wouldn't happen to know anything about post-modern existential hermeneutics, now would you?"

"No, I don't."

You can kiss my post-modern post-fucking arse is what I should have told him. There's one thing I've always been able to spot a mile away—and that's a bullshitter. And, from the looks of it, this guy could really spread it thick.

"A pity," he said, knocking his pipe against the nearest ashtray before making a big show of lighting it and sending puffs of smoke into the air. "I think I'd rather share an office with you than with good old Giulio."

"Thanks for nothing," I said. Then I turned and walked out.

"Come again," he shouted. "Our doors are always

open."

As I stepped out, the three brothers could tell by my shrug that Giulio was not in the philosophy department.

"We keep looking," Anton said, revving up the van. "Look, look, look!"

"Thank you," I say, that queasy feeling back in my stomach.

"But where to look," Anton said, as both he and his brother scratched their heads.

"Stanley Park," I said, holding my abdomen like something was going to fall out. "Wreck Beach."

Both Anton and his brother looked at me as if I weren't all there. Then Anton shrugged.

"Okay," he said. "We try."

Giulio's Journal

At first, I fear getting lost. But then, the closer I get to Stanley Park, the more I sense that every street seems to lead there. And, though every path may have veered and retreated somewhere along the way, it eventually comes to find its way there. Or perhaps it's only me. Perhaps, I've managed to reduce the world to that, to take all the objects within it—and reduce it to this one place. And, within this one place, there are only three possible categories, only three decisions to be made: You can be the murderer; you can be Torp; or you can be the bystander. As the murderer, you are the arbitrary judge; as Torp, you are the necessary victim; as bystander, you are the unwilling witness. And all three are heading to the place of execution, where one after another the Torps are crushed by hammer blows to the skull. And I take turns beating, receiving, watching—one moment Torp, the next the murderer, the third a bystander.

It's a vision that I'm totally unprepared for, a vision that should come at the end of the world, not on a grey day with ducks floating on the lagoon and children in yellow and purple raincoats swinging to the top, the very top, of the arc and then down again. I sit on that park bench for the good part of an hour, watching the blood from the continuous executions climb up higher and higher, washing up first to my toes, then my ankles, up to my knees, past my waist and neck. And then I let myself go, find myself swimming in it, swirling as if in the midst of a great turbulence, a powerful sucking away of all life till there is nothing left but me and sand and the red velvet-tipped fingers of ocean.

I realize then that what I've actually done is walk out into the water, that I've been swept back by the waves. But my backpack is high and dry on the beach. Thank God for that. I hug it to my chest and rock slightly, feeling the wet seeping through my trousers where I sit in the sand. Then, I stand up and move to the rockier, more sheltered part of the beach. There I'll have better protection from the spray. Several times, as I scramble over lichen-covered stones, my feet slip and I scrape my knee or bang an elbow. But it's nothing serious and I'm glad to be wedged at last into the outcropping. Some-one, anticipating my arrival no doubt, has stashed piles of dry wood there and, using the matches from the restaurant, I'm able to start a small fire.

I change clothing. But the chill doesn't leave me. I sit cross-legged, staring at the flames, steam rising from my drying clothes, the walls of the small cave reflecting a shadow of the heat and the darkness before me, going on forever. It starts to make me drowsy, to lull me to sleep. Out of no-where, I hear sounds coming from further down the beach, laughter and the crackling of a huge fire. This is no surprise. This is expected. I rise and walk towards it. Torp and his friends are there, like they've always been, and I can hear them talking. They talk of revolution and bombing, of unholy alliances in the halls of power, of greased money skidding under the table, helping to keep the world the way it is. They talk of changing the world, breaking up the hegemony. They smoke their numbing substances, take their mind-ex-panding materials. They sing their songs of youth and play their games of "what if".

Sitting in their midst and listening to the sweet voices, the flow of sound like that of the ocean it-self, one finds it almost believable, almost credible.

I see Torp head into the tent and I'm there as he makes love to shadows, to my wife, to me, to us, even more real now in his immateriality. I watch him come out again and go down the path, waving to his friends. And I rush after him, yelling at him not to go. But he can't hear me—he's never been able to hear me, it seems. And I re-live again and again the moment I rush through the trees, hearing that unnatural thwack, the glum thud, seeing Torp's body before me, the murder weapon crawling, bubbling, seething with blood, the final kiss sealing our fate, mingling our lives.

Each time, I'm certain I'll be able to prevent it, to circumvent it, to find some way to trip up the murderer, to distract Torp, to alter some essential factor in the equation so that it will come out differently. But it's no use. The result is fixed. The equation rights itself in order to always come out the same way. I suddenly realize how ghost-like (yet spiritless) I really am, how purposeless I've become. I want Torp back. Nothing else matters. This I understand each time we return to the beginning and I can see him once again in the tent, can smell his proud presence, can revel in his ability to please everyone, to make everyone a part of his eccentrically elliptical orbit. Without Torp, the most I can look forward to is a pleasant disintegration, the exploding of a mind overloaded with at best important trivia. And no hope of contacting the world, my real world.

And so, even though I know the outcome, I continue to "recreate the scene of the crime" time and time again, desperate, red-eyed, without a chance of succeeding, hoping that with enough effort I can at least lose myself, slip into the crack of another universe that isn't fixed the same way as this one, that takes chances Aristotle himself wouldn't understand. In the end, I'm on my knees in the mud at the spot where Torp has been bludgeoned, panting and dribbling like a beaten dog, clutching at vacant air. For he has been bludgeoned, despite the lack of a body. I'm certain of it now. I'm certain he'd never leave us of his own free will. And when I lied to Nicole back at the flat, I was also telling the truth. Then, I'm up again, chasing ravenous shadows down the beach, shadows that leave behind a fetid odour, that sizzle and turn the sand to glass. And behind me the friendly laughter of Torp's friends, innocent, unaware, strong in the belief that a few well-placed bombs (or well-written poems or well-sung verses or well-explained philosophic conundrums) will solve everything, will bring back the natural order of things.

Help me, I scream, reaching out to them. You've got to help me. But shake them all I want, I have as much effect on them as I've had on preventing Torp's death. Selfish bastards, I yell out. You call yourselves revolutionaries; you call yourselves changers of the world. But do you know what you are? You're nothing but … nothing but …. And I really can't make out what they are, really can't say. For I don't know what I am and from where it is that I speak. And that's how I find myself a few moments later, curled up in the sand, feeling the rain as it soaks through my back, the words "Help me" caught in my throat. I sit up and look around. Torp's friends are gone without a trace, leaving behind not even the ashes from their bonfires. Torp's friends were never there, you fool. And neither was Torp. You may wish him dead but he's not about to accommodate you.

I'm all alone again, the rain now whipping sideways against my face—and not even a raincoat to protect me. No one else is foolish enough to risk double pneumonia. I stand up and start to walk, practically staggering against the wind, Buster Keaton-like. I leave puddles in the sand where I step. The water is seeping in everywhere, smashing itself against the seawall, ready to engulf the whole world and to drown me in the process. On the hill ahead, I spot a figure. It's waving, calling out something I can't hear. At first, I think it's the figure from my dreams. But no. Is it someone coming to rescue me? To set me free? And then three more figures emerge behind it. Shimmering in the rain. They seem to be dancing, excited, pointing. Hello, I call out. I've been waiting for you.

*But the wind and rain are too strong. They blow
my voice back into my face. I wave my arms above
my head, hoping they can see me. Weariness over-
takes me. I struggle to keep my eyes open. I make
one last effort to go forward—and then collapse
face first onto the sand.*

At first, I couldn't believe it was him. It was like he had
aged several years in a day or something. And he was too
weak to stand on his own. With the help of the two brothers I managed to get him into the back of the van and laid
him down on a blanket. He was delirious and shivering
the whole time. Kept looking at Mr. Bedner and calling
him his saviour and stuff like that. He got angry when I
tried to tell him that it wasn't his saviour—only Mr. Bedner. He kept on insisting until I agreed with him just to
calm him down.

"Torp's not dead, you know," he said to Mr. Bedner.
"They couldn't kill him off."

Oh shit, I said to myself, what am I going to do now?
He's gone off the deep end and I'm going to be stuck here
trying to take care of him. He looked at me and repeated
the same thing, saying he had lied when he told me Torp
had been murdered. He said it had just been a fantasy of
his, that he was just covering up the "immense hurt" he'd
felt when Torp skipped out on us. Then he started to
breathe hard. I placed my hand on his forehead. He was
burning up with fever.

"We must get him to hospital," Anton said when he

too had felt Giulio's forehead. "Need doctor. No time to waste."

His brother, who was driving, nodded—and speeded up.

"Torp not dead," Mr. Bedner said gleefully. "Irena not dead." He clapped his hands. "Nobody dead!"

"Quiet, Harold," Anton said.

Giulio leaned against me, his head sliding down onto my lap. He looked so helpless. I felt sorry and guilty at the same time. Maybe I had been the one that had pushed him over the edge.

"It'll be alright," I whispered. "You're going to be just fine."

"The air is crystal clear," Giulio said. "The sea shimmers calmly in the distance. It's warm, practically summer warm. The gulls swoop down to scoop up the sand crabs, an oil tanker passes in the distance. The variables and the unknowns suddenly seem to know their places. It's time to take a chance, don't you think? What do you say, Aristotle?"

"Hurry, please," I called out. And suddenly I was crying, wiping tears from my eyes.

"Come with me, now," Giulio said. "There's a place I'd like to show you. Come on. It's in the downtown area, just around here somewhere. There's an alley I want to show you."

"No, Giulio, we can't stop now," I said. "We've got to get you to—"

"Stop!" Giulio shouted. "There's someone I know.

Someone I want to say goodbye to. He's here somewhere in one of these alleys. I know it. The alley that'll bring me back to that sunny spot where the wasps buzzed. You know it, don't you?" I shook my head. "You'll recognize him when you see him. He'll be wearing a faded and torn blue ski jacket. He'll have a dirty bandage wrapped around his head. He'll answer to the name of Torp—although that's not his real name."

We kept on driving. Anton's brother pulled the van up to the emergency entrance of the Vancouver General Hospital. Then, Anton and I helped Giulio out of the van and into the hospital.

I was frantic. Giulio ranted and raved about some guy he'd met. He kept on apologizing for beating the guy up. A couple of the orderlies put him on a stretcher and the doctor on duty came over to examine him. The first thing she asked was where Giulio had been. Then she said she couldn't be sure without more tests but she had a pretty good notion Giulio was suffering from at least hypothermia—and most likely some form of pneumonia. I asked if the hallucinations could be part of the symptoms and she said there was a very good possibility. Somehow, that made me feel better. He might die—but at least I knew he hadn't gone over the edge.

Giulio's Journal

Nov. 10: *I've just spent two weeks in a hospital bed. During that time, Nicole has come to visit me*

MICHAEL MIROLLA

practically every day and the secretary of the phi-
losophy department sent flowers. The other day,
Mr. Bedner and his two brothers came up. Anton
asked if I remembered what happened the day they
found me on the beach. I told him the truth: I re-
membered it all, every single moment of it. And
then we had a good laugh together. Mr. Bedner
patted me on the hand and said he had a "too too
nice" flat for us—and that he wanted us to meet
his wife who didn't speak any English.

That night, I had a dream—and I'm still not
sure whether it was pleasant or not. I'm back in my
room at my parents' place, listening to voices just
beyond the door. Son, my father's saying, as soon as
spring comes, as soon as the snow melts, I'll teach
you how to graft vines and we'll set up a beauti-
ful vineyard together. Now, son, one of these days
we'll have to have (to have to have to have)
a heart-to-heart (heart-to-heart-to-heart-to),
won't we? See what I've got here. It's a postcard
from that high-school teacher of yours. Remember
him? The Christian Brother from Newfound-
land? Sends you a postcard for Christmas every
year. It says, my father's voice continues: "Re-
member that Necessity is the Mother of Invention,
not the other way around. Merry Christmas.
The years have flown from whence we came upon
this earthly sleep and now their shortness should
make them all the more beauteous." Isn't that

299

pretty? my father asks. Wouldn't it be nice for all of us to gather round the Christmas table again? The whole family. Won't that be something?

And then later on the same night, another dream. This time, I'm back on the beach, still curled in the sand. I rise, leaving behind my curled impression. My rising is a bit unsteady, like that of a newborn fawn but it's a getting-up nevertheless and that's all that counts. I look around. It's a fabulously beautiful morning, the kind of late-October day we so seldom get here, full of gilt-edged sparkles on the water and letter-perfect gulls forming words and phrases and sentences in the sky. People are taking advantage of the weather to cycle one last time along the Park paths, to visit the zoo where the polar bears slide big-rumped into the water, to walk along the sea wall, to stare into the lagoon, to chat or run vigorously, or simply to sit on the benches reading and taking the sun. I see them all—as if I have all-penetrating vision. Then I stretch, look around at what must be familiar landscape. The night has been a long, hard one and my bones ache from the effort. But the sun soon warms me up, and I begin to walk, stopping only to take off my raincoat and cap, to put on the sunglasses in which the world is reflected in its own special way.

I walk along the beach, occasionally picking up flat stones to toss into the water. Suddenly, I look across and sense without seeing that there's someone else there. Someone following a parallel course to mine. Someone behind the line of trees. But I'm not afraid. Without being told, I know this person means me no harm and is only there to keep an eye on me. Only there because of a misplaced sense of responsibility. I round the tip of the bay, find myself almost beneath the bridge that arcs across towards the mountains. I look around for a moment. Then, I pull something out of my backpack—it's Torp's magazine. I hold it in my hands for a moment and then throw it carelessly away. I continue walking, scrambling up the side of the hill where the bridge's first pylons have been sunk. I make it to the top after slipping several times, make it by holding on to the roots of tiny trees that have begun to sprout there.

I'm standing there in the warm sun when I see someone behind me rush out suddenly from his hiding place in the trees. He's wearing a strange costume, almost like a cape. I watch him stoop down and pick up the magazine I've just tossed away. He cleans it off. Hey, he shouts. Hey! You've forgotten something, haven't you? This is yours, isn't it? Don't you want it anymore? I shake my head and walk slowly across the bridge. Across the bridge whose supports look eerily like those of a moat. A bridge whose other side is shrouded in eternal fog. A bridge that seems to be hanging in the air, half-finished, ready to snap shut like the

*jaws of a dragon. On the far side are two more fig-
ures waiting for me. They're hard to make out in
the fog. I walk towards them—and wake up just
before I'm about to vanish into the fog.*

*Several days ago, Nicole gave me the good
news: that I'd received a conditional acceptance at
the University of Auckland, pending the arrival
of the reference letters. She also told me she'd got
a job as a receptionist so we'd be able to save a bit
more money before heading out to New Zealand.
The doctors tell me I acted very foolishly, trudging
around all day in the cold and rain—and that I'm
lucky to be alive. Do I feel lucky? Yes, I think I
do. For one thing, I can now picture Torp before
me without either imagining him dead or getting
an uncontrollable urge to go hunting for him. For
another, I look forward to the day Nicole and I set
off for New Zealand. We've already talked about
it and decided we're going by ship. A leisurely
cruise Down Under. As Nicole put it: "It's the
romantic thing to do. Besides, we never did have a
real honeymoon, did we?"*

EPILOGUE

NICOLE

But one might complain of another if,
when he loved us for our usefulness or pleasantness,
he pretended to love us for our character.

—*Nicomachean Ethics*,
Book 9, Chapter 3

I worked right up to Christmas Eve. We were scheduled to sail the day after New Year's on a ship called *The S.S. Philonous*. Giulio said the name was a good sign … the name was … what was the word he used? … propitious.

"Don't you see," he said. "Bishop Berkeley argued that, because it relies on someone's perspective, shape can't be an essential feature of an object—or person. Philonous said that. Thus what something looks like can't be considered to be equivalent to what that something is."

As usual, I had no idea what the fuck he was talking about and couldn't care less as long as the ship floated and didn't leak.

"You guys are nuts. You wouldn't catch me in a boat, leaky or otherwise."

That was Raf. He'd finally made good on his threat and had shown up the week before Christmas, after I'd called him and let him know what had happened to Giulio. The three of us—along with the three Bedner brothers—had celebrated the holiday in grand style up in Mr. Bedner's house. With Raf's help, I put together a traditional meatless Italian Christmas Eve meal, complete with eels and codfish and cauliflower in batter. Anton reminisced about Christmases back home ("before the Red bastards") and the number of times all he'd received was a lump of coal; Anton's speechless twin brother, whose name we never learned, nodded and folded his hands across his chest; Mr. Bedner searched around for the plum brandy—"too too nice"—and insisted we sneak a couple of shots before his wife returned; Raf talked about setting up an office in Vancouver—the boom was coming, according to him, and he wanted to be smack in the middle of it; Giulio caressed the slim book I'd bought for him (with input from Reginald Worthington III, who turned out not to be the complete asshole I first thought he was)—*Phenomenological Hermeneutics and the Study of Literature*; I dreamed of the Pacific Ocean and the swells and the urgent rasping of a salty tongue between my waterlogged thighs; and the empty chair that would have been Torp's/Irena's gave off its own vibes. Then we all toasted to a long life and talked and ate and drank until it was time to attend midnight Mass. Giulio was reluctant but the rest of us insisted—and, skidding along the icy sidewalk, we all piled into the Bedners' van.

I'd been to lots of midnight Masses back home—my mother insisted we go because she said it was the French tradition and she wanted to keep up tradition. I think the real reason she did it was because she thought it might clean away all the sins she committed during the rest of the year. And my grandparents had taken me when my mother wasn't there. But I just couldn't enjoy myself, especially with that asshole of a priest looking down on me. This time, though, was different. Just a feeling. Nothing in particular. Nothing really definite. I looked around and noticed the gleam in the eyes of the Bedner brothers. They were like pure spirits or something. It still hurt me to think of what Giulio and I had done to Mr. Bedner. Strange how things happen.

The man we thought was our sworn enemy became a close friend—almost part of the family. And there was Raf beside me just being Raf. He leaned over during the sermon and whispered: "Wonder what this is going for per square foot." I giggled and jabbed him in the ribs. As usual, Giulio was lost in a world all his own. We still hadn't talked about that day when he'd taken off. Or Torp's vanishing. Was he dead or alive? I figured it was up to Giulio to bring it up. We had plenty of time. Besides, things were already complicated enough and I had my own stuff to work through.

On January 2, they all came out to see us off. The three Bedner brothers waved at exactly the same time in exactly the same way, like mechanical dolls. Then reached for old-fashioned handkerchiefs to dab their eyes. Raf did the thumbs up signal and blew kisses while shimmying back and forth on the slippery dock. We waved from the ship's deck. Would we ever see the Bedners again? Probably not. Raf? Maybe. Torp?

The seas were calm and there was plenty of time to relax and think things through. Several days out, after a few drinks too many at a candlelight dinner given by the *Philonous*'s captain, I finally got up the nerve.

"Giulio," I said, holding his hands in mine. "Do you love me?"

"Of course, I do."

"Why?"

"I'm pregnant."